Return to the Beach House

Books by Georgia Bockoven

Carly's Gift

Things Remembered

The Year Everything Changed

Another Summer

Disguised Blessings

The Beach House

An Unspoken Promise

Far from Home

Alone in a Crowd

Moments

A Marriage of Convenience

Return to the Beach House

GEORGIA BOCKOVEN

For Josi—thanks for hanging in there with me

This book is a work of fiction. References to real people, events, establishments, organizations, or locales are intended only to provide a sense of authenticity, and are used fictitiously. All other characters, and all incidents and dialogue, are drawn from the author's imagination and are not to be construed as real.

HarperCollins books may be purchased for educational, business, or sales promotional use. For information, please e-mail the Special Markets Department at SPsales@harpercollins.com.

FIRST HARPERLUXE EDITION

HarperLuxe™ is a trademark of HarperCollins Publishers

Library of Congress Cataloging-in-Publication Data is available upon request.

ISBN: 978-0-06-232689-8

14 ID/RRD 10 9 8 7 6 5 4 3 2 1

Acknowledgments

Thanks, Marcia. You came through for me yet again. I knew nothing about horses before I created a character who loved them. My confidence to plunge ahead came from knowing I had a world-class equestrian to go to with questions. And as always, you came through with the answers. If something slipped through, it's entirely my fault.

A second thank-you really needs to be added to the above—this one for being the world's best veterinarian and taking care of my literary companions with dedication and loving skill, even the one who showed no appreciation at all and had everyone at the clinic terrified to come near her.

A loving thank you goes to John, Sidney, and Cassidy for guiding me through teen waters. You're the best research assistants ever!

Finally, there's Samantha Spurlock, an extraordinary young woman who is an example of everything good and caring in her generation. You give me hope.

Prologue

The Beginning of May

A truly good face-lift is never obvious, whether performed on a sixty-year-old woman or a hundred-year-old home. The thought followed Julia Lawson from room to room as she made one more pass through her beloved beach house before heading to the airport to fly home to Eric and the kids.

She'd put off the work that needed to be done for too long, telling herself she was afraid of losing the charm that accompanied the decay, but in quiet moments of honesty she acknowledged that she was mostly terrified of losing the fragile memories of inconsequential moments with Ken and Joe and Maggie that, for her, were as much a part of the beach house as the tradition of summer renters.

Her heart still ached a little when she looked back. The burgundy-and-green sofa that now resided in the living room was beautiful and cushiony and inviting. But it wasn't the one where she had curled into the arms of her beloved first husband, Ken, and talked about the future while they watched flames dance in the fireplace. They'd never suspected or entertained the thought that dreams can be as fragile and vulnerable as sand castles built too close to the shore.

Year after year, through the emotional turmoil of learning to live without Ken and then finding her second soul mate, Eric, she had found ways to ignore the threadbare material. She'd even managed to cope with the holes that appeared in the armrests until the day the painful truth came tumbling out of the mouth of four-year-old Cassidy, the daughter she'd had with Eric: "Mom, this thing stinks."

The kitchen table where she had shared a hundred cups of coffee with Joe and Maggie had a loose leg that no amount of glue could coax back into a sturdy upright position. The sliding-glass door required muscle to get it to move, and the windows had an insulating factor somewhere between Shoji screens and gauze. The carpets were threadbare from decades of sand wearing away the fiber, and the walnut wall-to-wall bookshelves that Joe had made for his beloved Maggie when they owned the beach house were bleached and dried from the sun.

Still, even after Julia had finally decided she would not sell, she'd done nothing but the most necessary repairs, each year promising herself that next year she would get started. But then she temporarily gave up thinking about renovating when, almost twelve months to the day after she and Eric were married, she was pregnant. A year and a half later, surrounded by carpet samples and paint chips, she felt a familiar wave of nausea and realized she was pregnant again.

Always at the back of her mind was the knowledge that without a faucet so old it had come off in her hand she might not have met Eric, the extraordinary second love of her life. She wouldn't be the mother of two stepchildren and two preschoolers had she updated the house after Ken died. Would she be tempting destiny by making so many changes all at once?

Finally, after the birth of their second daughter, and with gentle nudging from Eric, she'd tried working with contractors, flying out from Maryland for periodic meetings, then going home more frustrated than when she'd left. Even the ones who had gained their reputations by restoring and maintaining the quaint multimillion-dollar cottages in Carmel failed to understand her attachment to decades-old shutters that hung slightly off plumb and brick walkways with cracks and chips outlined with bright green moss.

Understanding her almost paranoid reluctance to move forward, Andrew, her next-door neighbor, and one of Ken's best friends, had stepped in and volunteered to oversee the restoration. Julia trusted him the way she'd once trusted Ken and the way she trusted Eric now. With his intimate connection to the house, he understood why it was so hard for her to make even the most rudimentary improvements. More importantly, he understood why it was necessary for her to be able to return after the work was completed and walk through the door feeling as if she'd come home.

And she had.

Almost.

Fresh paint inside and out, and new rugs over the refinished hardwood floors were in keeping with the character of a house that had been built over a hundred years ago. Then vacationers had arrived via horse and buggy, an almost inconceivable contrast to the hybrid car that sat in the driveway now.

She'd involved Eric and the kids by giving them the job of picking out the material for the curtains and bedspreads in the bedrooms. Fitting their personalities, the fabrics were busy and brightly colored and not something Julia ever would have chosen. They would take some getting used to, but that feeling would come. It wasn't that the now colorful rooms weren't attractive, they were just different. So different she could no longer imagine Ken or Joe or Maggie living in them.

The craftsman quality of the refinished walnut bookshelves in the living room had given her pause when she first arrived. It wasn't that they looked new, it was that even through all the polish they were as familiar as the sound and feel of the ocean outside the new triple-paned windows. For just that moment she had wondered if she'd actually been looking for a way to escape the memories that tied her to the beach house.

And then she had gone into the kitchen, where she had felt an instant, almost overwhelming sense of emotional betrayal. How had she ever convinced herself that granite and stainless steel could or should replace subway tile and you-can-have-any-color-you-want-as-long-as-it's-white appliances? What had she been thinking?

The kitchen had gone from an old sweater you loved but changed out of when company was coming to a designer blazer. What would Joe and Maggie think? And Ken? He'd loved everything about the house just the way it was.

Or had he? Was he reluctant to make changes because he was afraid of offending Joe and Maggie? No matter how long he'd owned the house, he always thought of it as truly belonging to them. But he'd died unexpectedly—a man who'd never even had the flu—and left the caring about such things to her without telling her what she was supposed to care about the most.

And then, less than a year later, Joe and Maggie died, taking the dreams and hopes and desires of their lives with them. Reeling from her loss, Julia discovered that grief is a color—white. It is the gathering of other colors and combining them until the joy of yellow, the passion of red, and the calm of blue disappear. She was left with nothing but the daily effort to go on.

When Eric fixed her broken faucet and over the summer became a part of her life, he not only restored the primary colors but reopened her world to violet and orange and green. Gradually, carefully, she moved out of the shadow of white and back into sunflowers and grass and ocean waves. When their daughter was born two years later and they were alone for several minutes in her hospital room while they waited for the attendant to bring a wheelchair to take her to the car, a sliver of sunlight escaped the curtain and bounced off her wedding ring, spraying the opposite wall with miniature rainbows. Julia had never believed in signs or portents—until that moment. A tear slid down her cheek and landed on her baby's blanket.

Whatever sorrow had lingered in the depths of her heart was gone, replaced by the understanding that she was exactly where she should be and with the people she should be with.

Julia did a final sweep of the house, taking pictures with her iPhone that she would send to Eric and the girls while she waited at the airport for her flight home. As she tried to angle herself for the best shot of the master bedroom, she stopped to pay attention to the wash of afternoon light coming through the window. This was the room she had lived in with Ken, the room where Joe and then Maggie had died, and the room that she and Eric used now whenever they came west during the winter. She put her hand out and turned the diamond on her wedding ring to catch the sunlight. The room danced with color.

There should have been ghosts, but all she saw were rainbows. The house had accommodated change the same way she had . . . aware of the memories and love behind them, but unwilling to miss one moment of the journey ahead.

But she still didn't like the kitchen.

The End of May

Andrew Wells tried the front door to the beach house and, as he'd hoped, found it unlocked. He should have started looking for Grace here instead of at her usual beach and forest haunts. He took off his shoes and stepped into the foyer. "Grace?"

"In the kitchen," she called. "I'm going over the counters one more time before the Kirkpatricks arrive."

Julia had dropped the professional housekeeping service she normally used and hired her cash-strapped, eager-to-earn-money-for-college next-door neighbor, Grace—the adopted daughter of Andrew and his wife Cheryl—for the summer.

Not only was Grace supposed to take care of the house before and after the renters arrived, she was their contact person while they were there. It was her job to make sure the renters had whatever they needed and to handle any problems that might come up. She took this responsibility seriously, preparing for any eventuality as diligently and thoroughly as a mother otter grooming her pup, making lists of everything from an automobile repair shop to twenty-four-hour doc-in-a-box clinics.

Seeing that she'd already vacuumed, Andrew was reluctant to cross the plush Aubusson area rugs and leave footprints. "Are you about ready? We're leaving in a few minutes."

Grace popped her head around the corner. "No problem. I can do the bookshelves when I get back."

After glancing at the gleaming walnut wood, Andrew noted that not even a speck of dust reflected in the sunlight coming through the sliding-glass door. Julia could not have found a more dedicated or fanatical caretaker for her beloved beach house. Responsible, caring, loving, and dedicated, Grace was the antithesis of her biological mother, Rose, and had survived years of neglect and callous indifference—basically raising herself while her mother indulged in the "free" life of a vagabond.

Only it wasn't free. Grace had paid a heavy price in her deep-seated belief that if she'd only been better or prettier or smarter, her mother wouldn't have abandoned her so many times. When Grace was eight and Child Welfare entered the scene, Rose handed her over without so much as an alligator tear. Three years and four foster homes later, Grace came to live with Andrew and Cheryl. It took eight months before she flashed a genuinely spontaneous smile and an entire year before she could get into the car without asking if she would be coming back.

Grace crossed the room, skirting the carpet with the dexterity of a gymnast on a balance beam. Dressed in cutoff jeans and a tank top, her thick, sun-bleached hair cascading over her shoulders, and her face glowing with the unique light of youth, she looked like the iconic Super Bowl advertisement of a seemingly ageless Cindy Crawford reaching for a Pepsi.

Since she had turned fifteen two and a half years ago, total strangers had approached her to tell her how beautiful she was. At first the attention had scared her. Now she simply ignored it. Andrew reacted, however, with a fierce protectiveness, no matter how many times Cheryl tried to convince him that not every man who looked at their daughter was consumed with carnal longings. He just wished Grace was a little more like her older sister, Rebecca, who had learned through her time in the foster care system—before being adopted by Andrew and Cheryl—how to stop unwanted attention with a withering look. Instead, no matter how obnoxious the behavior directed at her, Grace was unfailingly polite, far too trusting, and painfully eager to please—an ulcer-producing combination for a father of daughters.

Grace dug her keys out of her pocket and locked the door. "Tell me again what time the Kirkpatricks are arriving tomorrow."

"The best estimate I could get was sometime after noon. Is there a reason you need an exact time?"

"I thought I'd go by the nursery and pick up a couple of phals. If that's okay with you. I saw some whites and a couple of yellows in the back room that still looked pretty good."

Andrew grew orchids commercially, shipping stock throughout the United States and Canada. He specialized in phalaenopsis, not only because they were long-lasting and shipped well, but because he loved growing them. The back room was where he kept the plants that didn't meet the shipping standards because they either were too far along in their blooming cycle or had unattractive color breaks. More often than not, after a second bloom, the color deviants ended up in the trash. But there were enough surprises in the process that Andrew found it hard to just automatically dump them.

"I think that's a great idea," he said. "Rebecca is getting an order ready to ship. I'll have her set a couple aside for you, and she can bring them home tonight."

"She's not going to the airport with us?"

"Trust me—your mom doesn't expect a major send-off, and all your brother cares about is getting a window seat. It's perfectly okay with them to be dropped off at the curb." Andrew put his arm around his daughter's shoulder and gave her a hug. Grace worried more about hurt feelings than Bobby's preschool teacher did with a roomful of four-year-olds on their first day in class.

"Well, it's important to me."

"A-mariachi-band-and-balloons important?"

She laughed. "Close. But I'll compromise with parking the car and walking them to the security gate."

"You know Bobby is going to have a fit if you try to hug him in front of all those people."

"I can handle a five-year-old."

Andrew unlatched the garden gate. "You bribed him, didn't you?"

She acted shocked. "Would I do something like that?"

"If it's chocolate, your mom will shoot you." Bobby reacted to an ounce of chocolate the way most people reacted to downing half a dozen Red Bulls. And of course, he was the kind of kid who ranked chocolate above any other food, including pizza.

"Hmm . . . I could slip him some M&Ms and they wouldn't let him on the plane."

Andrew's heart broke a little at her attempt to use humor to cover her fear of people she loved leaving her. "They're only going to be gone a month," he said tenderly. "You'll be amazed how fast it passes."

"I just don't like good-byes," she admitted.

"I don't like them either. I'm just better at hiding it." He tapped his finger on the end of her nose. "And it helps that they're only going to L.A., not across the country."

For what had to be the tenth time, Grace asked, "Why did this happen? What makes someone's brain stop working the way Grandma's did?"

"Figure that one out and you'll not only be richer than Bill Gates, you'll save a hell of a lot of heartache."

"Do you think Grandma April knows what's happening to her?"

"She knew in the beginning. I doubt she does anymore."

"How sad to watch someone you love disappear like that. Especially your own mother." She leaned into Andrew as they crossed the space that separated their house from Julia's. "At least Mom knows Grandma April isn't leaving her willingly. I guess that's something."

PART ONE
June

Chapter 1

BREATHTAKING.

Alison Kirkpatrick was at a loss for any other way to describe the view from the back deck of the beach house. She considered calling her friend Linda to tell her about it, but Linda had little interest in the world west of the Hudson River.

Alison needed new friends. Especially now that her best friend, her widowed daughter-in-law Nora, had remarried, and her grandson Christopher was about to go away to college. There were nights it was all she could think about. No matter how long she stayed in bed, sleep was as likely as any real bipartisanship in politics. She either grabbed her iPad and read one of the books she had on her digital bookshelf or wound up in the kitchen digging through the freezer for the Ben and Jerry's she liked to tell herself she bought for Christopher. She'd never understood people who turned to alcohol for solace when there was ice cream.

As weary of her self-imposed moodiness as she was her increasingly boring life, she purposely put aside the reason she was spending the next month in what had turned out to be a surprisingly delightful rental with an incomparable view and went back into the house to finish unpacking. The doorbell rang before she made it to the bedroom.

Standing on the porch, flashing an orthodontist's dream smile, was a girl Alison guessed to be near the same age as Christopher.

"Mrs. Kirkpatrick?" she asked.

"Yes . . ."

"Hi. I'm Grace Wells. I live next door"—she pointed to her right—"the house on the other side of the walkway."

"Hello, Grace Wells," Alison said. "How can I help you?"

"Hopefully, I'll be the one helping you. Not that I expect anything to go wrong," Grace added quickly. "But if it does, I'm your contact person while you're here." When Alison didn't respond, Grace prompted, "For the house? In case you have any questions? Or problems?

You know—like how something works or what the dinging sound coming from the refrigerator means. By the way, the dinging means one of the doors is open."

"Oh yes. I remember now. Your name was on the contract Julia sent. I was expecting someone . . . a little older." More to the point, she'd expected a rental agency with limited hours and voice mail. How nice to discover she'd been wrong.

"I have backup should anything really big need fixing. And my dad's really good with the smaller stuff." She shifted from one foot to the other. "I just came by to introduce myself and give you this." Grace put her hand on the binder she had tucked under her arm.

"Would you like to come in?" Alison opened the door wider and stepped to the side.

Grace hesitated. "If you're busy, I could come back later."

"Actually, your timing is perfect. I'd like some company." Alison led the way into the living room. "I assume you're the one I have to thank for the orchids?"

"My dad has a commercial nursery in the valley. The yellow phals are my favorites. He has a thing for the whites."

Alison indicated a chair beside the fireplace. "I'm sorry I don't have anything to offer you except water. I haven't had time to go to the store yet."

"I'm fine," Grace said, settling on the edge of the cushion.

Alison sat on the sofa and pointed to the binder. "You brought that for me?"

"It's nothing special," Grace said dismissively. "I made up some lists of places I thought you and Mr. Kirkpatrick might want to visit while you're here. There's the usual tourist stuff, but I included places no one writes about, places the natives go, like Garrapata Beach. It's great for picnics and not nearly as crowded as the beaches by the wharf. Or if you're into golf, according to my uncle, DeLaveaga is one of the best public courses in California. And someplace hardly anyone goes is Fremont Peak State Park. It has the best views from anywhere around here, especially if you're into photography. My sister won first place at the state fair with a picture she took there."

Grace put the binder on the coffee table and opened it to the first page. "I made a list of restaurants too. Since I don't have a lot of experience eating at really expensive places, I had to ask my parents' friends for recommendations." She smiled. "Don't worry, they're the kind of friends who go to the snooty boutique wineries for the new releases and read the *Wine Spectator* the way an evangelical reads the Bible." She added, "My dad's words, not mine. Anyway, these people know good restaurants."

Alison had never been interested in anything about wine beyond whether it was red or white, or sweet or dry. She glanced at the sample menus in the vinyl sleeves as Grace slowly turned the pages. Some were prix fixe, not the best choice for a soon-to-be-eighteen-year-old suddenly grown finicky. Others offered more standard yet elegant fare, everything from portabello sliders to wild-caught salmon with Béarnaise sauce.

Grace turned several pages at once, skipping the last of the high-end restaurants. "This next section has places I know really well and can recommend because I've been there. For instance . . . you can't do better than Pizza My Heart. It's a chain, but don't hold that against it." She flipped the page. "And hands down, the best place for a hamburger, fries, and milkshake is Carpos. They have a great salad bar too.

"I saved the best for last," she said with a grin. "The bakeries. We have a lot of them around here, but I've whittled it down to the ones that are so good you don't care how many calories are involved."

Alison glanced at the dividers that had been labeled with Day-Glo tabs. It was impossible not to respond to Grace's enthusiasm. "Do you have recommendations for the mundane things too, like grocery stores?"

"In the back." Grace flipped the pages to the final tab. "It's in the section called 'Necessities.' You'll find things like pharmacies and cleaners, and there's a couple of camera stores too. I included some maps to the best organic farmers' markets. At least the ones my mom thinks are the best."

"I'm impressed." Alison smiled. "I don't know how to thank you for all the work you've done."

"It was fun." Grace stood. "Let me know if there's anything else I can do. Or if there's anything else you need."

"I can't think of anything. But if I do, I'll call you."

Grace had already made Alison's time at the beach house infinitely easier than if she'd had to discover all these places for herself. Then it hit her. She'd spent the morning trying to arrange a rental car for Christopher and had come away from every agency, even one that was the equivalent of Rent-A-Wreck, not only frustrated but empty-handed. She either had to get creative or spend the next thirty days wearing a chauffeur's hat.

"You wouldn't know a good used-car dealer by any chance?" Alison asked.

"Sorry, no. But my dad might know someone. He and my mom are recycle fanatics and bargain hunters. They hardly ever buy anything new. I'll call him and let you know what he says."

She headed for the door, then stopped and turned back. "I almost forgot—if you or your husband are into surfing or would like to hire a boat for the day, I have a lot of that kind of information that I didn't include in the folder. I also have a book with maps of hiking trails I'd be happy to loan you."

There it was—the husband thing. It was a natural mistake, but one that Alison always dreaded. She took a deep breath—might as well get it over with.

"I'm a widow." Even after more than a dozen years, her throat still tightened a little saying the words, knowing the question that would inevitably follow. "The other Kirkpatrick you were told to expect is my grandson, Christopher. He'll be here in a few days."

Before Grace had a chance to say any of the usual platitudes, Alison immediately went back to her need to find a car. "Whatever you can come up with that would interest an almost eighteen-year-old boy would be appreciated. I'd love to entice him away from the horse stables he's come here to visit. At least for a few days."

"Horse stables?"

"He competes in dressage. His favorite horse went lame a couple of months ago, and he hasn't been able to find one to take her place. His coach heard about a couple of horses out here that were considered promising and capable of going to the next level with Christopher. So here we are. Well, here I am. Christopher had a show he had to attend before he could join me."

"So you're not actually here on vacation?" Grace asked. "You came all this way to look at a horse?"

"That's why Christopher is coming. I'm here to keep him company." If Alison were being completely honest, she would admit that her "company" explanation wasn't as altruistic as it sounded. She'd jumped at the chance to spend what would probably be her last full summer with her grandson. Once he started college, his life and the demands on his time, even the focus of his thoughts and energy, would change. In her heart she knew he would always think of her as his second mother. But he'd been sitting on the end of the branch strengthening his wings in mock flight for a long time now. He was ready for his first journey. Solo.

Grace shook her head. "I knew there were places around here where they raised horses, but I had no idea the horses were anything special. I need to pay more attention. Horses like that must be—never mind. It's none of my business."

"Expensive?"

"It really is none of my business. It's like I have a loose wire between my brain and mouth sometimes, and there's a disconnect where it's supposed to tell me about things like boundaries. My mom has these hand signals she gives me when I'm headed in that direction."

Unconsciously, Alison ran her thumb over the base of her ring finger, as always, feeling a quick jolt of surprise to find it bare. "I'm wired the same way. I can't tell you how many times I've said something at a dinner party that turned a lively conversation into dead silence." She gave Grace a smile accompanied by a what-can-you-do shrug.

"I honestly don't know what price level Christopher's coach had in mind when he sent him out here. I leave that sort of thing to him and his mother. What I do know is that dressage horses are a little like cars—they go from the equivalent of a Smart car all the way up to a custom-made Bugatti. Maybe when Christopher gets here he can explain to both of us why he had to come all the way to California to find a horse when there are trainers up and down the Atlantic coast with rink-ready animals for sale."

"I'd like that. What I know about horses you could put in a tweet and have a hundred and forty characters left." Grace stopped to clear a eucalyptus leaf from the porch with her foot. "I almost forgot—the gardener comes on Thursday," she said. "He usually shows up right after lunch. And the water runs on Tuesday and Saturday at four o'clock in the morning. I've never been in the house when the sprinkler is running, so I don't know how loud it is. If that's too early, I can have my dad make it later. But not after ten. The city has rules about when you can water."

"I'm sure it will be fine." Grace's intense attention to detail reminded Alison of what it was like to revel in the trust and responsibility of a first job.

Grace gave a quick wave and headed down the moss-covered brick pathway through the flower garden and out the gate. Alison watched her leave, mentally noting how she seemed to glide rather than walk the short distance between their houses.

On impulse, Alison followed the same brick walkway Grace had taken, opened the gate, and turned left to go down the wooden stairs to the beach. With the exception of a scattering of sunbathers, the beach was nearly deserted. They, too, would undoubtedly disappear if the fog sitting offshore rolled in.

The half-mile-wide cove was bordered on each side by rocky outcroppings, lending to the feeling of isolation. A half dozen logs washed in by past storms lay high on the beach, mute testimony to the power of the waves that had deposited them.

Despite the presence of other cottages ringing the cliff and another set of stairs a couple of hundred yards to her right, she sensed that this was a beach bypassed by most tourists, one where she could leave footprints that wouldn't be disturbed until the next high tide played eraser to a constantly transformed shore.

She left her sandals at the base of the boulder-reinforced embankment, then headed for the shoreline.

A salt-laden breeze tousled her pixie-cut hair, a style she'd only lately adopted and was still getting used to. Christopher said her new look "rocked," and Nora insisted she looked fifteen years younger.

How she wished that were true. How differently she would live her life if she had those last fifteen years to do over. Especially the first two when Dennis and Peter were still alive—when she was still a wife and mother, in addition to a mother-in-law and grandmother. She would make love more often—spontaneously and with abandon. The bedroom would be secondary to a secluded forest clearing, or the pool house at a friend's party, or in Dennis's office behind a locked door and in front of a window that overlooked the Statue of Liberty. She wouldn't stay home from a quick trip to London because she had a board meeting at the museum. Weekends with the family would be sacrosanct.

But without knowing what was going to happen, would she live those years any differently? Were there days or weeks or months she would change?

And what if she had known what was ahead? Could she have borne relinquishing even one day knowing it meant their time together was ticking away like some macabre clock? Could she have maintained her sanity?

Better that it happened the way it did. Impossibly naive in contentment one minute, devastated the next.

She came to the ocean's edge and stopped to let a wave wash over her feet. It was cold. No wonder there were so few people in the water. She thought about the current that had brought the frigid water to sunny California, how it had swept past glaciers and picked up calved ice filled with microscopic nutrients. It was the beginning of a food chain that ended with the largest mammal on earth, the blue whale.

Looking past the obvious was a gift Dennis had given her. He'd been one of those rainbows-are-your-reward-for-going-through-the-rain kind of guys who remembered a hike not by how long or rigorous it had been, but by what he had seen. He took as much pleasure watching a hummingbird gather spiderwebs for her nest as he did witnessing a female lion introduce her cubs to the pride for the first time.

She'd met him her first year of college and hadn't understood then any more than she understood now what he'd seen in her. She was his complete opposite, caught up in fashion and parties and determined that her college years would be the best of her life. Dennis saw college as a means to an end and carried more units in a semester than she did in an entire year. Working the same shift at the campus bookstore served as their introduction. A shared, off-kilter sense of humor led to a first date.

When she fell, she fell hard, waking up one morning and realizing she didn't want to be anywhere he wasn't. Their love never followed the prescribed ups and downs for such things. There wasn't a day she longed for a break or a day she didn't miss him when he went home to see his parents.

When he died, she immediately understood what she'd lost. It was the irony of losing Peter too that almost destroyed her. Dennis had gone to work early that day, September 11, 2001, to welcome the firm's newest employee—his son, his only child, his beloved Peter.

She would not have survived the loss had it not been for Christopher and his mother, Nora. The depth of their need provided the lifeline to her sanity.

Alison hugged herself as she gazed at the horizon, her vision blurred by unbidden, achingly familiar tears. It had been months since she'd had one of her private meltdowns. She knew what was happening now, and why, and allowed herself these brief, self-indulgent moments, though she was careful not to do so around Nora or Christopher.

She shifted her gaze to a line of pelicans skimming the water and heading north, fleetingly indulging the fantasy of what it would be like to join them.

We're going to make it, Dennis. I'm not unscathed, but I'm able to see the beauty of a sunrise that you promised would be even better when I turned sixty.

Nora met someone, just when I was beginning to think she would never get over losing Peter. His name is James Howard Duggan III. Luckily, he's not as stuffy as his name, and he adores Nora. He arrived too late to be a father to Christopher, but they've managed to become friends, and I think he will be a good grandfather, if and when the time comes.

What I'd hoped for and feared at the same time happened six months after they met. Nora and James were married in a small, private ceremony at his summer home on the coast of Maine. I cried, but you would have been proud of me. I had no trouble convincing everyone they were happy tears. And for the most part, they were.

I'll miss my time with Nora. Once we got past that really rough period, the six months after you and Peter died, she became more daughter to me than daughter-in law. Even though she's found the second love of her life, she's determined that nothing will change between us.

But how could it not?

Now I have to figure out how to keep her from feeling guilty when the inevitable happens and she becomes so busy that we go days instead of hours between phone calls. Guilt is the fertilizer that feeds resentment. I can't let that happen, no matter how much I miss her.

I could use some of your sage advice about now. Is there any way you could give me just a small sign that you're paying attention? Of course, you're going to have to tell me where to look for this sign. You know how obtuse I can be at times.

A sanderling chased a receding wave and came running back toward her with its prize, almost stepping on her foot. She inwardly smiled at its antics as she carefully moved out of the way.

One more thing—while you're helping me get through this stretch, could you figure out a way to keep Christopher frozen in time? Not forever. Just long enough for me to get used to losing him too.

Other than those first few weeks after you died, I've never been alone. Not once in fifty-nine years have I faced going home to a house that I know will never shelter anyone full-time but me. Would you mind adding that to the list of things I could use your help with?

Chapter 2

Alison stood on the sidewalk across the street from Tanner Motors in Monterey. It was the fifth used-car lot she'd visited that morning, and she was pretty much convinced she was on a fool's errand. The salespeople who had attached themselves to her the instant she entered each lot had wandered off as soon as she told them what she was after. Not only was no one interested in talking to her about a month-long lease, but two of the salesmen had actually laughed at her when she'd offered to buy a car outright—if they would put it in the contract that they would buy it back in thirty days.

She thought she'd handled everything that they'd need to make sure Christopher could use his New York driver's license in California, even making an appointment for him to get his nonresident minor certificate at the Department of Motor Vehicles within the required ten days.

But she hadn't expected the other stumbling blocks she'd run into, and if she didn't get them worked out, she was going to spend a good part of the next thirty days hauling Christopher around the countryside trying to entertain herself while he looked at horses—not exactly her idea of a great vacation, or Christopher's. She loved watching him compete and had never complained during all the years she'd sat in a lawn chair reading a book while he practiced, but she drew the line at the long, drawn-out process of testing and buying a new horse. And he drew the line at knowing she was sitting and waiting for him everywhere he went. He needed his space, and luckily she'd learned to give it to him. It had kept their relationship going despite the forty-plus years that separated them.

Just the thought of spending her days going from trainer to trainer was enough to goad her to get moving to find him a car. She checked for traffic and crossed the street, saying a quick prayer that jaywalking tickets weren't a primary revenue source in Monterey.

While Tanner Motors had the same basic setup as every other used-car lot she'd visited that day—red, white, and blue bunting flapping in the breeze, the price of the car or an upgraded feature written on the windshields, the "Hot Deal of the Day" sitting on a rotating raised platform—one thing was missing: a salesman.

With that in mind, she took a deep breath and entered the dealer's office, a converted modular home tastefully decorated in earth tones and early Spanish artwork.

A man just shy of six feet tall, with salt-and-pepper hair and a pair of reading glasses perched on the end of his nose, smiled as he pushed his chair back from his desk and rose to greet her. "Good morning," he said as if he sincerely believed it was. "How can I help you?"

"I'd like to buy a car," she said.

"Hopefully, I can help you with that." He dropped his glasses on his desk and held out his hand. "Kyle Tanner," he said. "Owner, chief salesman, and part-time financial officer of this fine establishment." It was said with an appealing twinkle in his eyes.

She put her hand in his, expecting a softness that wasn't there. Somewhere, at some time, Kyle Tanner had led another life that had nothing to do with sitting behind a desk. "Alison Kirkpatrick," she replied.

"How about we start with what kind of car you have in mind."

"Something for my grandson."

"A gift?"

"Not exactly. We're renting a house in this area for the next four weeks and won't be going in the same direction most days. It would be nice to have two cars." She considered his question again. "Does it matter?"

"Only in giving me an idea whether you're looking for a car that would look good with a big bow sitting on the hood or one that will keep money in his wallet when he pulls out of the gas station."

The phone rang. He looked to see who it was and let it go through to voice mail. "I'm going to assume you've already tried the standard rental route and there was a problem?"

"It's his age. He won't turn eighteen until August."

"And no one will rent to someone that young," he said, nodding. "Why don't we start by taking a look at what's on the lot. That way I can get an idea of what you think would appeal to your grandson."

She followed him out the door. "I should tell you up front that I'd like to work something out that you'll buy the car back thirty days from now—at a fair profit for you, of course, plus something for your trouble."

"I guess that would depend on the car you choose. Pick one of the losers I've been trying to move for six months and it's going to be pretty hard to talk me into allowing it back on the lot." He softened the words with a chuckle. "I seem to wind up with a disproportionate number of vehicles with only a couple of years left in them. If you want to sell me a used car, attach a sad story to it and I'll fall for it every time. I keep the better ones around for people who need cheap transportation. The others I junk."

"Then I'll try to pick one that you're sorry to see leave."

He stopped beside a Subaru. "Is this going to be your grandson's first car?"

"Yes."

"Is he more the athletic or academic type?"

"Both, actually. But I really don't care what we get as long as it's reliable. It's a thirty-day romance, not a marriage."

"What's his sport?"

"Dressage." The only sport where the contestants competed in top hat and tails.

"Ah, that must mean he's come to California looking for a new horse?"

"Yes," she answered, surprised that he knew enough to ask. "Judging by the scores he received before his horse was out of commission, his trainer thinks Christopher should move to the next level. That requires a horse capable of moving up with him."

"Word is that there are a couple of exceptional Dutch and German warmbloods at Harden Stables. I imagine they're on his list?"

She wasn't sure whether they were or not. Christopher did most of his own research and negotiating using his trainer for advice when he felt he'd gotten in over his head. She limited her involvement to enthusiastic spectator. "You're a rider?"

He shook his head. "Just a longtime friend to someone who is. He and my daughter were engaged, but it didn't work out. I think she got tired of coming in second place to a horse."

"I've seen it happen," she said.

Alison stopped to look at a metallic blue 2006 Mustang convertible. It was what Dennis would have called a muscle car, owned by someone who considered his transportation an extension of his personality. She tried to picture Christopher behind the wheel and couldn't. He wasn't the muscle car type. She started to move on when it hit her that maybe it was time her grandson tried something new. "How much is this one?"

"Twenty."

"*Thousand?*"

"This isn't a six-month car. It has less than twelve thousand miles on the odometer, and according to the mechanic at the shop where I have everything checked, it's not only show-room quality, it's as sound as a twenty-dollar gold piece. I could ask another three or four grand, and it would still be gone by the end of the week."

"If you were going to buy this for your grandson—"

"I wouldn't."

She frowned. "Why not?"

"It's too much car for a seventeen-year-old. Especially a first car."

She peered through the window at the interior. It looked brand-new. "He's very responsible."

"I have no doubt. Kids who do well in school and ride dressage rarely have enough time to get into trouble." He pulled a yellow cloth out of his back pocket and used it to wipe a set of fingerprints off the hood. "Give that same kid a car that pouts if it's driven under seventy and thirty days with little to do but run around looking for something to do, and you're just asking for trouble."

"Christopher isn't like that," she insisted.

Kyle laughed. "*Every* guy is like that. It's in our genetic makeup, the same way it's in the genetic makeup of preteen girls to be attracted to Justin Bieber. Neither one makes sense, at least not to me, but there you have it."

She was tempted to tell him that even as a young girl she'd never been drawn to the "pretty" Bieber type, that it was the raw sexuality of Bruce Springsteen that made her toes curl, but that was the kind of conversation you had with longtime girlfriends, not a man you'd just met. "Okay, you have my attention. What kind of car would you recommend?"

He thought a minute. "How involved is he in the care of his horse?"

"If he could, he would spend all day every day at the stables." If it didn't come across sounding so melodramatic, and if they hadn't just met, she would have told him the truth—riding had saved Christopher's life.

After his father and grandfather died, he'd pulled deeper and deeper into himself until there was nothing left of the little boy who had charmed jaded cab drivers in Manhattan as easily as he'd captivated the men and women who worked in Dennis's office. Struggling with their own grief, Alison and Nora did what they could to help Christopher, including sessions with the top child psychiatrist and grief counselor in Manhattan. Nothing stopped his decline.

Finally, unable to fill her own void, Nora went back to work, leaving Christopher's day-to-day care to Alison. He was eight, and on the verge of being lost to them forever, when Alison was invited to spend a week at a friend's house in Dutchess County, near Rhinebeck.

There, Christopher met Ransom, a black-and-white tobiano pinto pony rescued from a roadside petting zoo. Too proud and too stubborn to be trained with a whip, Ransom had been neglected, then starved, and finally abandoned to die in his stall. The magic moment between Christopher and Ransom had happened as gently as a fall leaf floats through the air.

Ransom had crossed the paddock, stopped in front of Christopher, and nudged his hand. Christopher straightened his fingers and offered his apple, smiling for the first time in months when Ransom worked his muzzle to move the apple into his mouth.

Somehow Ransom had recognized a kindred spirit in Christopher and was enticed to open his heart one more time. They formed what would become a lifelong bond at that first meeting. Before she and Christopher were headed back to the city at the end of the week, Alison had found and put a deposit on a neighboring horse property. At the time, she thought of it as a retreat from the city, a place where she and Christopher and Nora could escape old memories and create new ones, if only on weekends.

She'd dipped into an account she hadn't touched since Dennis died to pay for the property and house and full-time caretaker. To her surprise, she discovered that she liked seeing and experiencing an investment far more than looking at numbers on an investment account.

Not for a moment had she considered the possibility that the house would become a home for her and Christopher or that she would slip into the role of surrogate mother when Nora started traveling again and found her own escape in fourteen-hour workdays.

Kyle brought her back to the present when he pointed to the back of the lot. "I have something I've been saving for the right buyer."

She followed him to a multi-stall garage, where he pressed a coded keypad. The door closest to them opened. Inside, Kyle proudly explained, was a 1949 Chevy five-window truck, a classic for a collector, especially one itching to do the minor restoration work remaining that would make it his own.

Alison managed to hide her disappointment as she walked around the truck, noting the small dings and scratches and chipped paint that went with a vehicle that was over sixty years old. Why would he offer her something like this? "A little on the tired side, wouldn't you say?"

"Wait for this." He popped the hood and stood back with a broad grin. The engine compartment and motor looked brand-new. "It belonged to a friend of mine who had to liquidate for a divorce settlement. He worked on it frame off, personally cleaning, replacing, or restoring every piece. He was getting ready to send it out for paint, but put it back together to sell. Everything's done but the body."

So the truck wasn't a loser he was trying to get rid of. "I'm not sure why you think Christopher would be attracted to something like this," she said, sincerely puzzled. "I've never heard him express interest in anything older than six months—not clothes or music or movies. He's like his friends—waiting for what's next, not looking back to what was. This truck is almost as old as I am."

"That's not possible."

"What part?" she asked, a smile playing at the corner of her mouth.

"You can't be over fifty."

Sincere, or part of the sales pitch? "I'm sixty. Or at least I will be in a couple of months."

"There are half a dozen things I could say to that, but let's just leave it where I started. You don't look a day over fifty."

Alison laughed. "I remember when I thought fifty was ancient." Focusing on the truck again, she said, "I don't know . . ."

Kyle ran his hand over his chin. "I'll tell you what I'll do. You show him the truck, and if he can't see past the cosmetic, bring it back and we'll get him in something he likes better."

"Just not the Mustang," she said, offering him a conspiratorial smile. She looked inside the cab. Like the engine, it was the product of loving hands. "All he really needs is something that will get him from point A to point B for the month we're here."

She spoiled Christopher. He was as aware of it as she was, and they both knew why. He tolerated it the way he tolerated his work-addicted mother's need to keep busy and his own need to follow in his father's footsteps, from the sports teams he'd championed to the college he would attend in the fall. In a perverse way, even the riding was a result of his father's influence. Christopher had turned to the ring as an escape from a world where he had no control.

"I'll make this as painless as possible," Kyle said on the way back to the office.

Before going inside, he took a minute to wave to a middle-aged couple wandering around the lot. "Most of the new ones are on the back row," he called to them. "Let me know if you have any questions. If you want to take one of them out for a spin, you know where the keys are."

They returned his wave and said they knew where to find him.

"Kind of high-pressure, don't you think?" Alison teased.

Kyle indicated the chair on the opposite side of his desk. "They're at the planning stage right now."

She sat and waited for him. "Which means?"

"Deciding what kind of car they're going to buy when Fred is employed again. They come in every couple of weeks to see what's new. If there's anything that appeals to them, I give them the keys and they take it out for a test drive. It's a way to kill an afternoon."

The kindness of the simple gesture touched Alison. She was going to have to reconsider her prejudices about used-car salesmen. "That's incredibly generous, considering there's no chance for a sale."

"I've never given anything that hasn't come back tenfold."

Suddenly, and with inexplicable reasoning, Alison hoped Christopher didn't like the truck. It was the only legitimate reason she could come up with to see Kyle Tanner again before the end of her thirty days in California. "So, how are we going to do this?"

"I'm going to give you the keys, and you're going to show the truck to—?"

"Christopher."

"—to Christopher, and if he likes it you're going to come back and put down whatever mutually agreed-upon deposit we come up with to cover one month's use. I can't see any reason to do all the paperwork for a sale and then have to redo it at the end of the month."

She liked his plan. She especially liked knowing she would see him again before she left at the end of the month.

Now, what to do with the other twenty-five days.

Chapter 3

Alison saw Kyle a lot sooner than they'd arranged. The plan had been for him to follow her to the beach house, driving the truck while she drove the rental car, and then she would take him back to the car lot—a minimum of three hours out of his day. When he suggested she use the truck so that she could become familiar with any of its idiosyncrasies, she did fine right up to the point of putting the key in the ignition and reaching for the shift.

A quick glance at the floorboard where there were three pedals instead of the familiar two was like dropping a lead weight in the pit of her stomach. Christopher's plane arrived in six hours, and she'd hoped to meet him with a grand flourish of implied independence when she handed over the keys to his own vehicle. "I haven't driven a stick shift since I was a kid," she said, fighting to keep the disappointment from her voice.

"It will come back. It's like—"

She turned to face him. "Don't you dare say it's like riding a bicycle. See this?" She pointed to her cheek. "Under all this makeup is a very ugly scar that I got when my husband convinced me I could go on a sunrise bicycle ride down Haleakala Volcano in Hawaii. He said it didn't matter that I hadn't ridden in years, it would all come back."

"Then I guess we better get started with a crash refresher course." He tried not to laugh, but failed. "Nothing implied by the 'crash' part." He scratched his chin and ran his hand across his face. "I should have thought to ask—what are the chances Christopher knows how to drive a stick shift? I don't want you stuck with a truck no one can operate."

"I don't know for sure, but I have a feeling they're pretty good. He helps out at a neighbor's farm, and a lot of their equipment is really old."

"Then for the moment we'll concentrate on getting you comfortable driving one again."

"You don't have to do this. I can drive the car and make a fool of myself when I'm alone. Besides, don't you have work to do?"

"When I'm the only one here, I have a sign I put in the window telling people to call my cell if they need something. Otherwise, they can wait for one of my salespeople to show up. I call someone before I leave," he explained. "It's one of the perks of owning the place."

Still, Alison protested. "There's a beach parking lot not far from the house where I'm staying. I can practice there. And if I don't have the stick shift mastered by the time I'm supposed to pick up Christopher, I'll take the car and work on learning how to keep from dropping the transmission later."

"Then let's get this show on the road."

Fifteen minutes later, and a couple of miles from the car lot on a reasonably wide country road, Alison hiked herself up and settled in the driver's seat, waited for Kyle to get settled in the passenger seat, took a deep, determined breath, and turned the key. The engine started instantly, purring like a cat curling up in its own patch of sunlight. She looked at Kyle. "So far, so good."

Initially, she killed the engine whenever she tried to stop on a hill. Then she remembered how to play the clutch. The transmission survived going from first to third several times, and she and Kyle survived almost jamming their heads into the windshield before she got the feel of the sensitive brakes. At the end of her lesson, she felt a little like Rocky Balboa after he'd climbed the steps of the Philadelphia Museum of Art. She actually experienced a twinge of regret when Kyle announced there was nothing more he could teach her.

She dropped Kyle back at the dealership, and because she still had time before she had to leave for San Jose and the airport, on impulse she stopped by an office supply store where she bought a sheet of lime-green poster board and a set of Day-Glo felt-tip pens. Sitting in the car in the short-term parking lot at the airport, she made a sign with Christopher's name on it, ignoring the mental warning that what she was doing might embarrass him. He needed to lighten up a little too.

Christopher burst out laughing when he saw his grandmother standing behind a huge sign with his name on it. People looked around for the pseudo-celebrity and quickly realized the sign was a joke. He went to her to give her a hug.

"Been hitting the bottle, Grams?" he asked, putting his arm around her shoulders as he slipped the sign out of her hands and into a nearby trash can. She loved that he was demonstrative, his hugs coming as easily as his smiles.

She slid her arm around his waist and matched his steps as they headed to the luggage carousel. "How was the flight?"

"Okay, I guess. I slept most of the way." He'd been stuck in the center seat from New York to Denver between two preteen girls who flatly refused his offer to trade places so they could sit together. For the first half of the flight they were up and down, communicating with their parents who were several rows back; the second half they played the same Nickelodeon movie a minute apart on their iPads. With their headphones at maximum, sleep and his own headphones were the only escape from the echoed inanity.

"Have you talked to your mom today?"

It didn't matter how many times he told his grandmother that he was okay with his mother getting married again, she mentally hovered, looking for signs that he needed to talk about the changes in their lives. Maybe it was because she knew he still hadn't connected with James in any meaningful way. How could he? They had nothing in common except his mom. Bottom line, despite his mother's attempts to find ways for them to "bond," he didn't know James well enough to like or dislike him.

What he did know was that he was tired of being the center of his mother's and grandmother's world. He was a month and a half shy of eighteen, and two months away from starting his first year at Penn State.

College was supposed to be his escape. He'd applied for and been accepted into schools as diverse as Middlebury, Bowdoin, and Carleton. On a lark, he'd even applied to Harvey Mudd, one of the Claremont Colleges, knowing full well there was no way his mother would agree to his going there, no matter how high the school ranked or how difficult it was to get into. Harvey Mudd was in California, all the way across the country.

In the end he had settled on his father's alma mater, Penn State, not only to follow in his father's footsteps, but because he knew it would please his mother and grandmother. At least Penn State had a great equestrian program.

"She left a couple of messages on voice mail," he said. "I was going to call her back when we landed in Denver, but forgot." He didn't have to look at his grandmother to know she wasn't happy. "I'll do it in the car."

"It's three o'clock in the morning in Rome," she gently chided.

"I'll leave a message. She just wants to know that I got here all right." He spotted his duffle bag and lifted it off the conveyor belt. "Did my saddle arrive?"

"It came yesterday. The outside of the box was a little battered, so I checked inside. It was fine. So was your helmet."

"What about the box with my riding clothes and tack?"

"The box looked like the pilot had hand-carried it."

"Great." He shouldered his bag and turned to leave.

"You only brought one suitcase?"

"An extra pair of jeans and a couple of shirts—what else do I need?"

"Socks and underwear?"

"We're in California, Grams. They don't bother with things like that out here."

"I hate to burst your bubble, but not everyone in Santa Cruz is chasing a wave."

He pulled her to him and planted a kiss on the top of her head. "Are you shrinking?"

"Could it be you're growing again?"

"Impossible. Didn't Dad reach his full height by the time he turned sixteen? How could I possibly be different?" She covered it well, but he could see the quick flash of pain his flippant remark had created.

"You're not a carbon copy of your father," she said, at the same time offering him a sad smile.

"Since when?"

She put her hand against his chest. "Let's not do this—okay?"

"Sorry." Because it was the millionth time he'd apologized for this kind of remark, or something similar, didn't mean it wasn't sincere. The older he got, the more he felt trapped in a box without even a pinhole of light to show him the way out. His grandmother was the only person who seemed to understand, the one person who would forgive and forget his outbursts.

"I have a surprise for you," she said, doing what she always did when he backed himself into a corner, changing the conversation.

"First, I have one for you." He took her in his arms again and gave her a long, intense hug. "I really am sorry. I promise to work on my attitude and not screw up this vacation for you."

She touched his cheek. "It's okay. I remember how hard it is to be a teenager."

"Really?"

She gave him a questioning look.

"I mean it's been soooo long."

She couldn't help but laugh.

Almost at the end of the row in the parking lot, Christopher looked around, confused. "Where are we headed?"

As Alison pointed at the truck she realized there was no way he could see anything but the chrome bumper and a small portion of the back curve of the fender.

"You rented a *Hummer*?"

"Not even close." But something almost as bizarre, she abruptly realized. "Look behind it."

He moved closer. "The Jeep?"

She shook her head, not sure if he was teasing her or was too incredulous to even consider the truck a possibility. "Look again."

Puzzled, he stared at the truck, at her, and then at the truck again. What started as a low chuckle ended with a laugh so deep and uninhibited that he had tears in his eyes before he stopped. "Rent-a-Wreck, I assume?" he asked, wiping his eyes with the tail of his T-shirt. "They saw you coming, Grams."

"You don't like it?"

"You're serious?" When she nodded, he added, "What were you thinking?"

"That I'm tired of being predictable," she said with stark honesty. "So it needs a paint job. Use your imagination. Picture it candy apple red."

He tossed his bag in the back and took his time circling the vehicle, examining everything from the whitewall tires to the rims to the windshield wipers to the beautifully restored wooden bed. He held out his hand, and she gave him the keys. "Okay, so I can see the potential," he acknowledged. "And since you got here in one piece, I'm assuming it will hit freeway speed without falling apart."

"To be honest, I was a little surprised at how well it drives."

He cocked an eyebrow at her.

"It does," she insisted. He unlocked the passenger door and waited for her to climb inside. "You'll see."

She snapped the seat belt closed and adjusted the length while she waited for him to get in the other side. She used to be able to read his moods as easily as she read the morning paper. Now she was never sure about his moods, or about him. She remembered the summer before she left for college as one of the most exciting times in her life, being filled with a mixture of anticipation and angst and the sweetly melancholy knowledge that nothing would ever be the same. Half the time she bristled at still being treated like a child, the other half she spent terrified of being on her own.

As far as she could tell, Christopher took it all in stride—with the exception of his beloved horse, Josi, turning up lame just before a qualifying competition that last May. When none of their regular vets could find a reason for the lameness, Christopher had trailered Josi to Tufts University Veterinary School in Massachusetts. The vets at Tufts performed a spiral CT scan that revealed a cyst in the coffin bone. The treatment involved injecting stem cells grown from Josi's own bone marrow. While everyone told Christopher the prognosis was good for a full recovery, he needed another horse while he waited.

Christopher had ridden borrowed horses for the next two competitions, and his scores were the lowest they'd ever been. After several failed attempts to find a horse on the East Coast he felt drawn to the way he'd been to Josi, his trainer had tracked down a couple of promising leads in California.

Christopher settled into the driver's seat and stared at the dashboard. "Sweet," he said softly.

A smile played at the corners of Alison's mouth. "Wait until you see the house."

Chapter 4

"Sweet," Christopher said for the second time that day. Now it was in reaction to the view outside the sliding-glass door in the living room. "I could live here."

"I've been on the beach every morning since I arrived," Alison said. "You know your father had a real connection to the ocean too. He even insisted that when he retired he was—" She caught the look in Christopher's eyes, and her heart sank at her thoughtlessness.

"I'm sorry." She touched his shoulder. "I really am trying to do better." Her voice a gentle plea, she added, "Don't give up on me."

He shrugged, dislodging her hand either by accident or on purpose. "It's no big deal."

But it was. Enough so that he'd walked out of his own graduation party three weeks ago when she'd made the seemingly innocent comment about how much he looked like his father in his cap and gown.

With foolish certainty that she was doing the right thing, almost from the moment Christopher's father and grandfather died, Alison set out to do everything she could to ensure they wouldn't be forgotten. She talked about Christopher's father, Peter, and his grandfather, Dennis, as if they were about to walk through the door at any moment. Every day, sometimes every hour, she found something about them to integrate into the conversation, from their favorite books and movies to their favorite food. Reliving memories of birthdays and Christmases and vacations became second nature to her. She even used the weather—Peter loved rain, Dennis hated fog. Nothing was off-limits.

Eventually this behavior became her unconscious pattern, a quilt she cut and sewed and put together as easily as she breathed.

"You said there were bikes in the garage?"

"Yes."

"And we can use them?"

"Yes."

"Mind if I take off for a while?"

A half dozen warnings darted through her mind like bees at a hummingbird feeder. She'd planned to have him take her to Monterey to pick up her car, but it could wait until after dinner. Kyle had purposely parked it at the back of the lot in case she got tied up and couldn't get back earlier.

"Of course not," she managed.

He grinned. "Good job, Grams—not one 'be careful' or 'wear your helmet' or 'be sure to take a water bottle.' "

He'd started calling her "Grams" six months ago instead of the more formal "Grandmother" he'd used all his life. She was getting used to it, but that didn't mean she liked it. "I've got my finger in the dam. You better get out of here before it breaks and all my tired clichés start rushing out."

He leaned over and kissed her cheek. "Would it help if I told you I'll be careful and that I'll turn on my phone in case you need to reach me?"

"Immensely."

Before heading to the garage, Christopher dropped his duffle bag in the bedroom and changed into an old pair of shorts and a faded T-shirt with ROCK THE VOTE printed on it.

His grandmother had texted him a dozen pictures of the house and the beach, but none had done them justice. There were views of the ocean from every room at the back of the house. For a kid who'd lived his first eight years in New York and the next nine in the middle of farm country north of the city, he'd never understood why being near the ocean felt like coming home.

He went to the window and stared out, seeing up close what he'd caught glimpses of from the plane as it circled in a holding pattern, waiting its turn to land. The shore here wasn't like Long Island, where he and his mother and grandmother had spent at least part of their summers every year in a rental house. This was more like the part of Maine where James had his summer home, where he and Christopher's mother had been married.

From what Christopher had been able to glimpse on the ride to the beach house from the airport, the shoreline was covered with rocks, with an occasional narrow ribbon of sand—a long way from the Hollywood version of California.

This was the first place he'd gone where there would be no stories of his father or grandfather. Virgin territory. According to his mother, neither of them had ever spent any time on the West Coast. That gave him at least three states where he could be himself, where he could find the Christopher who was nothing like his father or grandfather. Where he could explore and discover the bits and pieces of himself hidden behind the need his mother and grandmother had to see the men they loved reflected back at them whenever they looked at Christopher.

The doubt that kept him awake at night was the scary possibility of discovering there wasn't anything to find.

Expecting bikes rescued from a secondhand store, Christopher was impressed when he discovered two brand-new Novaras, the same bike he used at home. A cupboard over the bikes held an assortment of helmets, and a note tacked to the cupboard door warned that helmets were mandatory in California.

Starting out slow in order to take in his surroundings, Christopher stopped at an overlook and sent a text to Alison telling her that he was heading south to do a little exploring and would be back before dark.

"Dinner?" she answered. "I could go to the store and pick up anything you'd like. Is there something you've been craving?"

"Sandwich is good."

"I have a book that says there's a bike trail that runs along the shoreline. Great views. Should b amazing. Have fun."

"Already am."

"It's been too quiet. I'm really glad u r here. Any plans for tomorrow besides taking me to Monterey to get my car?"

"Me too. Talk about plans L8R."

"Yes. Of course. You need to pay attention to traffic. Lots of people on bikes around here, but lots of tourists who don't pay attention too. Pls be careful."

"K."

"Bye."

Knowing she would wait for a response that none of his friends would expect, he texted: "B4N."

It had taken him six months to get her to use her iPhone for something other than making calls, and another six months to get her to give Angry Birds a rest and send a text. She'd taken to it faster than he'd expected, but he still had a ways to go in teaching her the benefits of brevity.

The traffic light turned red. He turned right and three blocks later was at the ocean. Right away he spotted the trail his grandmother had told him about that ran along the top of the cliff. This time he turned left and a couple of miles later wound up in a large parking lot filled with SUVs, vans, and cars with racks on their roofs. Half had surfboards being loaded or unloaded by people in various stages of putting on or taking off wet suits. A quick look at the shoreline confirmed that the other half were in the water.

Christopher threaded his way through the gathering, looking for a place where he could lock the bike and watch the action. Here was the sand and surf he'd anticipated. And it was everything he'd hoped it would be.

For him, this was the California of his dreams. He had no trouble ignoring the Hollywood scene or the cities that had songs written about them. He could even take a pass on Yosemite and the other parks that drew bumper-to-bumper tourists. And it wasn't as if he'd never seen an ocean.

What he'd imagined when he found out he was going to California was the freedom to wear his hair long or grow a beard or bus tables at a seaside restaurant where everyone understood it was more important to hit the waves when the surf was up than it was to clear dishes.

If he was ever consumed by any real ambition other than riding, he wanted it to be lit by a fire of his own making. He didn't give a damn about controlling the money in the half dozen investment accounts that would come to him when he turned twenty-five. It wasn't his money. He hadn't earned it. And yet he was going to spend the next five years learning how to make that money grow even faster than it already had—and the rest of his life doing the same thing for others.

It didn't matter whether it was bars of gold or an elephant sitting on his chest, the result was the same. Suffocation.

"Hey, just like my friend's. What do you think?"

Christopher looked up to see a kid with a wet suit unzipped to his waist checking out the bike.

"It's okay," he said, high praise in his circle of friends.

The kid was a walking, talking California advertisement—the kind Christopher had pictured when he thought about what it would be like to grow up out here. He had sun-streaked blond hair that hung below his shoulders, a surfboard tucked under his arm, and a look that said his dream was to ride the biggest badass waves on every continent that had them.

"I have a friend who's selling his," he said, "but I think he wants too much for it."

"Wish I could help, but as long as it gets me where I want to go, I'm satisfied."

"Yeah, that's all I'm looking for too."

"What's it like out there?" Christopher asked.

"Mostly ankle-snappers, but you take what you can get."

"No—I mean, what's it feel like?"

He studied Christopher for several seconds. "I wouldn't have picked you for one of the summer people."

Christopher decided it was a compliment—of sorts. "Thanks. I guess."

"It feels like I'm able to take a deep breath for the first time in months. A little like fresh powder in backcountry. And a whole lot like being with my own people again. But you have to understand, I spent the last nine months on a campus filled with people who think if you're not batting or throwing or kicking a ball, it's not a sport."

"Where back east?"

"MIT. Stanford was my first choice, but MIT was my dad's." He grinned. "He said he thought I should see what another part of the country was like. He was worried about me cutting classes whenever the surf was up. My mom was terrified I was going to dump school entirely and work the waves at Ghost Tree and Cortes Bank until I got good enough to be invited to Maverick's."

"Were they right?" Christopher knew Maverick's was a premier, invitation-only surfing competition up the coast from Santa Cruz, and he assumed the others were places with waves big enough to give surfers a chance to make a name for themselves.

"Yeah, probably. I'm going to give it another year, and if I still haven't found anything that makes me want to stay, I'm going to transfer to Caltech. Cost's about the same, and if this is supposed to be such a great time in my life, seems to me I should at least like where I'm going to school." He picked up his board. "Gotta go. My friend's loading up."

"Take it easy," Christopher called after him.

"You too."

"Thanks."

Christopher went back to studying the surfers, ending up with far more questions than answers. What determined how far they paddled out? How did they know which wave to catch? At what point did they leave the wave? And why did some surfers face right and others left?

It wasn't long—or at least it didn't seem like a long time—before there were only a handful of boards still on the water. Christopher turned back to the parking lot, saw that it was almost empty, and realized how late it was. He unlocked the bike and reluctantly headed back, reaching the house at the same time a van pulled into the driveway next door. A girl with incredibly long legs wearing flip-flops and short cutoff jeans came around the van and opened the cargo door. She reached inside for a bright yellow, three-fin surfboard.

She caught him staring and stopped what she was doing. "Hi. You must be Christopher."

Plainly Grams had been talking to the neighbors. "That's me."

She carefully leaned her board against the house and came toward him. "Didn't I see you at Manresa earlier?"

How could he have missed her? "Yeah, that was me too."

She stopped and stood with her feet slightly apart, her hands in the back pockets of her shorts. "So, do you surf?"

"Not much opportunity where I come from."

"Want to learn?"

He blinked in surprise. It was one thing to strike up a conversation with a guy at the beach, but having a girl who looked like she belonged on a magazine cover offer to teach him to surf was tantamount to being asked by Robert Ballard if he wanted to join him on a sub to check out the *Titanic*.

"Yeah, as a matter of fact I do," he said before he took the time to reason it out. "You know someone who gives lessons?" He didn't want to take anything for granted and wind up looking like an idiot if she hadn't been offering to teach him herself. She smiled, and his knees felt like someone had hit them from behind.

"Me?" When he didn't say anything, she added, "Unless you'd rather go through one of the shops.

I used to do freelance work for a couple of them and know which ones are the best."

"You're fine. I mean, sure, I'd like you to teach me."

"Great." She ran her fingers through her wind-blown hair, trying to control the strands that covered her face. "Now what?"

"First we'll have to get you fitted for a rental board and wet suit, and then we hit the beach."

"Just so I know up front, how much do you charge?" He choked on a groan when he realized how stupid he sounded. "Not that it matters. I just need to—"

"It's okay. I pay attention to things like that too. Tell you what. Why don't we trade. You can teach me how to ride a horse, and I'll teach you how to ride a wave. To keep things from getting complicated, you can arrange the horse stuff, and I'll take care of the board and wet suit."

"How did you know I'm into horses?" He shook his head. "Never mind. I can guess."

She laughed. "Your grandmother is really proud of you. I think it's great."

There were a hundred things he could say, but he settled on the one that counted. "You free tomorrow?"

"After one o'clock. I work at the nursery until then." He must have looked confused, because she added, "My dad grows orchids."

"Oh, that kind of nursery. I pictured you with a bunch of little kids." He loved that she was so easy to talk to. "Should I pick you up here? Or do you want to meet someplace?"

"How about Carpos? It's in Soquel. They make the world's best French fries and milk shakes. The hamburgers aren't bad either. My treat."

"Why?"

"Because I asked you. When you ask me, you can pay."

He nodded. If she was an example of what California girls were like, they were a whole lot different than the girls he knew in New York. "One o'clock. Harpos—"

"*Ca*rpos," she corrected him.

"Carpos," he repeated. "In Soquel."

"If you forget, call me. All my information is in the binder I gave your grandmother."

He wasn't even going to ask. "I guess it would be good to know who I'm going to give riding lessons to."

"Grace."

"Nice name."

"Thanks." She took a step backward. "Gotta go. I told my dad I'd fix dinner, and he's going to be home soon."

"See you tomorrow." He turned his bike toward the garage. It wasn't until he was sure there was no way he would be seen that he allowed the grin that had been building from the moment he'd seen Grace to transform his face.

Christopher found some rags in the garage and wiped down the bike before putting it away. The second he opened the door into the house and smelled his grandmother's spaghetti sauce, he realized how long it had been since he'd eaten. He headed for the kitchen.

"It smells awesome in here," he said in lieu of a greeting.

"I figured you would be hungry for more than a sandwich when you got back." Alison gave the pot a final stir and taste and put the wooden spoon on a plate. "How was your ride?"

"Great."

She leaned her hip into the counter. "Where did you go?"

"South—along the shore." Spotting a loaf of crusty bread, he broke off a piece and offered to share it with her.

Alison shook her head. "I'll wait for the garlic butter." She reached for her glass and took a sip of the red wine that had been left over from making the sauce. "I've been looking at a couple of maps of the area and thought we might do a little exploring tomorrow by car. I've always wanted to see the Big Sur area and thought the middle of the week might work out better than fighting the rest of the tourists on a weekend."

"How about the day after? I just made plans for tomorrow."

She tried, but couldn't hide her disappointment. "I thought you were going to take a couple of days off before you started making the rounds of the stables."

Christopher felt heat rise from his neck to his cheeks. He was like some friggin' flashing light whenever he was embarrassed about something. *Just like his dad. Or his grandfather. Or both. He never could remember how it went.*

"I met someone who's going to teach me to surf, and I'm going to teach her to ride."

Alison took another sip. "That should be fun."

Christopher laughed out loud. "You really need some lessons on subtlety, Grams." He broke off a second piece of bread. "But just because I'm a nice guy, I'll let you off the hook this time. She's not some hot surfing chick I picked up at the beach. She lives next door."

"Grace?" Alison smiled in relief. "I like her."

"Oh, so now it's okay that I'm bailing on you?"

"Give me a break," she said, refusing to respond to his baiting. "I could have asked to meet her parents."

"Which probably means you already have."

She gave him a sheepish look. "Just her father and sister. Her mother and younger brother are in Los Angeles for the month."

"Anything else I should know?"

"Not that I'm going to tell you. You'll have to find out for yourself." She picked up the spoon again. "Speaking of parents, you need to call your mother."

He glanced at the clock on the microwave. "It's five-thirty in the morning there. Besides, I thought we already had this conversation at the airport."

"That was before she called again when you were out. She's having a lot of trouble with jet lag, and there's not much to do there in the middle of the night. She said she was going to try to reach you on your cell. I take it she didn't."

Christopher took his phone out of his pocket. He checked the switch on the side of the phone. "I forgot to turn it on." There were two missed calls and seven missed texts. Both calls were from his mother. The texts were from friends.

"When you call, tell her that I've changed my mind about the pottery and that I'll text her tomorrow with a list of the pieces I want her to buy for me."

"And she's going to know what I'm talking about?"

"She found my pattern in a little shop in Deruta. It's a travel brochure kind of town almost exactly in the center of Italy. I've wanted to go there since your grandfather bought me my first ceramic bowl."

His grandmother had a tendency to give too much information, using a paragraph when a sentence would do.

"According to your mom, there are a couple of new pieces that are stunning. She's going to go back tomorrow to see if they'll let her take some pictures of the new releases to send me."

"Wow," he said with heavily feigned enthusiasm, "I can see why you're so excited. You'll get to shuffle everything around in the cabinets when you get home." Not until the words were out did he realize he sounded mean rather than teasing. "I'm sorry," he said. "I didn't mean that the way it came out."

The apology did nothing to stop a shimmer of tears from forming along her lower eyelashes. She worked to blink them away. "I know you didn't." She forced a smile. "You're just worried about me turning into one of those little old ladies whose life revolves around her 'things.' "

"Actually, I like your pottery. It's those freakish ceramic dogs that drive me nuts."

"Your grandfather gave—"

"Yeah, I know. But that was a long time ago. Did it ever occur to you that he might have grown tired of them by now too?"

The question brought her up short. "I never thought about that. Oh my God . . . do you know what this means? I can get rid of the dogs and put my new ceramic pieces in their place."

"I'm proud of you, Grams. Always thinking."

She took out a pot for the pasta. "Go make your phone call."

He headed down the hall to his bedroom. If it really was possible for his grandmother to let go of something his grandfather had given her, maybe there was hope that she could let go of him too.

Chapter 5

After Alison saw Christopher off the next morning to check out a stable that had horses to rent, she poured herself a cup of coffee and took it out on the back deck, along with the binder Grace had given her. Determined not to yield ground to the twinge of self-pity that had come over her that morning, she'd decided she had a choice. Either she could find a bookstore and stock up on the books she'd intended to read for the past year, living someone else's fantasies, or she could take her first steps toward dealing with the independence being thrust on her. Being surrounded by enticing covers and promising blurbs on the backs of books was enormously appealing still, though she knew that one day she'd convert to reading on her iPad. Just not yet. For now, she loved the feel of an actual book in her hands. She even loved the smell of the paper and ink.

She'd never been the kind of person who went places by herself. Movies were supposed to be shared and talked about afterward. The same with dinner at a fine restaurant. She even enjoyed a book more when it was one she read with her book club.

But either she could learn to enjoy traveling alone or she could become content to confine her world to her neighborhood.

Dennis would have been appalled at the idea of her allowing herself to become a recluse.

But in reality, she was the one who should have been appalled. Thirteen years ago, Nora and Christopher had needed her, and she'd been there for them.

But fair or unfair, they didn't need her anymore. And it was breaking her heart.

In the back of her mind, she could hear Dennis telling her that she still had places to see and people to meet. She'd always wanted to work on an archaeological dig and had even looked up possibilities on the Internet on nights when she couldn't sleep. She could learn to speak more than rudimentary Italian and go to Dureta herself. Holding an actual conversation with the men and women who made the pottery she loved so much would only make her collection more meaningful.

Whatever she came up with, she wanted it to be outside her comfort zone. Linda had suggested a travel club, hinting that Alison might meet someone interesting on one of the trips. But Alison wasn't interested in meeting someone new—or interesting. She just needed a stronger backbone to get out and do some exploring on her own.

She opened the binder Grace had made and went to the section labeled "Things to Do." Fifteen minutes later, she'd settled on a self-guided walking tour of the historic buildings of Monterey. Lunch would be on the wharf at one of the seafood restaurants Grace had suggested.

But before she did anything else, as soon as Christopher returned, she had to stop by the bank to transfer the money to pay for the one-month rental and then go back to Tanner Motors to pick up her car, finish the paperwork, and give Kyle a check.

"Hola," a startlingly pretty young woman said to Alison as she entered the sales office. "How may I help you?" she added.

Alison worked to hide her surprise. "I'm looking for Mr. Tanner."

"Mrs. Kirkpatrick?"

"That's me."

The young woman came around the desk and held out her hand. "Benita Vargas. I'm Kyle's part-time accountant and one of his fill-in salespeople."

Alison hesitated. "It might be better if I came back this afternoon. Mr. Tanner and I have an out-of-the-ordinary arrangement for the truck I'm using this month."

"That's not necessary. Kyle filled me in before he left. I can handle the paperwork and have you on your way in a few minutes."

Alison worked to keep her disappointment from showing. It was one of those moments when she didn't realize how much she had been counting on something until it was gone.

"Unless you'd like to talk to him about something else?" Benita added. When Alison didn't say anything, Benita returned to her chair.

"I have the papers for you to sign right here. The contract is a little unusual, what with it being more of a rental than an outright sale, but otherwise it's pretty straightforward. If you'd like to take a seat, we can go over everything."

It took less than ten minutes for Benita to detail the expenses, including a thirty-day insurance policy Kyle had arranged.

"This is a first for us," Benita said as she gathered the papers and put them in an envelope. "To be honest, I hope Kyle doesn't make it a habit. It's been a bit of a pain. He almost had to strong-arm the insurance agent to get him to cover the truck." She handed Alison a paper to fill out. "This requires your grandson's signature too. Please have him stop by as soon as possible. It's a law in California that if you're stopped for any reason, you have to show proof of insurance. You're free to use your regular insurance company, of course. Kyle just wanted to save you the trouble."

"Please tell him how much I appreciate all that he's done." While her insurance agent was thorough, he could be frustratingly slow. She took out her checkbook. "Now that my grandson has decided he's going to take up surfing, it's even more important for him to have his own transportation." She smiled. "At least it is for me." Alison handed Benita the check. "Do you need ID?"

"No, this is fine."

After filling out the insurance papers, Alison picked up the envelope with the duplicate papers inside, stood, and slipped her purse strap over her shoulder. "I'll see you, or Mr. Tanner, at the end of the month."

Benita came around the desk to walk her to the door. "If you have a minute, I just saw Kyle's car pull around the corner. I know he'd want to thank you personally for your business."

Alison gave Benita a sideways glance. "Even if it was a pain?"

The younger woman shrugged. "What can I say? He likes challenges."

Alison went outside to wait for Kyle.

He held open his arms in greeting and gave her a smile that heated up the air around them another ten degrees. "What great timing," he said. "I would have been upset if I'd missed you."

"I was hoping to see you too," she said, moving toward him. "I wanted to thank you again for everything you've done. And to let you know that Christopher loves the truck."

"He's okay with the standard transmission?"

"Turns out I was right about our neighbor letting him drive the farm equipment. I just had no idea that it's been going on since he was thirteen."

"Most farm kids are behind the wheel of their dad's tractor the day they can reach the pedals."

"I'm glad I didn't know. But I'm also glad he had the opportunity to be a normal kid. I have a tendency to hover."

"I assume Benita took care of you and that everything was in order?"

Alison nodded. "She also told me about the insurance. Thank you for that too." On impulse, she added, "Would it be okay if I took you to lunch sometime? To thank you." Where had that come from?

He didn't hesitate. "I'd like that."

"When?" If she didn't move fast, she'd lose her nerve.

"How does today sound?"

"Great. What time?"

He checked his watch. "Eleven-thirty?"

"Okay. I was thinking about someplace on the wharf. Do you have any preferences?"

"That depends on whether you're more interested in the food or the view."

"The view first, the food a close second."

"Then why don't you let me take care of the arrangements."

"Okay." She couldn't think of anything else to say and was afraid if she did, it would be something dumb. She headed for her car, stopping to call over her shoulder, "Eleven-thirty?"

He was still watching her. "I'll be here. And I'll drive. Traffic around the wharf can be a real pain that time of day."

She backed toward her car. "I'll see you in a couple of hours then."

"Looking forward to it."

She believed him, and it felt wonderful.

Alison started her walking tour at the Pacific House Museum, where she picked up additional material to add to the brochures Grace had put in her file. She'd been an information junkie all her life, with a passion for discovering obscure bits of trivia about the places she visited. There were times she was sure she'd seen Dennis's eyes glaze over when she insisted on sharing what she'd learned, but he'd never complained.

Having been raised in Connecticut, she hadn't been taught much about California history beyond the gold rush era and the mission settlements. The tribes she learned about in school were the Apache and Navajo and Lakota; even though the Indians who'd inhabited California before the mission settlements were also a part of Western lore, what she knew about them wouldn't fill the pages of a toddler's picture book.

Between the cattle grazing that depleted the traditional food sources of the Rumsien Indians and the diseases the Spaniards brought with them that wiped out entire villages, the native people who'd lived in the Monterey area for thousands of years were gone in less than two hundred years after the Spaniards arrived. The last-known speaker of the Rumsien language was a woman who died in 1939.

Alison hated the word "last." Last dinosaur, last passenger pigeon, last Javan tiger, last kiss, last good-bye, last words on a voice-mail message. . . .

She had a list of things she loved too, like puffy white clouds in a brilliant blue sky, songbirds announcing spring, Christmas trees laden with memory-rich ornaments, wistful memories that made her smile, and the sense of freedom she'd experienced since coming to California.

At home everyone knew her, even people she'd never met. After thirteen years, she and Nora and Christopher were still gossip fodder. They were classified the way doctors and lawyers and actors and politicians and criminals were labeled, *who* they were being lost in *what* they were. Her name forever carried the tag: *You know, she's the one who lost her husband and son in the World Trade Center attack.*

When her friends insisted it was time for her to start dating again and she'd finally agreed to give it a try, just to let them see she wasn't turning into a recluse, she hadn't dated one man whose eyes didn't cloud with his own memories when he found out how she'd become a widow. Once anyone, man or woman, knew who she was, they were more interested in her story than they were in her. She'd come to the conclusion that 9/11 was a wound that needed more time and an entire new generation to heal. The scar would never fade for those who had lived through that day.

She glanced at her phone. She still had another hour before she met Kyle. Plenty of time to go to the nearby Custom House and discover a wealth of information that fascinated her and bored her friends to tears.

Chapter 6

When Alison arrived, Kyle was standing beside a Chevy sedan talking to a young couple with a baby in a backpack. She caught his attention and pointed toward the art gallery next door. He excused himself from the couple and caught up with her. "Are you ready?"

"I can wait."

"Not necessary." He nodded his head in the young couple's direction. "They're just looking. He works the late shift at one of the restaurants on Cannery Row. They come in two or three times a month to see what's new and make plans—same as the couple you saw the other day. It's cheap entertainment and a reason to get out of the house. Best of all is that I get a kick out of talking to them." He turned and waved as they wandered back to their seventies-era Toyota. "One day he's going to own his own restaurant and he'll be shopping for a new car. Until then, I'll keep them and their baby in inexpensive, safe transportation."

"You have an interesting way of doing business."

"I started out liking money," he said, reaching up to rub the back of his neck. "Now I like people." He guided her to his car, a model she didn't recognize.

"What is this?" She took a minute to look the car over before getting inside.

"A Tesla Roadster. I know the guy who makes them and couldn't wait to get my hands on one."

There wasn't any noise when he started the engine. "Kind of like a Prius," she said.

He laughed. "A little. But this one's all battery. It never switches over to a combustible engine because there isn't one."

She ran her hand over the dashboard. The car might be pure economy to drive, but she'd bet her pottery collection that it hadn't been economical to buy. "Impressive."

She wasn't the only one impressed. As they made their way through the city the car drew serious and comical attention from the people they passed, everything from appreciative whistles to honking horns to thumbs-ups to a young man at a stoplight who got down on his knees, put his hands in a pleading position, and begged Kyle to adopt him.

Kyle took it all in stride, acknowledging the attention with a smile or wave and laughing out loud at the kid on his knees. "He's the kind of person I like to have working for me," Kyle said. "Makes the day more fun just being around people like that."

"Pure California," Alison said. "Or at least what I've come to think of as California. That isn't something anyone would do where I come from."

"Really? That's too bad."

She considered what he'd said. "I don't know if it is or not. I like knowing what to expect from the people around me. But then maybe it would be different if I drove a flashy car."

"Ouch."

"I'm sorry," she said. "I didn't mean that the way it sounded."

"Yes, you did, and it's fine. I put you on the defensive and got exactly what I deserved."

"Then tell me, why do you drive a car like this?"

"Lots of reasons. The most important being that I'm a car guy. I love everything about them, even the old ones like the '59 Cadillacs with those ludicrously huge fins. I went to a car show once that had nothing but homemade amphibious cars. I came home all excited about making one of my own, but Jenny put an end to that about as fast as she closed down my sailing solo around the world in a twenty-foot boat.

"She was the practical one in our marriage, which allowed me the occasional bits of craziness that made me feel young and adventurous. I didn't appreciate how important a part she played in allowing me my sense of freedom when she was alive. It wasn't until I took over raising the girls and saw what it meant to be the responsible parent that I finally understood the gift she'd given me." He paused, then added, "Of all the things I've had to learn to deal with, hindsight is the worst."

"And the words 'if only,'" Alison said.

"After everyone had gone home from the funeral, I told the girls that they had my permission to use any swear words they could string together to express their frustration, but that I wouldn't allow 'if only' to be spoken in our house."

"Wise man. Did it work?"

"It did what I'd intended. I didn't want them looking back with regret or guilt."

A car pulled up beside them, the passenger trying hard not to be obvious in his perusal of the Tesla. As he pulled away he gave a thumbs-up signal.

"Is it always like this?"

"Pretty much."

A lifelong conservative, Alison was a little disappointed to discover this flashy side to Kyle's personality. "It is a pretty car . . ."

"It's so much more than that. It's the future. Or at least it should be. Can you imagine the difference it would make if all our cars ran on batteries that were charged by solar panels?"

"I never gave it much thought," she admitted.

"It's pretty hard to ignore around here. We take this stuff seriously."

"So the only reason you drive a Tesla is the environment?"

He smiled. "It's not the *only* reason."

She sounded like she was about to tie him to a chair and shine a light in his eyes. "Can we start over? This is supposed to be a way for me to thank you for all you've done. I have no idea why I'm being so aggressive about your car."

"Could it be that I don't fit in your comfort zone?"

Oh great, he was a mind-reader too. "What makes you say that?"

"Because you're not the same person you were the other day, and I think that person is the real you."

Just like that she was crying. Was it possible for her to make a bigger fool of herself? She dug through her purse for a tissue. "You know—I think it might be better if we did this another day. Plainly I'm not fit company to be around today. Certainly not in a fancy restaurant."

He reached over and gave her hand a quick squeeze. "And what makes you think it's a *fancy* restaurant?"

She looked at him, at the twinkle in his eyes, at the half-cocked grin, and couldn't help but return his smile. "Jenny was a lucky woman."

"My kids insist I'm a nicer guy now than I was when she was alive, but Jenny and I had a good thing going for a lot of years. I just didn't have the sense to realize how good until it was gone."

"How long has it been?"

"Ten years."

"You're a nice man. I'm surprised you're still single."

He chuckled. "It's not for lack of trying by my friends. I can't imagine you haven't been going through the same thing. How long has it been for you?"

"How did you know?"

"Lots of little clues, but mainly the fact that you never once mentioned bringing anyone else into the decision-making process about the truck. It's obvious you've learned to do this kind of thing on your own."

"It's been thirteen years. And I have a suspicion I'm still single for the same reason you are. Haven't met anyone I wanted to be around more than a couple of hours at a time."

"Yeah, it's not a great sign when you're looking at the clock on the mantel instead of the door to the bedroom."

She glanced out the car window and realized they were passing the wharf. "I think you missed the turnoff."

"Change of plans."

They drove past signs directing them to the Monterey Bay Aquarium, then west for several blocks before turning right on Seventeenth Street. Kyle pulled into a parking lot next to a small park, got out, and walked around the car. "We're here," he said, reaching for her hand.

The "here" was the top of a rocky outcropping with a panoramic view of the ocean and the bay. There was a small beach in a cove on one side and more rocks with barely enough sand to build a castle on the other. Waves hit the outlying rocks with a force that sent foamy salt water thirty feet into the air.

"Wow," Alison said appreciatively.

A man wearing an apron with a picture of two crabs holding claws on it got up from one of a pair of lawn chairs on either side of a small picnic table. "Ciao, Signore Tanner. You pick a beautiful day for your picnic. No fog." He looked toward the ocean. "At least not yet."

He shook hands with Kyle and turned to Alison. "And who is this lovely lady?"

Kyle brought her forward by putting an arm around her shoulders. "Alison Kirkpatrick, this is Antonio Formisano, extraordinary chef and even better friend."

Antonio took Alison's hand and brought it to his lips. "Bella," he said.

"Grazie," she replied.

He tilted his head and looked at her. "Parli Italiano?"

She laughed. "Molto poco. I had a set of CDs that promised I'd speak fluent Italian in six weeks. I either didn't go enough places in the car or the CDs promised more than they could deliver, because not even my Italian grocer can understand anything I say."

"I wish I had the time to give you a lesson today, but sadly, I must get back to work. Perhaps next time. Buon appetito."

"What's this?" she asked Kyle when Antonio was gone.

"You said you preferred the view over the meal, but I didn't think you'd mind if we had both."

"I can't remember the last time I went on a picnic. What a terrific idea."

"I used to go on them all the time with Jenny," he said as he guided her to the lawn chairs. "I nearly forgot how much fun they can be." He glanced at the advancing clouds rolling in with the waves. "Even in the fog."

Before sitting down, she went to the short rock wall that provided a safety railing at the top of the cliff and looked over the side. Most of the waves broke before hitting the jagged rocks at the base of the cliff, releasing their energy on barrier rocks farther offshore. Still, there was enough force to create swells of rushing water and foam that swirled around and over the tenacious vegetation.

Another life lesson—learn when to hang on and when to yield.

"I love how something can be so scary and so beautiful at the same time." She came back, sat down, and adjusted a clip that anchored the checkered tablecloth to the small table.

"It's an intoxicating combination," he agreed. "A little like skin diving and having a great white shark brush against your leg."

"That happened to you?"

"Once." He chuckled at the memory. "Once was enough."

Kyle reached into the basket and brought out a covered dish and checkered napkin. Inside was a triangle of artfully arranged crab cakes. After handing her the dish and napkin, he pointed to the area on the other side of the outcropping and said, "If you look closely, you'll see otters in the kelp bed. A lot of them are mothers with their pups." He poured a glass of white wine, offered it to her, and when she took it, poured a short splash for himself.

"Do you come here often?" she asked, squeezing the muslin-wrapped lemon over the crab cakes.

"I used to. Whenever I could manage time off in the middle of the week, we'd have at least one lunch here at the park. Rain or shine." He chuckled. "There was one time we couldn't drink our wine fast enough to keep it from being more water than wine. Best picnic I ever had with Jenny. Now that I actually live here full-time, I'm more likely to make a reservation at the restaurant. There are some things that are better shared."

He studied her for several seconds. "Truth be told, I haven't wanted to come back."

"Too many memories?" She would take her cue about how much or how little he wanted to tell her from his reaction to her question.

"Something like that."

Alison took a forkful of crab and dipped it in the sauce. "Oh my God," she sighed. "This is amazing."

"Antonio doesn't believe in cans. If he can't get something fresh, it's not on the menu. I could live on his wild mushroom soup."

"And he still has time to fix a picnic basket and sit around the park waiting for us to show up?"

"He's a special friend," Kyle said. "But I had no idea that he'd come himself rather than send one of the staff, or I wouldn't have asked."

Kyle opened a third napkin held together with a length of raffia tied into a bow. "Forgot the bread," he said, holding the napkin open so she could take a piece.

A heated stone had kept it warm. There was a lovely bite to the smell that let her know it was sourdough freshly baked. She topped the bread with a slice of the accompanying brie and took a bite. "It's a good thing I don't live here. I could wind up as round as I am tall without giving it a second thought."

Kyle laughed. "My kind of woman."

She couldn't remember the last time she'd blushed. "So you like your women plump."

"I like a woman who isn't obsessed with how she looks." He offered to refill her wineglass, but she declined, and he put the bottle back into the basket without taking any for himself.

They finished their lunch, ending with strawberries the size of lemons that had been dipped in melted sugar. The crisp, translucent outer layer was a window into the perfectly formed and perfectly ripe strawberry inside. Alison looked at the exquisitely simple creation, was tempted, but was also convinced she didn't have room for one more bite of anything.

Until Kyle bit into the strawberry and she saw the look on his face.

Chapter 7

"Well?" Grace said, waiting for Christopher to move his saddle and helmet from the front seat to the back of the truck.

"Okay—it was a good hamburger."

She climbed in the cab and snapped her seat belt. "Just *good*?"

Christopher laughed. "Better than good."

"Try this on for size: 'Grace, that was the best hamburger I've ever eaten. And those fries? To die for. Then there was the olallieberry milk shake. I've never had a milk—' "

"Enough," Christopher said, holding up his hands in surrender. "I've never had a meal as good as the one I just had." For good measure, he winked and added, "And the company was *almost* as good."

Grace stuck out her tongue. She'd spent half the night wondering if she'd made a mistake trading surf lessons for riding lessons. It was a lot of time to spend with someone she didn't know, especially someone she didn't have a clue if she'd like when she did get to know him. She was good at getting herself into these situations, bad at getting herself out.

Christopher started the truck. "Where's your car?"

"I had my dad drop me off." What if she and Christopher wound up hating each other, and his grandmother said something negative about her to Julia?

He reached across her to open the glove box and pulled out a hand-drawn map. "How are you at navigating?"

"If I'd been with Columbus, he would have found China."

"Just so you know, I'm not interested in going to China." He handed her the paper. "See what you can do with this."

She recognized streets from all the running she'd done in the hills behind Watsonville when she was on the cross-country track team. "Okay, I know where we're going."

"And how to get there?"

"One way or another."

"You do remember we have a two-thirty lesson."

"I thought you were going to teach me."

"They insisted on handling the basic stuff at the stable, but I'll take over when we're on the trail." He stopped at the curb and fanned his hands out from the steering wheel. "Which way?"

She pointed toward the stoplight. "We're going to go south on 101 for a couple of miles and then get off on Sea Cliff Drive."

Grace felt a flutter of excitement in the pit of her stomach. All her life, or at least all that she could remember, she'd imagined herself horseback riding. First on a unicorn, then on a palomino, and then when she came to live with Andrew and Cheryl, on a gleaming black horse with a perfect white star on its forehead running along the beach. She'd come to believe the dream was so impossible that she'd never told anyone, not even her sister Rebecca. And now here she was, headed for her first up-close-and-personal meeting with a horse. How was she going to keep from acting like a kid who'd been told there was no Santa Claus only to wake up Christmas morning with a dozen presents under the tree?

"You need to get in the other lane," Grace said, forcing herself back into the present.

Christopher changed lanes, turned, and merged onto the highway. "Mind if I fill you in on what to expect when we get there?"

"Please. I've heard horses can smell fear."

He took her concern seriously. "Not fear so much as hesitancy. The horse expects you to know what you're doing and gets nervous when you do things that let him know you're a beginner."

"Like?"

"Gasp, shriek, giggle, scream—making any loud sound when he does something that surprises you or that you're not expecting. I've asked for their best beginner horse, and the woman I talked to described one that sounds perfect, but that doesn't mean he's going to put up with a lot of rookie mistakes."

"Such as?"

He held up his hand and started counting off with his fingers. "One—clamping your legs against his sides like a vise because you're afraid you'll fall off. You're looking for the same kind of balance you use on the surfboard. Brute force just throws the horse off his stride. Two—yanking the reins. This will really piss him off. He might put up with it a couple of times, but he won't be happy. That doesn't mean it's never appropriate, just that you and the horse need to know it's intentional and that you mean business. Three—it's tempting, and feels natural, but don't ride on the ball of your foot. Ride with your heels down. You'll get in all kinds of trouble later if you don't do this. Which is why

I told you to wear boots with a heel that you can fit into the stirrup. Four—when you're on his back, don't look at the horse, look at where you're going. Preferably pick a spot between his ears and then focus on the area thirty to forty feet in front of that. Five—don't ever walk behind a horse without letting him know you're there. In the wild, predators attack the back legs and thigh to bring the animal down, and then they go for the throat. If you surprise him, he's going to try to protect himself and you're going to wind up on your ass and possibly in the hospital."

"Makes sense."

"None of that makes you want to rethink getting on the back of a horse when you could be out riding a wave?"

"Nope," she answered, turning her face to the side window to hide the huge grin of anticipation she hoped he couldn't see reflected in the glass.

Christopher came up beside Grace and ran his hand down the flank of the horse she had been riding. She was still talking to Louis, the owner of the stable. After first asking him if he ever traded labor for lessons, she was now caught up in learning everything she could about the horse she'd just ridden. One ride and she was hooked. Louis insisted she was a natural.

From the moment she was settled in the saddle, it was as if she'd always been there.

Christopher had left when the negotiating started, eager to look at a couple of Danish warmbloods he'd spotted being worked in the back paddock. One was a chestnut with perfectly matched white stockings, the other an almost black bay with a small star in the middle of his forehead. Both were well over sixteen hands and had near-perfect conformation. Neither was on the list Christopher's trainer had given him.

He returned a half hour later and discovered Grace still in deep conversation with the owner. Christopher casually slipped the reins from Grace's hand and started toward the barn.

"Hold up," Grace called, running after him. "I want to watch how the groom puts him away." She hadn't stopped grinning the entire time they'd been at the stable. "I know it's not something they'll let me do right away, but I might as well learn what's expected."

"So you got the job?"

She nodded.

"Congratulations." He handed the reins back to her. "When do you start?"

"Not until August. I won't get to do much with the horses until they see that I know what I'm doing, and I won't get many hours until the people who work here throughout the summer go back to school. But I will get free lessons whenever they have an opening. And I can hang around the stables and ask questions whenever I have free time."

Her excitement was contagious, and he did something he rarely did with anyone outside his close circle of friends in the dressage world. "As soon as we're through in here, there are a couple of horses out back that I think you should see."

"Dressage horses?"

He liked that she'd picked up enough clues to know there was a difference between the horse she'd just ridden, the horses in the far paddock that were being worked for barrel racing, and the kind of horse he rode. "They could be hunter/jumper-trained, but I'd be surprised if they don't have dressage in their background."

A groom took the horse from Grace and secured him to a hitching post. He removed the tack, then took out a brush and thoroughly went over the horse's coat. He gave him a drink and then a piece of apple and led him into the barn.

"I can do that," Grace said to Christopher.

"Not all horses are like this one. Some can be downright cranky." He started toward the back paddock. "And they're smart enough to do mean things on purpose if they don't like you. Or it could have nothing to do with you. It could be that they've had a bad day."

"What do you do then?"

"Like everything else, you play it as it unfolds. Horses are like humans—each one is different. You need to learn how to read them. Sometimes you can speak their language, sometimes it's Klingon."

"You realize you're not being very helpful."

Christopher laughed. "Okay, here we go again." He held up his hand with the fingers splayed. "First, when a horse that's new to you sticks out his nose, that means he wants to smell you. Let him sniff the back of your hand. Second, don't ignore a horse that's pawing the ground. He's either trying to get your attention because he's bored, or he's spoiled and wants you to do something for him, like give him a treat, or he's letting you know that something is bothering him. Until you know which it is, be careful around him. Third, never forget you're dealing with a thousand-pound animal. Steel-toed cowboy boots work a whole lot better than something fancy like Uggs when it comes to a shoving contest."

"Voice of experience?" she asked as they neared the paddock.

"Unfortunately, it was my mother who learned the hard way. She stopped by one of my practice sessions on her way home from work, and when she tried to get a horse to move so she could see better, she wound up in a cast for six weeks."

"Ouch."

"She tried to convince everyone that ruining her Jimmy Choo heels hurt more than hurting her foot. But then she's one of those women who has a thing for shoes." Christopher looked around to pick an advantage point to watch the rider who had just come out of the stable area on the black stallion. He held his hand out to Grace and led her to the top of a grassy mound.

"Are you going to tell me what's going on?" she whispered.

He leaned back on his elbows. "Is there nothing that doesn't interest you?"

She leaned back with him. "If there is, I haven't found it yet."

An hour later, Christopher's phone vibrated. He checked to make sure it wasn't his grandmother—she had a thing that was a mile past normal about not being able to reach him. It was a text from a friend back home. Without reading the message, he stuffed the phone back in his pocket.

"It's getting late," he said. "Do you have to get back to fix dinner?"

She shielded her eyes from the low-hanging sun. "Not tonight. It's Rebecca's turn." She reached for her own phone. "But I should tell her what time I'll be home." She looked at him expectantly.

"How long does it take to get there from here?"

"Half an hour."

"Make it an hour from now." He stood and brushed off his jeans. "So, what did you think?"

"I'm impressed," she said, finishing her text. "The black horse seems a little full of himself, but I would imagine it's because he's still so young."

She couldn't know this. It had to be a lucky guess. "What makes you think that?"

She shot him a sideways glance. "Really want to know?"

"Yes."

"Louis told me."

He shook his head. "I should have guessed."

"You have to admit, I had you going for a couple of minutes." She followed him to the truck. "So, are you interested in the black one?"

"I could be. But he's young and not very well trained."

"Why do you suppose he's not on your list?"

"Could be because he's not for sale."

"Are you going to ask?"

Christopher stopped and looked at her. "What's up? Why all the questions?"

"No reason. I was just wondering about actually buying a horse out here. How are you going to get it home?"

"By plane."

She frowned. "You're kidding, right? That would cost a small fortune."

"Three or four thousand. Maybe a little more."

"Is it safe?" She climbed into her side of the truck. "For the horse, I mean."

"It's actually less stressful than trailering it that far."

"Why?"

"They're not very good travelers. They stress out easily, and that lowers their immunity system, which makes them prone to respiratory infections. Once you get where you're going, it can take days for them to regain their strength."

"Can you imagine the first time they put a horse on a plane? I'll bet there were some nervous people at the other end of that flight."

"I don't like thinking about one of my horses boxed up in the belly of a plane," he admitted. "But if I ever get good enough to compete in Europe, I won't have much choice."

"*One* of your horses? How many do you have?"

"Right now I'm down to three. Only one gets shipped anywhere. The other two are too old for anything but a slow stroll along the trails around my house."

Grace wished he hadn't told her about owning three horses and buying another one and shipping it home in an airplane. Normal people didn't have that kind of money. And she wanted him to be normal because she liked him.

"Do you need me to give directions?" she asked.

"I think I've got it. I'm pretty good at getting back from someplace." He glanced at her. "You okay?"

"Yeah, sure. I'm fine. Why are you asking?"

"You're not going to go all weird on me just because I have a couple of horses, are you?"

"Maybe," she admitted. How did he know?

"Well, don't." He gave her a lopsided grin. "You still owe me a surfing lesson."

Grace stared at him long and hard. "You busy Friday?"

"I thought we'd settled on Wednesday."

Of course he'd think she was talking about surfing. "There's a party on Friday. One of my friends is leaving to spend the summer in France."

"All by herself? Not shipping any animals to keep her company?"

She laughed. "Do you want to go or don't you?"

"Yes—I want to go."

"Good—all the other guys I know have turned me down."

"I sincerely doubt that."

She took off her boot and brought her foot up to tuck under her leg. "I'm going to give you the name of a rental shop in Santa Cruz that will fit you for a wet suit and a board. I'll tell them you're coming and that I'm going to be there at noon to pick you up. They'll take good care of you."

"I assume you want me to go there Wednesday morning?"

She nodded. "They usually show up around nine, but if the surf's up, they may not be there until ten. If you have to wait, there's a great coffee shop and bakery around the corner."

"Are we going to Manresa?"

"Those aren't novice waves. You want to start where you can learn the basics without fighting the water. Cowell's is a great place to learn if it's not too crowded. It's to the right of the pier as you're facing the ocean."

"What pier?"

She laughed. "I guess that would help—the Santa Cruz pier."

Chapter 8

Christopher considered himself in decent shape, but he couldn't remember ever being as sore as he was when he woke up Thursday morning to the sound of the doorbell ringing. "Grams?" he called.

She didn't answer.

He stumbled out of bed and grabbed a blanket to wrap around himself. The doorbell rang again before he was halfway down the hall.

"I'm coming," he shouted, wondering who in the hell would be at their front door at this hour. . . . He glanced out the sliding-glass door and realized it was later than he'd thought.

"Hi," Grace said when he peered outside. "Dude—you look awful."

He opened the door wider. "Dude? No one says that anymore."

"In case you haven't noticed, this is California, and we're not into caring what the rest of the world says or doesn't say." She came inside.

He brought the blanket closer. "I thought you were working this morning."

"And I thought you had an appointment to look at a horse."

"Been postponed until tomorrow. There was some emergency with one of the colts."

"I realize this is none of my business, but you don't seem all that excited about finding a new horse."

"Why would you say that?"

"Aren't there other places you could be looking?"

"I have appointments for all the horses my trainer felt I should see while I was here."

"And that's it?"

"Pretty much. Horses at the level I'm looking for are hard to find. Which is why I'm free today. . . ."

"The shipper can't pick up our order today, so I've got the day off. I saw your truck outside and thought I'd come by and see if you wanted to hit the waves."

He yawned as he ran his hand through his hair. "Sure. Just give me a couple of minutes."

"In case I forgot to tell you, you did great yesterday," she called after him.

"I felt like a total spaz."

"Everyone does their first time out. It took three years before the guys around here stopped calling me Gidget."

"I don't have three years."

"Then what do you care what someone calls you?"

He came back wearing his standard cutoffs and T-shirt, this one a faded lime green with a bird falling out of its nest screaming TWEET.

"Are we in a hurry or is it okay if I eat something first?"

She glanced at her watch. "We have an hour before the tide's good at Cowell's. And the fog should be burned off by then."

"You want something?"

She followed him into the kitchen. "Like?"

He opened the refrigerator. His grandmother had picked up the basics, but little else. "Bacon and eggs?" He checked the cupboard. "Cereal? Toast?"

"Go for the protein. I don't know why, but it helps with the cold."

He fixed the bacon while she scrambled eggs and put a couple of pieces of bread in the toaster. They ate sitting at the counter. "When does your school start?" he asked.

"First of September."

"Where are you going?"

"Cabrillo—it's a community college. I'm going to get the basics out of the way and then, hopefully, transfer to either UC Santa Cruz or UC Los Angeles. I want to major in marine biology, and they have a couple of the best programs in the country. What about you?"

"Penn State."

"Because?"

"They have a great equestrian program."

"Something tells me that's not the only reason."

One of the things he liked best about Grace was her lack of guile, but it was also one of the things that drove him nuts. "My dad went there."

"And?"

"What do you mean?"

"You need a major. Something you're interested in. At least that's what's been pounded into me for the last four years."

"Economics."

"One of my best friends is an economics major, and you're about as much like him as a frog is like an alligator." She picked up their plates and took them to the sink. "What's the real reason?"

"My dad and my grandfather both graduated with economics degrees." Christopher wondered if it sounded as lame to her as it did to him.

"And you're following in their footsteps. Have you ever thought to ask them if they're happy economists or if there's something else they'd rather be doing?"

"That would be pretty hard to do. They're both dead."

Surprising them both, she glared at him. "That was just mean," she said. "You let me go there knowing I would make an ass out of myself by asking."

Christopher hadn't told a lot of people about his father and grandfather, but there were some he'd purposely wanted to embarrass as punishment for their blatant, insistent curiosity. He'd never had anyone have the nerve to react to his rudeness the way Grace had.

"You're right. It was mean. I'm sorry."

She put the plates in the dishwasher. "I'm sorry too. I know what it's like being where you are and how sometimes you just want to scream at everyone to leave you alone. What is it with people who think it's okay to poke and prod for every private detail of someone else's life?"

"I'm going to take a chance here, but how do you know what it's like? Is your dad dead too?"

She shrugged. "To know something like that I'd have to know who my dad was."

"Then what did you mean?"

"If you consider death an abandonment, then to have been purposely abandoned by someone who's still alive would be like a train that runs on the same track, don't you think?"

Christopher frowned. "I'm confused."

"Andrew and Cheryl adopted me. I was taken away from my biological mother when one of the neighbors turned her in for leaving me alone while she went on the road with her boyfriend."

"How long were you by yourself?"

"When I was little, it would be for a day, but then as I got older, it turned into weekends. By the time I was seven, it could be an entire week. The last time was twelve days. That's when the neighbor stepped in."

"How old were you then?"

"I was eight when they took me away. The first time she left me—that I remember—was the day of my fourth birthday. Breakfast was a Hostess cupcake with four candles. She made a big deal out of leaving to get my present. When it was bedtime and she still hadn't come back, I figured it must be a really special present. I waited outside her bedroom door for her to get up the next morning to surprise me, but she'd forgotten. She was sorry and said she'd make it up to me, but she never did.

"After a while, I started picking up the clues when she was about to take off. Most of the time she'd buy one of those enormous jars of peanut butter, a loaf of bread, a half gallon of milk, and a big box of cereal. No matter how long she was going to be gone, she'd leave a twenty-dollar bill stuck to the refrigerator with magnets. As I got older she got more creative and sometimes there'd be four five-dollar bills perfectly lined up so that Lincoln was facing the same direction. One day, for Valentine's Day, she left twenty one-dollar bills arranged in a heart shape.

"I think she was relieved when Child Welfare took me. She knew she never should have had me, and to her credit, she never had another child. At least none that I know of."

"Was she into drugs?" Christopher asked.

Grace shook her head. "I never saw her high. She was just one of those people who wasn't meant to be tied down. They write romantic songs about men who are wanderers. Women they crucify."

"She should have given you up for adoption when you were born."

"Yeah, I've thought about that too. But if she had, I wouldn't be where I am now. Andrew and Cheryl wouldn't be my parents, Rebecca and Bobby wouldn't be my sister and brother. And I wouldn't have the friends I have." She shot him a quick smile. "And I wouldn't have met you."

"I'm no prize," he said.

"What makes you say that?"

"It's a long, boring story. I'll save it for another time. Right now, there's some waves that we need to catch—*dude.*" He raised his hand for a high-five.

"Awesome," she said, hitting his hand with enough force to make a slapping sound. "Next lesson—what are ankle-snappers?"

"Small waves."

"Bumps?"

"Small waves that you can still surf." Christopher grabbed his keys and wallet and the towel he'd left on the back of the chair.

"Mahalo?"

"It means 'thank you.'" Christopher stopped at the front door and turned to Grace, looking into her eyes. "Mahalo, Grace."

"What for?"

"Everything."

She shrugged. "I haven't done—"

He came forward and gave her a kiss, quick, but in no way misdirected.

Grace leaned back and stared at him. "What was that for?"

"Because I felt like it. Actually, I've felt like it since I saw you unloading your surfboard from the back of your dad's van."

Seconds passed before she came up on her toes and kissed him back. Her kiss was longer and executed with the assurance that it was welcome. "Mahalo to you too, Christopher."

"What for?"

"Listening. But most of all, not judging. I know my mother wasn't perfect, but in her own way she loved me. It took a long time for me to realize that sometimes that's all we get. And it's okay."

No, it wasn't. She deserved so much more. His mother and grandmother hadn't deserved what happened to them either, nor had he. Nor had the kid he'd seen in a wheelchair at the beach the day he'd gone bike riding who'd been staring at the water with a longing Christopher couldn't begin to fathom.

"Give me a minute," he said and headed down the hall toward his bedroom. When he came back, he'd changed into jeans and boots and had his saddle over his arm.

"Change of plans," he said. "We're going riding."

"Why?"

"Because I like the way you look on a horse."

She folded her arms across her chest. "No—I really want to know why."

"If you're going to be working at the stable, I think you should know as much as you can about horses. And I want to be the one who teaches you."

"Okay, but this isn't part of the original deal. I pay my own way from now on."

"Then forget it." He shifted the saddle higher on his arm.

"Why are you being so stubborn about this?"

"Me? It's you who's being stubborn."

"Give me one good reason you should pay my way."

"Because it's how I was raised."

"Maybe when you take someone out on a date, but this isn't a date."

"Since when?"

The question stopped her cold. She opened her mouth to say something, then closed it again. Finally she found the words she wanted. "Okay. But only if you let me buy lunch."

"How is lunch not part of the date?"

"Don't push it," she warned.

"Carpos?"

"Nope—Pizza My Heart." She thought a minute. "You do like pizza, don't you?"

"I consider it one of the basic food groups. But I should probably warn you, I'm partial to New York pizza."

"Yeah, and you thought you knew what a real milk shake tasted like before I took you to Carpos."

He glanced at his watch. "We better get going. I have the horses reserved for one-thirty."

"When did you do that?" she asked, blushing with pleasure.

"When I was getting dressed."

"Awesome. Thanks."

He grinned. "No problem."

She opened the door and headed for her house to change clothes. "I'll meet you at the truck."

Christopher watched her go, a warning echoing in his mind that his involvement with her could easily turn into a huge mistake, one that he would regret for years to come. She wasn't like any of the girls he'd met at summer camp. Believing for an entire month that he'd met the love of his life, he'd swear he would keep in touch and then promptly forget all about the girl as soon as the car door opened at home and his best friend showed up to go riding.

He didn't know how he knew it, but Grace was different. She was the kind of girl you didn't forget, the kind his advanced-English teacher said famous writers immortalized in novels. It was a crummy time to have her come into his life. Why couldn't they have met a couple of years from now?

The thought that they could manage something long-distance flashed through his mind, but was gone almost as quickly as it had appeared. Things like that didn't even work out in movies.

Chapter 9

Kyle stopped to offer Alison a drink of water. They were on the outbound side of the loop to Pfeiffer Falls in Big Sur. It was the second hike they'd taken in the area in as many days. The redwood forest was everything Alison had dreamed it would be, with lush vegetation creating a thick bed of ground cover, streams running clear and cold, and waterfalls that made you want to put your hand out to feel their power. Best of all was sharing the experience with Kyle. He was the perfect tour guide, his eclectic interests covering everything from the history of the elephant seal in California to the best places to see wildflowers in the spring.

Being with him brought back memories of what it felt like to be with a man she liked. At one point she was stunned to realize she was actually flirting with him.

It made her feel so good that she didn't stop, even knowing the insanity of starting something she couldn't finish.

She took a drink and handed the water bottle back to Kyle. Pointing to an innocent-looking plant, she asked, "Is that poison oak?"

He nodded. "And that." He pointed to another cluster of leaves.

Alison gave the plants a wide berth. "How much farther to the falls?" she asked, spotting a sign with an arrow pointing straight ahead at the same time. Below the sign was a small metal plate warning to be on the lookout for mountain lions. She'd been watching for two days, but hadn't seen any. Still, even knowing the danger, she couldn't help wishing they'd at least catch a glimpse. Safely. She liked to think of herself as brave but not stupid. And she liked knowing Kyle felt the same way. He introduced her to bear spray, giving her a canister to carry and teaching her how to use it.

"Tired?" Kyle asked.

"Excited," she said. "The pictures at the information kiosk were amazing."

The day before, they'd spotted a couple of California condors riding the thermals near the entrance to the park. Even at a distance, their ten-foot wingspan made the birds look like soaring dragons. She'd watched them so long she'd gotten a crick in her neck.

Kyle kept insisting that he hadn't had as much fun in years. He loved showing her places no one else he knew wanted to see. She told him it was a little like all the New Yorkers who'd never been to the top of the Empire State Building or visited Ellis Island. It had seemed only natural that she would offer to show him her part of the country—should he ever find himself in New York.

Expecting a polite excuse for not taking her up on her offer, she was surprised when he asked, "Would fall be a good time to visit?"

The sun was headed for the offshore cloud bank that would be tomorrow's morning fog when they were on Highway 1 headed north again. A mile or so after crossing Bixby Creek Bridge, Alison's phone chirped, letting her know that she was back in service and that she had a message.

"Sorry," she told Kyle. "I need to check this."

"I understand."

She looked at her missed calls and saw that the first two were from Linda—undoubtedly filled to bursting with gossip after last night's charity ball. The third was from Nora and the fourth from Christopher. She listened to Nora's first and was relieved there wasn't any crisis—Nora just wanted to let Alison know that they were leaving Italy and headed for France. Next, she picked up the one from Christopher.

"Hey, Grams—I need to talk to you about all this running around you've been doing. Aren't you supposed to be taking care of me? Feeding me? Washing my clothes? Making my bed? What's up with you taking off like you're on vacation or something?

"Just kidding. I'm glad you're having fun. You are having fun, aren't you?

"I know we're supposed to have dinner together tonight, but I was wondering if it would be okay if we made it tomorrow night instead. I forgot that Grace invited me to a party at her friend's house and I said okay. Can you believe it? When was the last time I had a weekend I wasn't competing or traveling when I was able to go to a party?

"Call me."

Alison smiled as she used her shirttail to wipe fingerprints off her phone. "It appears I've been stood up. Christopher has a date tonight."

"Great," Kyle said. Realizing it might not be the best response, he added, "I hope you're not too disappointed."

"I'm thrilled," she said. "He's actually acting like a kid instead of a seventeen-year-old going on forty."

"So does that mean if I were to ask you to go out to dinner you'd consider it? Carmel has some of the best restaurants on the West Coast."

She looked down at her hiking boots and jeans. They were a good hour and a half away from Santa Cruz. By the time she picked up her car at Kyle's house in Carmel and drove all the way home to get cleaned up, and then all the way back again, it would be midnight and even the European-style restaurants would be closing. "I can't go like this."

"You're perfect for the place I have in mind."

And she was.

Kyle's house was perched on a rocky outcropping overlooking the ocean. It was one of the few Carmel houses on the ocean side of Scenic Road that had direct water access. The view was as open as structurally possible, which made the house appear larger and a part of the landscape. Alison had fallen in love with the rugged, volatile coastline that marked this area of California.

Inside, the house was decorated in tans, grays, and soft greens. The furniture was simple but classic, and beautifully finished to a soft shine. Alison had felt a welcoming warmth the minute she crossed the threshold, something that rarely happened in the overly decorated homes of her friends.

"Ready?" Kyle asked, joining her at the window.

"How did you do this?" she asked.

"What?"

"Create this feeling of peace."

He stood closer, their arms touching, their images reflected in the glass as if they'd stood that way a hundred times before. "It was important for the girls to feel a sense of home without seeing their mother everywhere they looked. I didn't want this house to be a shrine, but a place where they could and would remember her without being overwhelmed by those memories."

"And the furniture?"

"If it's wood, I made it, including the fireplace mantel. The girls picked out everything else."

"I noticed you don't have any pictures of Jenny."

"They're in the hallway and bedrooms."

Alison thought about her house and how every room had pictures of Dennis and Peter displayed on walls, tables, and bookshelves. With the exception of a couple of upholstered pieces, the furniture hadn't been replaced in twenty years. Without conscious thought, she'd created a shrine.

She forced a smile. "So you're a woodworker."

"Passed down from my father, who owned a cabinet shop for over forty years. When he retired, he and my mother moved to Africa, going wherever they were needed in over a dozen refugee camps. She's a nurse and works in the clinics. Dad spends his time building classrooms and teaching carpentry."

"And they're still there?" She did some quick calculating and realized they had to be in their eighties.

"They come home once a year, at Christmas. I arrange meetings with as many businesspeople, church leaders, and friends as I can so my mother can solicit funds to keep the clinics going. It's never enough, but people give what they can, and she's wonderful about keeping in touch so everyone knows exactly how their money is being spent."

"You and the girls must miss them."

"My mother finds a way to hook up to the Internet two or three times a month. She's convinced Skype was invented with her in mind." He leaned in close and nudged her playfully with his elbow. "Enough about me. Let's get out of here and see what's washed up on the beach while we were eating dinner."

She looked outside at the full moon sitting low on the horizon and at the shimmering path it created across the water. "Finders keepers?"

"If it bites, it's yours."

She laughed. "I can hardly wait."

They followed a path along the rocky crest. For the moment, there was no wind, only the sounds of birds gathering for the night and waves clearing the remnants of the day's footprints. At the end of another hundred yards, the path led them to a wider beach, as deserted as the first.

"The end to a perfect day," Alison said.

Kyle reached for her hand. "I'm glad you think so."

They walked that way for several minutes. "I realize we barely know each other," he said, "but I like the way I feel when I'm with you. I keep waiting for something to happen that will change my mind about what I'm feeling, but being with you every day just keeps getting better and better."

He stopped and looked into her eyes. "I'm going to go way out on a limb here and assume you feel the same way."

She did, but was hesitant to say so.

Kyle offered her an apologetic smile. "Too soon?"

It was on the tip of her tongue to tell him yes, that she needed time, when she surprised them both by saying, "No . . . I like the way I feel when I'm with you too."

"So what are we going to do about this elephant in the room?"

"The only thing we can—talk about it."

He nodded, but didn't say anything for a long time. "Should I go first?"

"Please."

He took a deep breath before he started, plainly going somewhere that wasn't an easy journey. "Jenny was the love of my life. From the day I met her I never strayed, either mentally or physically—wasn't even tempted. She was all I ever wanted or needed."

They came to a weathered bench nestled against a large rock retaining wall. Kyle cleared sand from the rustic wood as best he could. She sat down first and then he joined her.

"What happened?" Alison asked gently after they'd been there several minutes.

He leaned forward, his elbows resting on his knees. "You'd think after all these years the telling would get easier."

"There are times I feel like I'm going to punch the next person who asks me how Dennis died."

Even now, she continued to meet these kinds of people. No matter where she went at home, somehow someone found out she was one of "them." Either one-on-one, or in a group, the questions would start—which building, which floor were Dennis and Peter on, why were father and son together that day, were any of their remains ever found, how did she feel about the memorial, and on and on and on. After what should have been strictly personal details were revealed, inevitably the questions would continue with someone asking if she'd signed the papers saying she wouldn't sue the airlines, how much money was involved in the settlement—for some bizarre reason, this was always asked by a man—did the settlement change according to the life insurance payout, and on and on some more. It was as if bearing witness to her private grief would somehow lead to an understanding of something they couldn't comprehend any other way.

"It was a stupid accident," Kyle said. "Never should have happened." He leaned back again. "She'd stopped for a cup of coffee. The lid wasn't on tight. It spilled. When she tried to clean it up, she unconsciously moved the steering wheel to the right—not far, just enough to catch the front tire on a curb. The car rolled a couple of times and ended up on the opposite side of the road in the middle of oncoming traffic." He ran his hand across his face.

"Just like that, ten seconds—actually less, according to some witnesses—and her life was over. For a long time, I thought mine was too. Our youngest daughter, Caroline, was in the car, but in one of those ironic moments that make you believe in destiny, she managed to escape with only minor injuries. Even the bruises were gone in a matter of weeks. The rest wasn't so easy—she was affected mentally for a couple of years. Dangerously so. She and her mother had been arguing about a sleepover she wanted to go to, and the last thing she said before the accident was something hateful."

"How is she now?"

"Married with a couple of kids of her own. She says she's fine, but every once in a while, mostly during the holidays, I see that same lost look she had after the accident. It's pretty obvious, at least to me, where she's gone and what she's thinking."

"How many kids do you have?"

"Three. All girls."

"Were they home when Caroline was having problems?"

"The oldest, Karla, was in her final year at Stanford, and Sidney was just finishing her freshman year at UCLA."

"Did they come home?"

"For a semester, and then I insisted they go back to school. They were great about spending weekends with their sister, but she needed someone available to her full-time. So I sold my car dealerships in the Bay Area and brought Caroline down here with me. We moved into what had been our family vacation home, and I put her to work helping me remodel. It was the smartest thing I could have done. She needed to get away from the everyday reminders of home and from the friends who'd stopped calling. Most of all, I had to convince her that what happened wasn't her fault."

"How long ago was this?" Alison asked.

"Ten years last August."

"And now you're a grandpa."

"Times five. I'm still waiting on Sidney. I have a feeling it's going to be a long wait."

"Career?"

"She works for Apple in their design division and lives, eats, and breathes her job. She loves what she does so much we damn near have to kidnap her to get her to come home for the holidays."

"And Tanner Motors? How did that come about?"

"Boredom."

Alison knew little about car dealerships, but she did know there was a lot more money selling new models. "Why used cars?"

"I didn't want the headaches that come with new-car dealerships, especially the high-end kind that I'd owned before. Then when the economy took a nosedive and people started losing their jobs and then their homes, I figured it was time I did something to help out where I could."

"Which is why you handle the safe, affordable cars."

He put his legs out in front of him and crossed them at the ankles. "With a couple of exceptions."

"The Mustang being one?"

He nodded. "It's gone, by the way. Sold it to the family of a guy who spent his high school and what should have been his college years working the fields in Salinas to help put his brothers and sisters through school. It was a present from his family to celebrate the youngest sister's graduation from medical school."

"What a great gift."

"The best part is that it's his turn to go to school now. He needed the car for transportation, and his siblings felt it was time he had something that wasn't held together with duct tape."

"You're a nice man," Alison said.

He frowned. "What brought that on?"

She ignored his question and asked one of her own. "How big a loss did you take on the car?"

He stood and brought her up with him. "I wound up a whole lot richer at the end of that transaction than when I went in. I wish you could have seen the look on Francisco's face when his family showed up on the lot and his brother handed him the key."

"Like I said, you're a nice man." She came up on her toes and kissed him. She liked that he was the first man since Dennis who'd let her initiate the first kiss between them. Most of all, she liked the way kissing him made her feel, especially when he got over the shock and kissed her back. His lips were soft and yielding as the kiss deepened. Desires she thought she would never feel again spread through her midsection with a sweet ache of longing.

Dennis cupped her face with his hands. “Before this goes where I want it to go, we have unfinished business.”

At first she didn’t understand what he meant, and then it hit her. “Here or back at the house?”

“Doesn’t matter. The elephant is going to follow us until we set it free.”

“I could use a cup of coffee.”

He put his arm around her shoulders and started back, following their footprints, creating a path just wide enough for them to travel together.

Two hours and a pot of coffee later, Kyle said, “It’s hard to let go and rebuild your life when you’re not allowed to move past your grief in private.”

Alison saw an understanding and compassion in his eyes that she’d received from no one else. “I hung on too long, and now I don’t know how to let go.”

“Sure you do.” He took her hand, slowly opened her clinched fingers, and kissed each one, ending with her palm.

She caught her breath, torn between wanting him and terrified at the thought of leaving the imperfect world that had sustained her for the last decade. How could she walk away from the only shelter she knew?

God, she was such a coward.

Chapter 10

Alison tossed Christopher a head of lettuce. He dropped it. "Good thing it's wrapped in cellophane," she said as he dove to retrieve it from under the table.

He unwrapped the lettuce, broke it in two, and put the smaller piece under the faucet. "How hungry are you?"

"What you've got there will do." She put on an oven mitt and checked the salmon. "Five more minutes."

"I thought you told me a couple of days ago that you were going out for dinner."

"I postponed it until tomorrow. I told Kyle I wanted to spend some time with you tonight. We haven't had a chance to really talk since you got here, and I wanted to catch up." She poured two glasses of water and put them on the table.

"You didn't have to do that. It's not every day you get asked out on a date," he teased. "As a matter of fact, I can't seem to remember you ever being asked out."

"How could you forget Charles?" Her friend Linda had fixed her up with a man she said she was willing to bet her $14,000 Manolo Blahnik alligator boots would be the one to get Alison back into the dating scene again. Since Alison didn't wear anything that had to die to satisfy fashion, Linda had always known her boots were safe. Instead, when it turned out that everything about Charles was a lie, from his alma mater to his hairline, Alison insisted Linda make a donation to Planned Parenthood.

"You count him?"

"Not willingly—only to make a point." She checked the salmon again, this time with a fork. She was after crisp on the outside and still pink and moist in the middle, which was sometimes a matter of seconds. "Besides, I know I didn't have to stay home with you. I wanted to. Wasn't that supposed to be one of the reasons for this trip? So we could spend some time together before you take off for school?"

Christopher tore the lettuce into bite-size pieces, added the tomato, green onions, carrots, and celery he'd been cutting, topped it with croutons, dressed it, and put the bowl on the table. "It's not like I'm leaving as soon as we get back."

"And it's not like I'm trying to guilt you into spending time with me now." She reached up to brush a strand of hair off his forehead and then gave him a kiss on the cheek. "I happen to enjoy your company."

He leaned his hip into the counter and took a bite of lettuce. "Oh yeah? Seems to me you're spending a lot of time with this car guy."

"His name is Kyle Tanner. You're too young to have this much trouble remembering someone's name."

"Okay, so what's up with you and this Kyle Tanner guy?"

"I like him." She purposely busied herself getting the salmon out of the oven, but managed a glance to see how he'd reacted to her statement. "He's fun to be around."

" 'Like' as in, 'he's a great guy who gave me a good deal on a car,' or 'I can't wait to get my hands on his hot body'?"

"Oh, *definitely* the last one." She could feel herself blushing and knew if she didn't do something to discourage him, Christopher would be all over her with questions. She nudged him out of the way with her elbow. "You know I always go for the ones with the hot bodies."

"Oh my God, Grams. You really do like this guy. When did this happen? You've only seen him a couple of times."

"It's been more than a couple," she admitted.

"How many?"

"Nearly every day since I bought the truck."

"Whoa—what's up with that?"

"Like I said, he's a nice guy. And only one of those times was a real date." She pulled the baked potatoes and salmon out of the oven and put the larger piece of fish on Christopher's plate. "Enough about me. Is surfing as much fun as you thought it would be?"

He held her chair, a nearly extinct social mannerism that he'd been taught by his mother, then sat down at the opposite side of the table. "I'll tell you in a minute, but first I want to know more about Kyle Tanner."

"What do you want to know?"

"Everything."

"I don't know everything. Just some of the important stuff."

"Why are you making me drag this out of you?"

"Because it's fun."

"Not for me."

She relented. "Kyle is two years older than I am. He has three daughters and five granddaughters. His wife died in an automobile accident over ten years ago, and he hasn't had a serious relationship since—mainly because he's been too busy taking care of his family. He lives in Carmel. His house is bigger than a cottage but smaller than this one. It has an uninterrupted view of the ocean. Which, I have a feeling, pushes it up a couple hundred thousand dollars in this real estate market." She sliced open her potato and added sour cream and chives.

"I'm only telling you that to let you know he's comfortably situated and can take care of himself," she added.

"Hmmm . . . 'comfortably situated.' Kind of a stuffy term, don't you think?"

"Eat your salmon." She took a bite of salad. "Now let's get back to the surfing."

"Not yet. I think I should know what you were doing at his house."

"We stopped by—" She realized he was teasing her. "He's just a friend, Christopher. Who also happens to be a lot of fun to be around."

"Have you kissed him yet?"

Her only answer was an immediate flush that spread from her neck to her cheeks—the second time she'd blushed in less than ten minutes.

"You *have.* I guess that means I'm going to have to give you the social diseases lecture."

She couldn't look at him. "I think I have it covered."

Christopher sat back in his chair and stared at her. Suddenly serious, he said, "Too bad he lives here."

Not until that moment did she realize that he was worried about her being alone when he left for school. Not just the surface things, like who would climb up in the rafters in the garage to get the holiday decorations down, but the important ones, like who would she share her day with over dinner. Her heart swelled with sympathy. She'd spent far too much time worrying about herself and what Nora's marriage and Christopher's leaving would mean and hadn't stopped to think how worried they might be about her.

"I'll be fine, Christopher."

"I know you will." He picked off a crispy corner of the salmon with his fingers and popped it into his mouth. "This is better than what we get at home."

"I don't know about better, but it's different."

"It's okay, you know."

"What?"

"That something might be better here. There are lots of things we have at home that are different than California. And that's okay too. It's not like this is some big competition. Not being the same is okay."

"Sounds like you've been giving this some thought. Any particular reason?"

"I want to travel and meet new people and see how they live—how they think."

"You travel now. You've been to almost every state on the East Coast."

"To compete. It's like being in a bubble that just floats from one location to another, carrying the same people with the same interests with the same background from place to place. You could drop me in the middle of Lexington and I'd swear I'd never been there. And how many times have I competed at the Kentucky Horse Park?"

"What about school?" she asked, afraid of his answer.

He ignored her question. "How did my dad wind up at Penn State? Was it because that's where Grandpa went?"

Alison got up and poured herself a glass of wine from the bottle she'd opened the night before. "Where did that come from?"

Christopher sat back in his chair and put his napkin on the table. "I wonder all the time whether I'm this clone of my father and grandfather because it's what you and Mom want me to be, or if it's really true. There has to be something different about me. There has to be some small part of me that's just me, a part that would be me no matter who my relatives were."

Alison didn't know how to answer him. How could she admit she purposely looked for Peter and Dennis in Christopher as a way to convince herself that the essence of her husband and son hadn't really died? Maybe it had been understandable and even forgivable in the beginning, but how had she let it go on for over thirteen years?

"Did you ever wonder how I could be half mom's kid and a part of you and none of it show? Doesn't it seem a little strange that the only genes I inherited were from the men in the family?"

How could she have done this to him? She drained her glass and refilled it again. Liquid courage.

"Would it help if I told you that your dad hated salmon?" she said, knowing it was wrong to try to lighten the mood with a stupid question, but unable to come up with anything she hadn't said a dozen times already. "I'm sorry. I shouldn't have said that."

Christopher let out a humorless laugh. "I've never told you, but I'm not that crazy about it either."

"Your dad was afraid of horses," she quickly added. "So was your grandfather."

He reacted as if she'd flung a bucket full of water at him, drawing back, his mouth open in stunned surprise. "No way."

"When your dad was five, he was invited to a birthday party where they had pony rides for entertainment. Peter fell off the horse, and when your grandfather went to pick him up, the horse kicked him. The hoof hit his forehead, and even though it really wasn't cut that badly, it bled all over everything—and everyone who tried to help them. Imagine your dad screaming, your grandfather bleeding, and the birthday boy crying. That was a party to remember."

"I can see why they wouldn't like horses after that."

"It didn't bother you when the same thing happened to Freddie. You just stuck his head under a faucet and wrapped a towel around him until the ambulance came."

"I'd forgotten about Freddie. I don't think he ever came back for another lesson. At least I don't remember seeing him."

"See? You are different. Especially from your grandfather. He couldn't handle the sight of blood."

He came forward again, propping his elbows on the table. "You're trying too hard, Grams."

"Okay, how's this—your dad hated being a broker. He wanted to be a musician. A bass guitar player, actually. He had no desire to be the front man, just wanted to be a part of the band."

"How could I not have known this?"

"Because no one told you. You were so young when he died. I didn't think it was important. It was a dream he had when he was a kid. I don't know how he felt about it when he was older because we never talked about it."

"What about Grandpa? What was his dream?"

"He wanted to sail around the world."

"I didn't know he had a boat."

"He didn't. I don't think there's a rule that dreams have to make sense. I'm sure he figured he'd have plenty of time to learn how to sail after he retired. You never noticed all those sailing books in the library?"

"Yeah, but I never paid attention to them. There's a lot of books about space flight too, but—" He pinned her with a stare. "Don't tell me he wanted to be an astronaut too."

"That was my dream."

"So why didn't you ever do anything about it?"

"I was in love with the idea, but wasn't willing to put in the effort. It was a different time for women back then, and I wasn't the bra burner type. I was content to go from my parents' home to the home your grandfather and I built together."

"What was it like for you when Sally Ride went up?"

"I cried," Alison reluctantly admitted.

"Why?"

"For what might have been. I was only twenty-nine at the time and didn't know myself well enough to recognize I would have made a terrible astronaut."

"I don't know, Grams. I can picture you up there with your face pressed to the glass looking at Earth and wondering if you forgot to unplug your curling iron."

Alison laughed. She wasn't ready to let go of him. What would she do with herself when he was gone?

He got up from the table and took his dishes to the sink. "I have dessert," she said.

"Maybe later."

"Going out?"

"I thought I'd hang around with you tonight."

"Oh, Christopher, you don't have to do that. I'm perfectly capable of entertaining myself."

"I know. But there are some things I want to talk to you about."

She cleared the rest of the table. Neither of them had finished their meals. "Such as?"

"I want to know more about my father and grandfather. I understand why you and Mom have only told me the good stuff, but I need to know who they really were. I used to think there was no way I could ever measure up to them, that one day the Vatican was going to announce they were candidates for sainthood. But then I got older and looked around, and there just aren't a whole lot of people who are like that. There must have been something about them that made them like everyone else—just regular guys.

"And then I started wondering if you were keeping something bad from me because you thought I couldn't take it."

It never once entered her mind that he could or would come up with anything remotely like this. It was long past the time she and Christopher should have had this conversation. "Let's leave the dishes for later. I'm going to open another bottle of wine. We can go outside and watch the sunset, and I'll fill you in on the good, the bad, and the ugly about your father and grandfather."

They settled into two oversize chairs with blue-and-yellow-striped cushions and put their feet up on the matching ottomans. She touched her glass to his canned soda and said, "To new beginnings."

When she'd settled back in the chair and taken a moment to absorb the beauty surrounding her, she began. "Do you want to ask questions or should I just pick something and jump in?"

"Jump away."

What were the important things, the ones that would make a difference in understanding two people Christopher would be tied to for the rest of his life but would only ever know through the eyes of others? With the same faith that accompanies a skydiver who steps through the open door of a plane, Alison took a deep breath and jumped.

"Your father ran away from home when he was thirteen. It wasn't the first time he'd sneaked out of the house with his valuables in a backpack, but it was the most serious. This time he was angry at me in particular, but his dad was a close second. We'd refused to let him transfer to a new high school, and he was convinced that if he didn't go he would lose the girl he'd fallen in love with that summer.

"Naturally, we combed the neighborhood where the girl lived, thinking he'd gone there. A day turned into three and then a week. There were police and private detectives involved in the search. We were frantic, as I'm sure you can imagine."

"Where did you find him?"

"St. Louis."

"No shit," Christopher said in awe. "He was only thirteen and he made it all the way to Missouri?"

"He was a very clever thirteen. And he could easily pass for a lot older mainly because of his dark hair and the fact that he was already shaving."

"Where was he going?"

"California." She glanced at Christopher, a "can you believe it?" look on her face. "He was going to support himself by playing bass guitar in a rock band after the money his grandparents gave him for his middle school graduation ran out."

"What happened?"

"He got mugged. And tired. And lonely. And more importantly, he got arrested for shoplifting from a grocery store after he lost all his money to the mugger. Suddenly living at home with parents who couldn't understand him didn't seem so bad after all. Dennis flew out to pick him up. I never asked what they talked about when he got there or on their flight home. It was enough that Peter was safe and willing to promise that he would never do anything like that again."

"My dad got arrested? How did that turn out?"

"He was taken to the Juvenile Detention Center and held there until your grandfather could bail him out. The shoplifting charge went away when your dad went to the store owner and apologized."

"And the girlfriend?"

"We were willing to yield on that, and as soon as he was home and settled we took him to the school so he could see it for himself—hoping, of course, that he would hate it. It turned out that I actually liked the teachers I met, and even though we believed it was a mistake, we agreed to let Peter transfer. It was one of the hardest decisions we'd ever made as his parents, but we figured that, if being with her was important enough for him to take such drastic measures, we had to respect his feelings and be there for him if something went wrong. He was beside himself and couldn't wait to tell Katie. He found her holding hands with another boy."

"Ouch."

"It was a rough winter that year, for all of us." She put her glass on the end table and stood. "I'll be right back. I'm going to get my sweater. Then I'll tell you about your grandfather's first job and how he got fired."

Christopher stared into the orange and pink sky and then at the people sitting on the beach doing the same thing. He'd always wondered at how slowly the sun seemed to move across the sky—until it reached the end of the day. Then, as if picking up speed from its downhill slide, there was a rush to end the day.

Was that what life was like? Was this what his grandmother meant when she said she could feel her days slipping by too fast? Was that the reason for her deep sigh whenever he insisted he couldn't wait to be older?

Chapter 11

Christopher stood on Grace's porch and rang the doorbell. She answered wearing her work clothes instead of the swimming suit he'd expected. After three weeks of lessons and conquering some decent-size waves, it was as hard for him to stay off the water as it was for Grace to stay away from riding the horse she'd fallen in love with. "I thought we were hitting the waves this morning."

She had tears in her eyes when she answered. "I can't. Two of the packers didn't show up for work, and my dad needs me at the nursery. He doesn't know that this is our last day together, and I didn't have the heart to tell him. He really needs me. If he doesn't get this order out—"

Christopher took her in his arms. "It's okay. I'll be back before you've had a chance to miss me."

"Don't do that," she said, hitting his shoulder with the flat of her hand. "You're not ever coming back, and we both know it. This is it. Our last day together. Ever."

Too many people had left Grace for her to believe anyone ever came back. He could tell her a hundred times that he would be ringing her doorbell within six months and it wouldn't make any difference. The only way to convince her was to leave and keep his promise. "Does that mean you'll stop waiting for me?"

"No." She lifted the bottom of his T-shirt and wiped her cheeks, then tried to smile. "I'll just add you to my list, along with my mother."

"Hey, that's not fair," he said, feeling both defensive and sad.

"I don't feel like being fair."

"When do you have to be at the nursery?"

"A half hour ago."

"Want me to drive you? That would give us a little time."

"What about tonight?"

He winced. "I promised Grams I'd have dinner with her. She's trying really hard to pretend she's excited for me, but she's not. And I think she's a little afraid of what my mother is going to say about her not keeping a tighter rein on me."

"I thought you were going to talk to your mom last night."

"I did, but it was pretty one-sided. No matter what I said, she kept telling me just to wait until she gets home in the morning before I take off. I kept telling her it wouldn't make any difference, but she wouldn't listen. She wants to talk about what I'm doing. Or so she says. What she really wants is to guilt me into doing what she thinks is best for me."

"Wow, sounds pretty ugly."

He let out a sigh. "Not ugly, just normal. She's having a hard time with me making my own decisions. Probably because it doesn't happen very often. For the last year it's been like she's standing in the basement and I'm standing on the roof. We can't hear each other, so neither one of us makes any effort to listen. Usually it's easier for me to go along with what she wants, but not this time."

"What did she say about not going to Penn State?"

"That put her over the top. I thought she was going to catch the next flight home. She started breathing again when I told her the woman in admissions had arranged everything so that I could take a yearlong leave and come back in the fall next year without any new testing or penalty. It helps to have your grandfather's name on a building when you want a favor."

"How's she going to feel when she finds out you lied to her?"

"I didn't lie. I just left out a couple of things."

"Like you're going to be applying to other universities and changing your major?"

"I figured she had as much as she could handle. I'll drop that one on her at Christmas. With any luck, she'll be so caught up in her life with James by then that it won't matter that I'm going to apply to veterinary school. She'll be happy just knowing I'm actually going back to school."

Grace's phone announced she had a text. "That's my dad wondering where I am." She went inside and grabbed her phone and keys, sending a quick "On my way" as she followed Christopher to the truck.

"Can I call you later for a ride home?"

"What time?"

"Four-thirty."

"I'll be there. Dinner isn't until seven, so that will give us a couple of hours."

They were settled in the truck and headed toward the highway when Grace said, "How would you feel if I could scrape enough money together to fly someplace to meet you for a weekend?"

"I'd love it. But I don't think your folks would appreciate you flying off to spend the weekend with a guy you've only known a couple of weeks, and I don't want them mad at me."

"I don't want you to go," she admitted. "I wish you could just stay here and ride the waves and figure out who you are and what you want to do with your life. Why do you have to go wandering around in this old truck? What's with that?"

"I'm running away from home," he said, more to himself than to her. "It's something I've wanted to do for a long time. I just didn't know how."

"Your dad was lucky. Think of all the awful things that could have happened to a thirteen-year-old kid."

"But they didn't. The awful thing waited until he was a grown man and supposedly protected by a great job and lots of money and thick concrete walls and steel beams." Christopher pulled off the highway and headed to the valley where several orchid growers had discovered the perfect climate to raise their product.

She was crying again. "I don't want to lose you."

He reached for her hand. "You won't."

Almost too softly for him to hear, she added, "I think I love you." Before he had a chance to answer, she added, "I know that's crazy. We've only known each other a month."

"How long does it take?"

"Don't tease me about this. I'm serious."

"I am too. I knew I loved you from the minute you shared your sweet potato fries with me at Carpos. I've never known anyone as outgoing and funny and easy to be around as you are. You don't give a damn who I am or how much money I have or what happened to my father and grandfather."

"Okay," she said with a sheepish smile. "You convinced me. But tell me again."

"I love you."

"For sure?"

"Yes . . . for sure. And for always." He could hear voices in his mind insisting that he was too young, too inexperienced, and too naive to know what love was. He knew without question that they were wrong.

"All right. I'll promise not to bug you anymore about when you'll be back. I'll even keep my texts below fifty."

"A week?"

"A day."

"What if that's not enough for me to tell you what it's like standing on the edge of the Grand Canyon?"

Grace caught her breath. "Save the Grand Canyon for when I'm with you."

"What about Yellowstone?"

"Oh—that too."

"This isn't going to work."

"I know. I'm sorry. I'll try harder from now on."

He pulled up to the side entrance of the nursery. Grace leaned across the seat and kissed him. She tasted like strawberry gum and smelled like lavender. "I'll see you later."

She looked up and saw her father waiting for her. "Gotta go." She kissed Christopher again, this time, for her father's benefit, with less yearning. She got out of the truck and disappeared into the greenhouse. Andrew smiled and waved as Christopher turned around to leave.

For the third time that morning he tried manipulating how many days he needed to get back to New York in time for his birthday so he could stay with Grace just a little longer. Birthdays were important to his mother, none more so than his eighteenth. According to Google, if he drove ten hours a day it would take him four and a half days, not counting delays or traffic or any of a dozen other possibilities. Five days seemed reasonable.

Driving twelve hours a day so that he could get there a day sooner, and giving him another day with Grace, would scare the crap out of both his mother and grandmother. He didn't have the patience to listen to the warnings that would rain down on him like the backside of a hurricane.

Simplifying his life was turning out to be more complicated than he'd ever imagined.

Chapter 12

Christopher pulled the truck into the back of Tanner Motors where Kyle had told him to park. Of course that was because Kyle thought he was there to return the truck and wanted it left where the mechanic could pick it up and look at it before it went in to be painted.

Kyle must have seen Christopher pull up because within minutes he came out of the office and headed his way. "Good to see you again," he called. "Are you in a hurry, or do you have time for lunch?"

"Lunch sounds great."

Kyle looked around. "Where's Alison?"

"She's not coming."

He cocked an eyebrow and studied Christopher for several seconds before nodding. "I hope you don't mind, but Alison has told me about what you've been going through."

"It's okay. She's told me a lot about you too."

"All good, I hope."

"For the most part."

Kyle chuckled. "I can see it's a mistake to lead with my chin around you."

"Sorry—couldn't resist. Actually, I'm pretty sure she likes you just the way you are."

"Nice to hear. Thanks. The feeling is mutual." He started back toward the office. "Give me a second to close up and we can get out of here."

Christopher hesitated. "It might be better if we took care of the paperwork on the truck first."

"All right. Although there's not much to do. Just a couple of things to sign and it's a done deal." He frowned. "Someone's picking you up, I assume?"

"I hope it's not necessary. I wanted to talk to you about buying the truck."

Kyle opened the door and held it for Christopher. "Take a seat," he said. "I'll get your file."

"You don't seem surprised."

"I told your grandmother that you'd fall in love with that truck, but she couldn't see it at the time. I'm not sure she can see it now. But there's just something about those old five-window beauties that pulls me in every time. I would have kept it myself if I'd had the room to store it." He tossed the file on the desk and sat opposite Christopher. "Would you like me to arrange to have it transported back to New York? I know a couple of companies that aren't too expensive and do a good job."

"I'm going to drive it. That was one of the things I wanted to talk to you about—whether or not you feel it's up to the trip mechanically. I haven't had any trouble around here, but it's over three thousand miles between here and New York."

"That truck could handle a dozen round-trips to anyplace on this continent, including Alaska."

"Alaska?" Christopher's eyes lit up.

Kyle sat back and studied Christopher. "Want to tell me what you've got in mind?"

Christopher didn't know how to express himself without sounding like he'd been smoking a peyote-filled pipe. Mostly, he didn't want to come across all mystic and new age. He hadn't been in California long enough to pull it off. "There's a lot of country I haven't seen and a lot of people I haven't met. I figure I'll never have another time or another opportunity to just take off and wing it. Once I start school, everything will change. I'll get caught up in my classes and grades and riding again."

He struggled to find the words that would help Kyle understand, realizing instinctively that he would be the person his grandmother turned to when she was trying to figure out what was up with her wayward grandson. "I want to know what it's like to come to a road and follow where it goes just because it looks interesting. For one year in my life I want to experience real freedom. Then I'll go back and do what's expected of me."

"Are you sure one year is enough?" Kyle asked. "What if you like that feeling of freedom so much that you can't give it up?"

"Not going to happen. Somewhere inside me I'm still my father's son. It would hurt too many people."

Kyle sat back and took several minutes to absorb what Christopher had told him. "I know a lot of good people pretty much all around this country. I'm going to give you a notebook with their names and addresses and phone numbers. If you need something, if you break down, if you're in trouble, you can call any of these people and they will be there to help you as soon as they can. Think of it as a kind of roadside insurance."

Christopher grinned and shifted in his seat. "Thanks. I appreciate it, but I hope I'm never in the position where I have to call on any of your friends."

"You never know. You just might get a hankering for a home-cooked meal. Any one of them would love to have you stop by. And I know your grandmother and mother would feel a whole lot better knowing there are people out there ready and willing to take care of you. Consider them part of the 'whole lot of people you haven't met yet.' "

"Is that what's called an ulterior motive?"

"It comes from being a parent and grandparent myself." Kyle changed the subject as he began sorting through the papers. "What about the horse you came here to buy? I thought Alison said you'd found one you liked."

"I bought him. I'm going to leave him here, and they're going to continue his training while I'm gone."

"That should go a long way to convince your mom and Alison that you'll be coming home eventually—but I have a feeling it might have more to do with you thinking about settling out here eventually." Kyle opened a file next to his desk and pulled out a sales contract. He tapped the stack of papers on his desk to even them, looking at Christopher over the top.

"I'm going to deny I told you this should you ever feel the need to pass it on, but I think this trip is the best thing you could be doing with your life right now. Hell, I'd be trying to bum a ride if it weren't for everything I've got going on around here—your grandmother included.

"Just be careful," he went on, trying hard to keep his words from sounding like a lecture and almost succeeding. "Not everyone deserves your trust. And no matter how much that mushroom growing in the forest looks like the one you get back home in the grocery store, don't eat it." He locked his gaze on Christopher's. "You get what I'm saying?"

"Stay away from drugs."

"And booze. Not only because you're too young to drink it legally, but because we're all too stupid when we're drunk to see when we're headed for trouble. There will be plenty of time to do that kind of stupid stuff when you get home. Stay away from it on the road."

With startling clarity, Christopher suddenly saw what it would have been like to grow up with a father and was filled with an ache that nearly choked him. Did Kyle's daughters feel the absence of their mother with the same longing Christopher felt for his missing father?

"One more thing," Kyle added. "Always look and act like you're down to your last twenty dollars. This country is filled with good people, but there are some bad ones in the mix. Don't tempt them."

"How can you tell the difference?"

"For the most part, you can't. The guy you meet nursing a cup of coffee at a hole-in-the-wall diner could turn out to be a gentle schizophrenic who's only looking for a kind word, while the happy-go-lucky fatherly sort who slides onto the stool next to you at that same diner could be reaching for your wallet while he's slapping you on the back."

"I hope you're not telling my grandmother this stuff."

Kyle laughed. "Not a chance." He passed the stack of papers across to Christopher. "Did Alison happen to mention that she's coming back after your birthday?"

She hadn't even hinted it was a possibility. "When did this happen?"

"This morning. She got a call from the woman who owns the house where you've been staying. Seems the couple who were supposed to be there in July can't make it after all."

His grandmother couldn't be staying because of him, not when he was leaving in the morning. Which meant it had to be Kyle. Somewhere in the back of his mind he had to have figured this out, but he'd been so caught up in his own world that he hadn't given hers more than a cursory thought. "This is turning into an interesting summer."

"We have some things to work out," Kyle said. "My life is here, and hers is in New York."

"It used to be in New York. Now, with my mother moving to Connecticut and me taking off, there's not much to hold her there anymore." The words were difficult, the idea even more so. The house he'd lived in for over half of his life, the horses and barns and paddocks, the town, the neighbors—these were home, the place he'd counted on always being there. But he had no right to ask or expect his grandmother to maintain a home just to accommodate his occasional visits. She deserved the same freedom he longed to experience.

"Memories are powerful magnets."

"I'm beginning to understand that." Christopher dropped his gaze to the papers in front of him. "Are you going to try to talk her into staying?" He wished he hadn't asked. Selfishly, he wasn't ready for her to start a new life. A huge part of his independence was tied to knowing his mother and grandmother would be there if he called.

"Yes," Kyle admitted. "I'm not crazy about the idea of a long-distance courtship. We both learned the hard way that you can't count on tomorrow."

Christopher tried to put a positive spin on his grandmother moving three thousand miles away. "At least I'll have family around if I manage to get into Davis."

"I thought you were going to Penn State."

"It's a long story."

"I have time."

Christopher began, reluctantly, telling Kyle about a dream he'd never shared with anyone until Grace. He talked about his long-standing friendship with the vet who took care of his horses and how he'd gravitated toward taking care of the large animals when he worked at his neighbor's farm. His first trip to Tufts University Veterinary School with his horse Josi had been an eye-opener. He'd left determined to talk to his mother about veterinary school and walked into a surprise party she'd thrown to celebrate his acceptance at Penn State. Everyone was there. Everyone was thrilled for him. His grandmother cried. His mother beamed. He put up good old Penn State's blue-and-white flag and surrendered.

"Why didn't you say anything before now?" Kyle asked.

"Because I didn't want to disappoint my mother and grandmother. It wasn't just their dream that I follow in my father's and grandfather's footsteps, it was their obsession. I can't remember a time when I didn't have a Penn State pennant in my bedroom or a T- shirt in my closet. We even have Nittany Lions ornaments on the Christmas tree and an exact granite copy of the Nittany lion on a pedestal in the garden. Growing up, the only homecoming game I ever missed was when I was in Lexington at a dressage competition."

"How would you feel if I were to put in a good word for you at Davis? It couldn't hurt to do your undergraduate work there."

Was it really possible for everything to fall into place this easily? Of course there was a wide river between a good word and an acceptance letter. "That would be great."

Kyle pushed his chair back from the desk. "Why don't we talk about this over lunch? We can take care of the truck when we get back."

Christopher followed him outside and waited while Kyle flipped the sign on the door and then locked it. "I can see why Grams likes you."

"And it's pretty easy to see why she's crazy about you too." As naturally and comfortably as if Christopher were his own son, Kyle put his arm around his shoulders and walked him to the garage stall holding the Tesla.

The next morning Alison stood beside the truck, her arms folded tightly across her chest, fighting tears while she waited for Christopher to come out of the house.

"I think I've got everything," he said, standing on the porch and staring at her. "Come on, Grams, you promised. No tears."

"It's the wind."

"It's foggy. There is no wind."

"Okay, so I got something in my eye."

"It's just a road trip. People go on them all the time. It's why there's so much traffic. Just imagine I'm going away to college."

"I'd rather imagine you pulling up to the house five days from now."

"Whatever gets you through the week."

She laughed as she wiped tears from her cheeks. "Wherever did you pick up that expression?"

"Grace's dad says it all the time."

"I saw Andrew this morning. He said Grace was crying too."

"I seem to have that effect on the women in my life."

"Only because we love you." She put her arms around him and hugged him tight. "Now go on. Get out of here. And before I forget, there's a present in the glove box."

"What is it?"

"A camera—something that takes pictures a cut above your phone. You're going to be seeing a lot of country I've never seen, and I want a full report, pictures included."

He settled into the driver's seat and rolled down the window. "Love you, Grams."

She blew him a kiss as he pulled out of the driveway. "Five days," she called after him.

Still facing forward, he put his arm out the window and waved one last time.

Alison watched until the truck disappeared into the eucalyptus grove before she headed back into the house to answer her cell phone. It was Nora.

"He's on his way," she said in lieu of a greeting.

In more ways than we might have wanted, and on a road that's sure to have more bumps and twists and turns than we would have wished, but it's his journey, not ours. No matter how much it hurts, it's time to let him go.

Alison carried the phone to the back deck only half listening to Nora's plans to try to talk some sense into Christopher when he arrived. They discussed last-minute details for his birthday party and what to do with the new ceramic pieces that had arrived the day before, then said good-bye with a promise to call each other as soon as either of them heard from Christopher.

She tossed the phone onto the chair and went to the railing, where she had a better view of the beach. The fog would be gone in another hour or so, and the beach would begin to fill. But for now it was nearly deserted.

Was this your doing, Dennis? I know I've been complaining about being lonely and that I've been worried about Christopher, but don't you think you went just a little overboard?

I finally decided you must have called Peter in to give you a hand with Christopher. That brave face I put on when I saw him off was about as real as the smile on the runner-up in the Miss America contest. I'm going to miss him all day every day and with every part of my being.

Is that why you sent Kyle in my direction? I like him. Maybe too much. But I think you'd like him too, so I guess it's okay. After all these years, I'm actually thinking about uprooting myself and doing something I couldn't have imagined a month ago. Can you picture me a California Girl? Well, okay, a California Woman.

Alison watched a mother and her five-year-old son cross the sand and settle near the shore, where the sand was wet and compact. The boy was carrying buckets and cups and scoops, equipment to build a sand castle. The mother had the towels and umbrella and water bottles.

Alison's eyes grew misty as memories of long-ago beaches and sand castles washed over her.

"For every thing there is a season," she said with poignant longing.

And we've reached the season of final good-byes, my beloved. It really is long past the time I should have moved on.

Her phone announced a text message. She considered ignoring it, but habit won out.

It was Christopher.

"Hey, Grams! Stopped for a burger and realized I forgot to say I luv u. I do. Luv u, I mean."

She pressed the phone to her chest and smiled as tears filled her eyes. She was okay. No, she was a whole lot better than okay.

"Thank you, Christopher," she texted back. Then she called Kyle to ask him if he would like to accompany her to New York to celebrate Christopher's birthday and to meet Nora.

His "yes" was filled with an enthusiasm that made her heart sing.

PART TWO
August

Chapter 1

"How long are you going to be mad at me?" Bridget asked, shifting lanes to merge onto the freeway after leaving the Sacramento International Airport.

Danielle shot her a glaring look. "I haven't decided."

"Could you at least try to understand?" There was an unmistakable plea in the question.

"No." Danielle ran her hand under the seat-belt strap that crossed her shoulder. She'd paid a premium on her current car for the sole reason that it had an adjustment to keep the belt from cutting into her neck. Now she was spoiled, even knowing, with all that was going on at home, that it was likely the last time she'd be able to afford this particular luxury.

Most of the time she didn't mind being an eighth of an inch under six feet tall because she'd made enough money over the years to afford the consequences of not fitting the norm, but now that she and Grady temporarily lacked an income since they'd lost the ski shop, she was going to have to learn to deal with things differently.

"You do realize I could do all the things that make people feel sorry for me. The minute someone realizes I've lost my hair to chemo, they're mine." Bridget gave Danielle a quick smile before she turned to look at oncoming traffic, slowed the Honda to match their speed, then eased into the flow behind a semi hauling trailers filled to overflowing with bright red Roma tomatoes. The tomatoes were headed to the factory to be turned into a paste that would become everything from catsup to pizza sauce, and the sight of the trucks on the freeway was as familiar as the rice fields.

"How was your flight?" Bridget asked, purposely changing the subject.

"Great. Right up to the minute I saw you with that rag on your head."

Bridget reached up to touch the scarf she'd wrapped turban style around her fuzzy scalp. "My mother made this."

"Makes sense. Your mother always did like your sister better than you."

Bridget laughed. "God, I've missed you."

"Just not enough to let me know what you've been going through?" Danielle tried, but couldn't help a welling of tears. "How could you not tell me?"

"It's taken two years for the four of us to put this trip together. And even at that, we're still a year past the five-year schedule we promised we'd never forsake—*no matter what.* There was no way I was going to give anyone an excuse to postpone again."

"Do you have any idea how lame that sounds? What could have been more important? One phone call and we would have been on the first plane to Sacramento—all of us. We would have worked something out."

"I thought about it, but Carrie was in the middle of a battle to keep the love of her life from walking out. You were knee-deep in that new project at work. And Angie . . . she never takes time off for anything."

"Did you buy all that stuff with Carrie?"

"What do you mean?" Bridget asked.

"I don't know . . . it seemed kinda fishy to me. She never even mentioned she was living with someone, and then all of a sudden she was terrified they were going to break up."

Bridget adjusted the air conditioner vents, directing them at her face. "Are you going to ask her what happened?"

"No way. I figure if she wanted us to know, she would have told us."

"Still . . . aren't you curious?"

Danielle laughed. "Don't even try. There's nothing you can say that will get me to go there with Carrie."

"You've never been shy about asking me about my love life," Bridget said.

"That's different. I didn't make a blood vow behind my grandfather's barn to never keep secrets from Carrie and Angie the way I did with you." Danielle and Bridget had been best friends since middle school in Atlanta, Georgia. They'd expanded their friendship to include Carrie and Angie when they were sophomores at the University of Virginia and created what had turned into a lifelong bond. Despite winding up living a thousand or more miles apart from each other, the four of them had remained best friends. Just not always as close as Bridget would have liked. Otherwise, Bridget never could have kept her cancer a secret from them.

Danielle knew where and to whom Bridget had lost her virginity. More importantly, she knew whether it had been worth the wait.

She had been the maid of honor at Bridget's wedding and was the first one at the hospital four years ago when Bridget had her second miscarriage, the one that ended any possibility she would ever be able to carry a baby to term. Danielle had arranged a flight, packed a bag, gotten to the airport, flown from Denver, and arrived in Dallas before Miles managed to leave his meeting in Houston.

Danielle had never liked him before; she actively hated him after that trip.

Bridget passed the tomato truck only to get stuck behind one hauling almonds. It was harvest season in the Sacramento Valley, and the freeways were filled with open and closed trucks hauling everything from watermelons to apples to peaches to plums. Later would come rice and olives and onions and garlic. "I knew you'd be upset when you found out about the cancer, but I was so sick, all I wanted to do was crawl in a hole and disappear."

"Did this happen before or after you dumped Miles?"

"I know how hard it is to accept, but you need to get over it. He dumped me." Bridget fought to show that she'd moved on, but the way her hands gripped the steering wheel, so tight her knuckles turned white, gave her away. She shrugged. "Pure and simple, he wanted kids and I couldn't have them. He felt it was not only his right but his duty to find someone who could."

"What about adopting?"

"Not good enough. Miles is convinced his sperm carries a genetic superiority that would be criminal not to pass on. He panicked when he read an article that said males have a biological clock too, and that his is ticking away his chance of producing wunderkinds. For a while he was willing to go the surrogate route if we could find someone suitable. But then I was diagnosed with breast cancer, and he said he simply couldn't take the chance that I would die and scar his children with my loss."

Danielle groaned. "I will never understand what possessed you to stay with that asshole as long as you did."

"I put it off to my warped idea of love. Even after the four of us stole Miles's car and we knew that if he ever found out what we'd done he'd see we all landed in jail, I made excuses for him. Not even you and Carrie and Angie pointing out all the reasons I should run like hell got through to me. Miles convinced me his screwing around had nothing to do with how he felt about me and that the love of a good woman—meaning me, of course—would change him." She laughed at the thought of ever believing something so far-fetched.

"And you have to remember," she went on, realizing the conversation was long overdue, "when Miles screwed up, no one apologized better. He had contrition down to an art form. Forget the wine and roses, with Miles it was tears and a ruby bracelet.

"Through it all, I managed to build a life that I could never have managed on my own. I loved the traveling and the opportunity to see museums and galleries. And on most of those trips, because of Miles's connections, I had VIP access to places the public never gets to see.

"Dubai was incredible. Our apartment was on the fiftieth floor of a marble palace. There were jaw-dropping views in every direction. I wore designer clothes and had live-in help. When Miles's boss discovered I was interested in art, he arranged a private tutor to accompany me on expeditions to the best galleries in the Middle East."

Bridget sighed. "I was living a fairy tale."

"Some fairy tale," Danielle said. "I will never understand why you married him. You are beautiful and smart and fun. Any man who thinks with the brain above his neck would be thrilled to have you in his life."

Bridget shrugged. "By the time it fell apart, I recognized that for all his faults, Miles had something I needed. He was emotionally safe because I no longer had expectations. I honestly didn't care. I knew he would be unfaithful, and I honestly believed he couldn't hurt me anymore. I was right about one and dead wrong about the other."

"We should have had this conversation a long, long time ago."

"To what point?" Bridget asked, sending Danielle a poignant smile. "My father screwed around on my mother the entire time they were married, and she chose to pretend it wasn't happening. She cooked and cleaned and ironed his shirts and slept with him when he was between lovers and full of promises that it would never happen again. I had no illusions about Miles. I knew exactly what I was going to get out of the marriage. And I wasn't wrong."

"Were you still sleeping with him after you found out?"

She shot a glance at Danielle. "Finally—something you'll like. I told him I wouldn't sleep with him until he brought me a doctor's report saying he was clean." She chuckled. "He threw a fit and called me a few choice names and even resorted to threats at one point, but I didn't budge. He gave in eventually."

"Why did he care when he could always pick up someone on the side?"

"Oh, he did, but he couldn't stand the idea that he couldn't have me too."

"I'm surprised he didn't just leave."

"Ah, there's the key to all of this. Divorce is frowned on at Kelly and Bascome. Too messy. Not to mention too emotional and time-consuming. It gave me leverage and, for the most part, a life that was better than living in a loft."

Danielle didn't believe her. There was too much pain in the telling for it to have been as simple as Bridget made out.

"But when Miles's mother got sick and he made a big deal out of exiting the fast track to rush home to take care of her, I thought things might be looking up for us. Then I found out his career was at a standstill and he had some major repair work to do to get back into the good graces of his boss, and everything slipped into place. Turned out that taking care of his mother was going to be my job while he perfected his role of self-sacrificing martyr."

Danielle frowned. "That's why you moved back to the States? Why didn't you ever say anything?"

"I was too humiliated. And I knew what you'd say."

"I remember her funeral. It was years after you came home."

"Turned out her death wasn't exactly imminent after all. Funny thing about heart disease. Get a doctor who knows what he's doing and he can put in a pacemaker that keeps even the hardest heart beating."

"What was it—two years she lived with you?"

"Three."

"Your life must have been hell." Danielle shuddered. "So where are you now, divorce-wise?"

"It's done. I'm set up to start school next spring at California State University Sacramento. Not exactly the top school for a master's in art history, but close to my doctors and the friends I've made while I was going through treatment. I wanted to give myself plenty of time before I jump into anything again." Bridget adjusted her scarf, slipping a finger underneath the lavender folds and scratching.

"Where are you with your treatments?"

"My doctor says I'm in complete remission."

"That's fantastic," Danielle said. When Bridget didn't immediately respond, she added, "It is, isn't it?"

"Of course it is."

"But?"

"But nothing." Bridget forced a smile. "I just need to get used to thinking of myself as a survivor."

Danielle put her hand over Bridget's where it gripped the steering wheel. "I'm so glad nothing got in the way of our getting together. It's obvious you need this. You need us."

"That's me—needy."

"You aren't the only one," Danielle said, swallowing another urge to cry. "So dish, girlfriend. I want to hear all about the divorce."

"Okay, but after this, I don't want to talk about it anymore. My gift to myself is to put the divorce behind me and explore the wonderful new directions my life is going to take.

"California is a no-fault divorce state, so there's not much to tell. Everything is automatically divided, including retirement accounts. He could have negotiated some of the stuff and I would have backed off, but he was so scared that he'd come out sounding like the self-centered son-of-a-bitch that he is by leaving in the middle of my cancer treatments that he just kept shoving stuff at me."

"Whatever you've gotten," Danielle said, "it doesn't come close to what you deserve." She toed off her heels and smoothed her slacks. "What did you have to give up to get him to go along with what you wanted?"

Bridget glanced at Danielle. "You know me too well."

"I used to. Or at least I thought I did."

"I can't write a memoir about our time together."

Danielle burst out laughing. "As if you'd want to. As if there was anything about him anyone would want to read."

"He's convinced he's going to be famous in the business world one day."

"For what?"

"He's still waiting for the revelation."

Danielle put her hand up for a high-five. "Way to go, girlfriend."

Danielle stared out the window at the fields of rich agricultural land being consumed by houses. She felt an almost overwhelming sense of guilt for not being a better friend to Bridget these past six years. She, Angie, and Carrie hadn't known about the cancer, but they couldn't hide behind the fact that Bridget hadn't told them. There were clues in the abbreviated emails they exchanged on a daily basis, and in Bridget's persistent nagging about the four of them finding a way to get together.

All it would have taken was a quick flight. Denver wasn't that far from Sacramento. She could have surprised Bridget on her birthday or just come for a day to take a friend to lunch.

"How long does it take to get from Sacramento to Santa Cruz?" Danielle said, struck by a sudden impulse.

"Who's driving?"

"Me."

"Three to four hours, depending on traffic."

"What time do we have to be in San Jose to pick up Angie and Carrie?"

"Not until tomorrow. Why?"

"I want to go shopping."

"In *Sacramento*? This is not the place someone comes to look for your kind of—"

"Stop right there. I'm not that big a snob." Danielle hesitated. "Well, maybe I am, but I can make do if I have to. You must at least have a Nordstrom."

"Several, but wouldn't you rather go to San Francisco? It's on the way, kinda."

"Well, yes, eventually. But before I take you anywhere, I'm going to get you some new scarves. And hats. And all kinds of fun things, including a sexy new bikini. It's my gift to see you on your way for this wondrous journey."

"I'd rather spend the time catching up with what's been going on in your life. You haven't told me anything about the store or Grady or the new puppy."

"The new puppy is completely egalitarian, peeing throughout the house with no regard for tile or carpet. I've turned him over to Grady and told him I won't be back until the two of them have worked things out. Then I want the house steam-cleaned from one end to the other."

"That takes care of Grady and the puppy, but what about you?"

"Same old same old." Not exactly the truth, but Da-nielle's problems were an anthill compared to Bridget's termite mound. And she really didn't care that she should be on a tight budget. She and Grady would work that out when she got home. "About the shopping—indulge me, okay? I'm going to outfit you in bright colors and flirty shirts and skirts. I want you stopping to take a second look every time you pass a mirror. Remember the fun we used to have creating haute couture from the sales racks at Marshalls? We could both use a day like that again."

Bridget smiled. "You were always a lot better at it than I was."

"You're just saying that because it's true."

Bridget beamed in delight. "I have a spare room. You want to move in?"

"If that puppy isn't housebroken pretty soon, I just may take you up on that."

"What kind of dog is it?"

"She's round and fluffy and unbelievably cute—when she's not chewing on cords or pillows or knocking over the hamper to steal dirty underwear. Her lineage is pure pound dog."

"I'm assuming she has a name?"

"We're saving that for the first time she asks to go outside to pee. Then we're having a naming ceremony."

"I'm assuming you brought pictures?"

"A couple. But they're all the same—me holding her at arm's length and making a dash for the back door."

Bridget laughed so hard she almost choked. She stopped just short of tears.

Chapter 2

Carrie Gordon glanced at her watch as she wheeled her fory-nine-and-three-quarter-pound suitcase through the San Jose International Airport to the Starbucks in Terminal A. She'd only gotten it under the weight limit and saved the extra charge by removing her jacket and wearing it on the plane.

Taking into consideration the time it would take for Angie to retrieve her own suitcase after her plane landed, Carrie figured she had an hour to wait. Then, unless for once in her life Danielle would be on time when she picked them up, it would add another fifteen or twenty minutes. Which meant the four of them should be at the beach house in time for drinks before dinner. Hopefully there'd be a dry white wine and not one of the fruity creations Danielle favored.

Carrie ordered her usual soy latte, this time making it a grande instead of a tall, and paid for it and a *New York Times* before settling into a chair she'd found that offered a 180-degree view of the passengers coming and going through the terminal. This way she could watch for Angie from both directions.

Even though the four of them had shared pictures when someone thought to nag, it had been six years since they'd been together. Six years was a long time when you were leaving your thirties behind, both mentally and physically. For Carrie, the highlights she'd used for almost ten years to disguise the encroaching gray had stopped looking like a fashion statement and started looking like what they were. Now she was back to a reddish brown that her hairdresser insisted looked stylish, not desperate.

At least she was waging the battle more successfully than Angie, who was the "baby" of the group. Apparently the requirements for being an Alaskan bush pilot included abandoning makeup and embracing any haircut that could be pulled into a ponytail and held in place with a red rubber band.

Two years out of college, Angie had met a guy who had a bug to move to Fairbanks, Alaska, to work on the management end of the pipeline. On a whim, and believing she'd found the love of her life, she gave up a coveted job with Intel to follow him. It only took one winter for the guy to discover he wasn't the wilderness type and for Angie to develop a connection to the wide-open spaces that went far beyond anything she'd ever felt for the boyfriend. He left, begging her to go with him. She stayed, not even trying to talk him into giving her and Alaska one more year.

She became a pilot, first in Fairbanks and then in Anchorage, making her living taking fishermen to camps that were inaccessible by road or boat, and photographers to even more remote locations. A few years later, with the help of an unexpected inheritance from her grandmother, she bought a fishing service company.

Carrie heard a squeal and looked up to see Angie maneuvering her way through a stream of passengers, a suitcase held together with silver tape wobbling off balance behind her. Carrie hardly recognized Angie the way she was dressed—in a navy blue jacket, matching slacks, and a bright yellow silk shirt. What happened to the plaid shirts, jeans, and lace-up boots?

Carrie braced herself to keep from being knocked over by Angie's wildly enthusiastic hug.

"Oh, my, God," Angie said, holding Carrie at arm's length. "You look fantastic. Nowhere *near* forty," she added with a teasing grin.

"You do too," Carrie said, meaning it for the first time in a long time. "I like your hair." It was short and curly and provided a perfect frame for Angie's narrow face.

Angie gave Carrie another hug before wheeling her suitcase next to the empty chair Carrie had saved for her. "I have to use the bathroom. Do you know where it is?"

Carrie pointed toward the sign.

"Be right back."

"Do you want a coffee?"

"Decaffeinated green tea, if they have it. If they don't, just get me a water."

"*Decaffeinated* green tea. What in the hell is that?"

Angie laughed. "It's something I'm learning to like. I brought my own in case I couldn't find any here."

Surprisingly, not only did Starbucks have it, but the barista acted as if it was their best seller.

Angie came back and reached for her wallet.

Carrie held up her hand to stop her. "My treat."

"My turn next time." Angie sat and put her feet up on her suitcase, showing off a pair of flats. Angie saw Carrie staring. "Cute, huh? I had a six-hour layover in Seattle, so I did a little shopping. There are times I miss wearing nice clothes."

"The earrings aren't bad either." The diamond studs were easily a carat each and so unlike Angie that Carrie found it hard to believe they were real.

Angie reached up to touch one before bringing her hair forward to hide it. "They're the main reason I had my hair cut."

"So you could hide them?" Now here was the Angie that Carrie knew.

"They were a gift, impossible to return, stupid to toss in with my junk jewelry, so what choice do I have but to wear them?" She reached up and touched the other stud. "Actually, at times, I forget I have them on."

"That's quite a gift. Must be a special guy."

"He is. But it's not what you think. It's a thank-you from a fisherman who had a heart attack two hundred miles from the nearest hospital. We were in the middle of a series of nasty storms that made picking him up a little dicey, and I was the only one willing to try. He's convinced I saved his life. His wife sent me the earrings a week after he got home."

"Obviously he lived."

"Surprisingly. He was in pretty bad shape. But he's a stubborn old goat—who just happens to own half the high-rise buildings in Toronto."

"Other than you demonstrating a complete lack of regard for your own life, how's the flying business going?"

Angie took a long drink of tea before answering. "Unbelievable. We're about to open a satellite office in Fairbanks. I stuck my neck out—way out—to take advantage of a deal someone offered me on three cargo planes, which are scheduled to be delivered by the end of the month. We already have five new pilots hired and contracts for hauling that will take us through the winter. Now we just need to get the office set up and operating and we'll be good to go.

"As far as the operation in Anchorage, the flight-seeing and fishing-lodge businesses have grown twenty percent in the past four years. Seems the people who could afford to come north before the recession still can. Only now they're bringing friends."

"Wait a minute," Carrie said. "Did I hear you right when you said 'we'?"

Angie shook her head. "I should have known you'd pick up on that."

"So spill."

"If I tell you now, you're just going to have to hear it all over again when we get to the house. Tell me about Chicago. Still love living in the Windy City?"

"I can't imagine being anywhere else. Dealing with the snow gets to be a little much around March, but then spring arrives and all is forgiven."

"I've decided I'm going to try to talk all of you into coming to Anchorage for our next reunion. I want to show you why I fell in love with Alaska."

"All those mosquitoes and outhouses—no thanks. If I'm going on a vacation, I want it to be someplace with a beach and beautiful, sexy waiters."

"I don't want to step all over your stereotypes, but I happen to have indoor plumbing. And I have triple-pane windows that look out to see beluga whales in Turnagain Arm. On the opposite side of the house, I get to wave good-morning to my resident moose and her baby."

"What about the grizzly bears?"

"*Brown* bears," Angie said. "When you come north, it's important that you sound like a local."

"Have you ever had a 'brown' bear try to break in through your triple-panes?"

Angie swirled the remaining tea in her cup, looked at Carrie, and grinned. "Personally, I think they're a lot less dangerous than the men who hand out beach towels at resorts."

Carrie glanced at the clock over the arrival board. "Time to go." She stood and shouldered her computer bag, then gave in to the spontaneous urge to hug Angie again. "Why is it I have no idea how much I miss you until I see you?"

Angie's eyes lit up as she returned the hug. "I know. Me too."

Bridget and Danielle and Angie were the sisters Carrie had never had but desperately wanted when she was growing up. They'd stood by her through heart-break, without knowing how or why or who had caused the pain, and through bosses who expected more than she was willing to give. They gave advice when she asked and never had their feelings hurt when she didn't listen.

She'd been the one who had made it impossible for them to get together the year before, putting up road-blocks for every solution. They were forgiving and understanding. She was going to need every ounce of both now that she'd finally decided it was time to tell them the real reason she had been such a pain in the ass about so many things for such a long time.

Chapter 3

Danielle searched the drawers for a corkscrew in the surprisingly state-of-the-art kitchen. When they'd arrived at the beach house, she'd been instantly charmed by everything from the rustic appearance on the outside to the attention to detail on the inside. She especially loved the English gardens filled to overflowing with a rainbow of blooms. The walkways through the garden and around the house were moss-covered brick, the garden gate a whimsical wrought-iron creation more art than function.

The house was bright and comfortable, with orchids in every room. The furniture, something between modern and antique, featured an overstuffed sofa and armchairs that encouraged lounging. The ocean view through the sliding-glass door provided the perfect background. Danielle could easily imagine herself curled up with her thoughts and a cup of coffee with the accompanying music of gulls singing soprano and the waves a steady baritone.

She loved Denver—the mountains, the plains, the skiing, the Broncos, the Nuggets. But she could easily be seduced into a summer affair with this place. The coast drive that she and Bridget had taken before heading for the airport to pick up Carrie and Angie had been beautiful.

Carrie, looking as stylish in shorts and T-shirt as she had in her Chicago business suit, held up an Ah-So cork puller. "Is this what you're looking for?"

"Well, no," Danielle said. "But it will do." Struggling with the tines, she added, "We open bottles the old-fashioned way in Denver."

"Let me," Carrie said, reaching for the bottle. "I had two and a half dates a while back with someone who was a self-proclaimed wine expert. Supposedly this is the only way anyone who knows anything about wine would take out a cork."

She slipped the two thin metal prongs between the cork and the neck of the bottle, gave the handle a twist, and brought out the intact cork. "And there you have it," she said.

Danielle lined up four large-bowled wineglasses while Angie added crackers to the cheese and fruit plate. When Danielle started to pour, Angie held up her hand, "None for me."

Danielle stopped and studied her for several long seconds, her eyes narrowed in thought. Finally, she announced, "You're pregnant?"

Angie let out an exasperated sigh. "*That* gave me away?"

An immediate chorus of shouts and laughter, gasps and whoops filled the kitchen.

"How did you really know?" Angie asked.

Danielle hugged her a second time while her emotions ricocheted between joy and jealousy. "The only time I've seen you turn down a glass of wine was when you were driving, and you're not going anywhere tonight. Hell, I've seen you drink wine in the shower. That leaves only one other thing that could get you to turn down a bottle of"—she held the bottle to read the label—"Kapcsandy Grand Vin Cabernet Sauvignon."

"There's always cirrhosis," Angie suggested, grinning as she tugged on an earring.

"Not for another decade. And now, maybe never." Da-nielle put the bottle on the counter and stepped out of the way for Bridget to give Angie another hug.

"That's fantastic news." Bridget leaned back and looked at her. "It is, isn't it?"

Angie laughed. "Yes."

Carrie put her hands on Bridget's shoulders and gently moved her out of the way. "My turn."

She held Angie tight, rocking her back and forth. "I'm so, so happy for you." Then she held her at arm's length and stared deeply into her eyes. "I'm assuming this wasn't an immaculate conception? Do we get to hear about the father?"

"Was he the one who gave you those ostentatious rocks on your earlobes?" asked Danielle.

"Time for that later," Bridget said, the tail of her new blue-and-yellow Hermes scarf artfully draped across her shoulder. She came forward and kissed Angie on one cheek and then the other. Soon they were all crying tears of joy.

"Thank you," Bridget said, wiping her tears with her hands and then her hands on her too-big shorts.

"For what?" Angie answered, honestly confused.

"For making us aunts. I've always wanted to be an aunt, but it's really hard when you don't have any brothers or sisters."

The tears turned to laughter again. And then another group hug. The hug didn't end until Danielle said she had to either break free to get a tissue or wipe her nose on Carrie's sleeve.

Chapter 4

"No gossiping without me," Carrie yelled from the back bedroom, where she'd gone to get a sweater.

Danielle added warmed Brie to the platter, then topped it with a mound of fig jam. "It took us a year to get Miss Chicago out here, and now look at her. She's acting like a mother hen tucking her chicks under her wing."

"Have you ever noticed how many of us wound up in cities that start with the first letter of our names?" Angie took plates out of the cupboard and added napkins from a tray on the counter.

"I can't say that's something I've spent a lot of time thinking about," Danielle said.

"It's just kinda strange, don't you think? I'm from Anchorage, Carrie is from Chicago, you're from Denver . . ."

"And Bridget is from Sacramento."

"But my middle name is Sarah," Bridget said. "That should count for something. Did I ever tell you what Miles called us?"

"I'm not sure I want to hear this," Danielle said.

"The Alphabet Girls."

The statement was met with loud groans.

Bridget laughed. "Don't worry, it wasn't said with affection."

Danielle balanced the two cheese trays with one hand, utensils and napkins with the other, and headed outside. Not knowing Angie was pregnant, they'd bought a large wheel of Brie at the gourmet grocery store where they picked up supplies that morning. Angie said she couldn't eat it, but as long as they kept the cheeses separate, it wouldn't be a problem.

The sun had slipped behind a low-lying cloud, changing it from ivory to a deep orange and creating rays of yellow and pink that escaped into the sapphire blue sky. For the first time in almost three years Danielle felt a sense of peace. And hope.

They settled into the cushioned patio chairs, Danielle and Carrie insisting Angie and Bridget take the ones with footstools.

"I'm pregnant, not an invalid," Angie said. "Look at me." She patted her stomach. "You can't tell whether this is a baby bump or one too many pizzas."

"Well, I'm going to take advantage of any pampering you want to send my way," Bridget said. "When my mother came out to take care of me, she had it in her head that if I didn't do as much as I could for myself I'd give up."

"How did you discover the lump?" Angie asked, her hand still resting on her belly.

"I didn't. I went in for a mammogram after my sister discovered she had the BRCA2 genetic mutation. Interestingly enough, I didn't have the mutation, just the cancer."

Danielle cut a wedge of Brie and put it on a wheat cracker, adding a drop of fig jam. "Why did your sister decide to get tested?"

"She read an article about families with a high incidence of premenopausal breast and ovarian cancer that said it could be tied to two inherited gene mutations. There's a lot of controversy about being tested if you don't have a high incidence of early cancer in your family, but my mom's cancer was enough for my sister, and once she found out she had the gene mutations, she opted for a double mastectomy. When you're married to a doctor, and that doctor is as paranoid as you are, it opens doors."

"What kind did your mom have?" Angie asked.

"Ovarian—in her late thirties. She was incredibly lucky that it was discovered as early as it was."

Carrie reached for a piece of smoked Gouda that she broke in half, skipping the cracker. She chewed slowly, as if counting every up-and-down movement of her jaw. Despite going to the gym three times a week and running on the other four days, it took a lot more effort to remain a size 0 now than it had five years ago. And in the work world she inhabited, there was an unspoken but recognized credo that success and appearance went hand in hand. The glass ceiling was for those who believed hard work alone was the road to power. She shuddered to think what she'd have to do to maintain this size when she turned fifty. "And you're okay now?" she asked Bridget.

"I should be."

As if able to satisfy her growing hunger vicariously, Carrie put three different cheeses and a variety of crackers and fruit on a plate and handed it to Bridget. "What do you mean *should* be?"

"Like everything else, there are no guarantees." Bridget tried to sound lighthearted, but with tears pooling in her eyes and the constriction in her throat from trying to hold them back, she couldn't pull it off.

"Is it really just a fluke that you got this, or is it possible there's something going on that's tied to that genetic thing?" Danielle was still standing, though at six feet tall, she might have been more accurately described as looming.

"That's the double Jeopardy question in the 'Mysterious Medical Facts' category," Bridget said. "I've seen more shrugs over that than any other part of my treatment."

Danielle moved her chair and sat down to face her friends rather than the van Gogh sky. "How do you function with that hanging over your head? Are you going to any support groups?"

Bridget looked around at her three best friends. "I have the best support group I could ever have right here with me now."

Angie unfolded her napkin and wiped her eyes. "We've been together less than half a day and I'm already dehydrated from all the crying."

"It's the pregnancy," Carrie said. "My cousin was on an emotional roller coaster the entire time. Up one day, down the next. Almost drove her husband nuts."

Bridget pulled the scarf off her head and ran her hands over her scalp. "This itching is going to drive me nuts."

"Let me," Danielle said, getting up to stand behind Bridget. She made a show of preparing, cracking her knuckles and then stretching before she ran her hands over what looked like a teenage boy's face a year before he required a razor. "Hmmm . . . this is kinda sexy. I think I'm getting turned on."

Bridget laughed. She didn't seem aware when the laughter turned to tears. "I've missed all of you so much." She reached up to take one of Danielle's hands. "Thank you for being my friends."

"Friends who will stop speaking to you if you ever keep something like this a secret again," Danielle said.

"I'm hoping there is no 'like this' again. But I do promise—no more secrets."

Danielle was trying to hide her own guilt when she saw Carrie cringe. For just a second. There was no doubt something in the exchange had made her uncomfortable. "And no more cancer."

Bridget wiped her tears. "I'll do my best." She looked down and saw broken bits of crackers scattered across her denim shirt and started picking them off one by one, gathering them in the palm of her other hand and then tossing the whole into the bushes. "I'm tired of talking about me. I want to hear all about this baby you're having, Angie. So tell."

"She, or he, is predicted to make an appearance outside the womb sometime between six and seven months from now. I have a feeling my doctor refuses to pin it down any closer than that because he thinks I'll be all over him if the baby shows up early or late." She grinned. "He's a good friend and knows me too well for me to get away with bullying him. He also knows I have a lot to do to get the business ready, including finding another pilot to cover for me for the two months I won't be flying."

"Two?" Carrie and Danielle said in unison.

"I'll fly until my belly gets in the way, and then when the baby is born, Darren and I will switch off child care with his mother and sister, who will fly in from Kodiak Island. That's where they live. I have a feeling his dad and brothers will be involved in the hands-on care too. They're that kind of family, and this is going to be the first grandchild."

"Darren?" a chorus of voices repeated.

She blushed. "Okay, so you got it out of me."

"And it was damn hard to do too," Carrie said, laughing. "Like sticking a pin in a balloon."

"We want to know everything," Bridget insisted. "This is a very big deal, and you're not allowed to leave out any details. No matter how small."

Angie tucked her hair behind her ears. The instant her index finger brushed against one of the diamonds, she fluffed her hair out again. "His full name is Darren Francis Langley Jr. He's a pilot—and the baby's father. We've known each other for a couple of years but didn't start dating until a couple of months ago. He's as excited about the baby as I am and keeps trying to talk me into getting married before she or he is born, but I'm—" She shrugged. "I don't know. I'm just not as sure it's the best thing to do right now."

"What's he like?" Bridget said. "Remember, I have to get my romance secondhand these days, so don't skimp on details."

"He's tall, has really thick, wavy black hair—and the most incredible blue eyes. He was born and raised on an isolated inlet on Kodiak Island and has four younger brothers and one sister. They're beside themselves that their big brother is going to be a daddy, especially his little sister. She and her mother have already started a baby quilt."

"Awww. . . ." Bridget sighed. "I like them already."

"What about Darren's dad?" Danielle asked. "Is he as enthusiastic?"

Angie laughed. "I'd been around him all of two hours when he told me that if Darren didn't get a ring on my finger before the baby was born, he and Darren's mom were going to make arrangements to adopt me."

"Wow," Carrie said. "Those Alaska people don't hold back."

"No, they don't. It's one of the things I love about being there."

"Back to the romance," Bridget insisted, tying her scarf around her head to ward off the cool breeze coming in with the tide.

"We didn't hit it off at first. Darren insists I was standoffish and totally oblivious to his charms.

My version is that he came across as cocky and full of himself."

"Known in some circles as being too self-confident," Danielle chimed in. "Been there, done that. So what happened that changed your mind?"

"He saved a little boy and his father when they were tossed out of their raft on the Mulchatna River. It was early in the first week of the salmon run, when the bears are testy. The rafters made it to a sandbar, where a couple of territorial brown bears kept them from going anywhere else. Rescuing them was a much bigger deal than it comes across in the retelling because there are so many nuances to the story. But basically, Darren had to land his plane on a sandbar that was too short and narrow to get off again with the added weight. He should have waited for help, but he was afraid the father was going to do something that would antagonize the bears, so he went in."

"Scary," Bridget said. "I'd worry about him every time he went out after doing something like that."

"The important part of this story is that Darren never said a thing to me or anyone else. I had to find out what happened from another pilot."

"About the baby," Danielle said. "None of my business, and feel free to tell me so, but failed birth control or intentional?"

Bridget sat forward. "Okay, I admit I'm curious too. But isn't that a little personal?"

Carrie and Danielle looked at her. Simultaneously they said, "Nah."

Danielle added, "If she doesn't want to tell us, she won't."

Angie laughed. "I'll tell you, but don't you dare tell Darren that I did."

"It's a deal," Danielle said.

"Wouldn't dream of it," Carrie added.

"Not even if he promised to introduce me to his brothers," Bridget chimed in.

"Darren was due back from a flight to Lake Clark, and he was over an hour late. I kept trying to raise him on the radio—but all I got was static. It was fifteen minutes to midnight, and because float planes fly by sight, not by instruments, he had to be back before sunset, which was less than ten minutes away.

"I went outside and started pacing, listening for the peculiar sound that particular plane makes. Finally, when I heard it, I was sick with relief. And I was furious at how Darren had scared the hell out of me. I thought about locking up and leaving as soon as he landed and waiting until morning to find out what had caused the delay."

She finished her tea and sat back, propping her legs on the ottoman. "Instead, I waited. Turned out to be a fateful decision. I planted myself on the pier so that

I'd be the first thing he saw when he pulled in. I stood there with my hands on my hips, doing my best imitation of a pissed-off polar bear, getting madder and madder the longer he ignored me. I saw him watching me out of the corner of his eye the entire time it took him to unload his gear. When he finished and came up the pier, he dropped everything at my feet, didn't say a thing, put his arms around me, and kissed me like I've never been kissed before."

"Oooh, I like this guy," Bridget said.

"What did you do?" Carrie asked.

Angie popped a piece of cheese in her mouth. "I kissed him back, of course."

"Good girl," Danielle added. "And then?"

Bridget laughed. "There's this obnoxious voice inside of me insisting this borders on voyeuristic. Give me a minute to choke the life out of it."

"This next part is so saccharine it will make you gag, but here goes. He swept me up in his arms and carried me into the office." Her mouth turned up in a Cheshire grin. "Let me tell you, by this point I was soooo glad I hadn't locked up. We tore each other's clothes off, he tossed a couple of sleeping bags on the floor, and—we made a baby."

Bridget sighed. "Not once, in all the time I was married, did I experience anything even close to this romantic."

Always the detail person in the group, Carrie asked, "Why was he late?"

"He had engine trouble and had to make a landing on one of the isolated lakes near Redoubt. The radio had stopped working, so he knew that even with the GPS he was in big trouble if he couldn't fix whatever it was and get airborne again. He said he spent a lot of time thinking about what he'd left undone and I was at the top of his list."

"What will you do if he decides he wants to leave Alaska?" Bridget asked. "I'm assuming that would be a deal-breaker for you."

"That's not going to happen. Darren's parents took care of that possibility by sending all five of their kids to the Lower Forty-Eight to go to college—whether they wanted to or not. Darren chose the University of Washington because he thought Seattle weather was the closest he could get to home. He hated it, but he stuck it out, then moved back the day he graduated."

"When was that?" Bridget asked. "My cousin went there."

Angie focused on the welting outlining her seat cushion as if it were an exhibit in the Museum of Modern Art. "I'm not sure."

"Approximately," Carrie nudged.

Danielle watched Angie squirm and wondered why. And then it hit her. "Did you bring a picture?"

Angie let out a resigned sigh. "Okay, so he's a little younger than I am."

"Doesn't matter," Bridget said. "If you're happy and he's happy, that's all that—"

"He's ten years younger," Angie said, interrupting her. "He thinks I'm crazy that it bothers me."

After several seconds of stunned silence, Danielle was the first to say something. "And you're sure his family still likes you?"

"That's what they claim." Angie put her feet on the wooden deck, her elbows on her knees and her hands over her face. "I don't know what to do. Darren insists he loves me, and I know he's thrilled about the baby, but that's how he feels now. What about twenty years from now when I'm sixty?"

"Haven't you heard?" Carrie said. "Today's sixty is yesterday's forty. No telling what it will be when you're actually there. Maybe even thirty-five. Whatever—you'll still be as beautiful and interesting and fun then as you are now."

"And if you aren't, there's always stress management and plastic surgery," Danielle added.

Again, there was stunned silence. Only this time it was followed by hoots of laughter.

Danielle stood. "Come on, Carrie. Let's start dinner, and leave these two invalids to enjoy this glorious sunset by themselves."

Chapter 5

When they were alone, Angie turned to Bridget. Even though they considered themselves a group of four, there were times when the four settled into twos. Angie trusted and loved these women and knew the feelings were reciprocated, but when she needed to share the most intimate details of her life, it was invariably Bridget she went to, Bridget who listened without judging.

"We were always so sure that nothing, not even time and distance, could make us drift apart. And yet look at us. How did we let this happen? Why didn't you tell any of us about your cancer? Did you have so many shoulders to lean on that you didn't need ours?"

"I could deal with Miles or I could deal with my cancer. Having both happen at the same time was too much. It isn't that I didn't want to reach out—I couldn't. For a while, just picking up the phone took too much emotional energy. Most days it was easier to crawl into a hole and try to disappear."

"I understand. But I still wish I'd known. I could have laughed through really bad movies with you while we were making a voodoo doll of Miles." Angie summoned an evil grin. "Imagine the places we could have put pins."

She finished her tea, stared at the rapidly disappearing sun, then shifted her gaze back to Bridget. "Why didn't I tell any of you that I was pregnant?"

"Because you knew we'd bombard you with questions, and you weren't ready to answer them. That's one of the problems with staying connected the way we do. We rarely have real conversations, something that goes deeper than what can be said in a paragraph." Bridget tucked the tail of her scarf under the wrap. "Like with me—how do you tell your best friends that your life is falling apart in fifty words or less? Especially when you've allowed them to believe for years that everything is okay?"

"You don't," Angie admitted. "Every once in a while I start to tell all of you about something that's going on with me, but then I think how busy everyone is and I wind up hitting Delete before I can send anything."

"Which is why it's so important that we get together in person."

"But it needs to be more than once every five years."

"How often do you think it would take to get back to the way we were in school?"

"We know too much and we've experienced too much to ever be what we once were. That kind of sweet naïveté is for the girls we were, not the women we've become." Angie didn't say anything for several minutes. And then a smile formed. "Even so, we could try for every other year and see what happens."

"I was thinking more along the lines of every year. Not for the three weeks we've gotten together in the past. That's too hard. Maybe go for a long weekend the way the guys I know are always taking off on golf trips."

"I like that. Any ideas how to convince Danielle and Carrie?"

Bridget gave her a sly smile. "A few months back, as I was heaving my guts out, it occurred to me that if I had to have cancer, I might as well get something out of it. When we talk to them, I'll casually let it drop that it's important for me to see as much of my best friends as I can for as long as I can."

"And you think they'll let you get away with that?"

"What do you mean?"

"Danielle will see it for what it is before you put a period on the end of the sentence."

Bridget laughed. "No doubt. But it will plant the seed, and that's all we need."

The spark left Bridget's eyes. "Six months ago, when Miles had one of his heart-to-heart conversations with me, he said he'd given it a lot of thought and decided it would be better for everyone concerned, me included, if I stopped fighting the cancer and died like the classy woman I've always been."

Angie gasped. "He didn't."

"Yes—he did."

"The son of a bitch."

"That's putting too much blame on his mother. As Miles likes to remind people, he's a self-made man."

"I can't think of any way to say this without it sounding macabre, but I'll never forgive you if you ever go through something this harrowing again and don't tell me."

"Don't worry. I've learned my lesson. I desperately needed all of you, and I was just too stupid and too proud to let you know."

"There's something else you're not telling me," Angie said.

Bridget's chin trembled as she tried to smile through welling tears. "I was scared. What if I asked and none of you came?"

"God, you can be such an idiot. How could you not know that we would have moved heaven and earth to get to you?"

"No one ever has." The admission was as embarrassing as it was painful. Bridget brought her knees up to her chest as if trying to make herself the smallest possible target for her own tortured thoughts.

Angie's heart ached. She had to consciously force her lungs to expand and contract through the pain. "I'm sorry."

"For what?"

"For not finding a way to show you how important you are to me—to all of us."

"There was no way you could have known."

"You mean other than picking up the phone every once in a while or catching an empty seat on one of the airlines that offers me deals in exchange for taking their VIPs to luxury lodges in the wilderness? I used to think about how easy it would be to meet you for lunch and still be home in time to sleep in my own bed that night."

"Planes fly in both directions. I could have flown up to see you." Bridget straightened her legs again, then tucked one under the other.

"Lesson learned."

"Hopefully."

"How about your mother? Has she been any help at all?"

"When she was staying with me, it was like I was the target of one of those machines that throw tennis balls. Only these balls were snippy bits of advice and great big blobs of criticism. When I'm feeling charitable, I tell myself it was her way of dealing with the thought of losing her daughter."

"And when you're not feeling charitable?"

"Then she's just a first-class bitch who was angry because she'd been inconvenienced—even though Miles paid her expenses and gave her spending money because he couldn't be bothered with taking care of me himself."

"Now I get it. I can see why you wouldn't want to call any of us for help and break up that lovefest." Angie made a grab for a napkin that had blown off the table and stuffed it into an empty glass.

"When did I become a mealy-mouthed little mouse who felt she had to ask permission to squeak?"

"Things like that don't have a start date. They happen so slowly you don't realize you've changed until everything falls apart. I worked so hard to build my flying business that somewhere along the line I forgot I wasn't just one of the guys. When I caught a glimpse of myself in a window I was passing and it took several seconds to realize it wasn't a guy looking back, I decided it was time to find myself again." Angie held up her feet to show off her shoes. "Thus the newly created fashionista."

"How long do you think this other you will be around?"

"Long enough to show Darren that I can be more than jeans and boots and plaid shirts and not give my customers a wrong impression. They're putting their lives in my hands when I fly them into the wild, and they're not comfortable if those hands have sparkly pink nails. As much as I'd like to wear something with a little lace and woven ribbons, my shopping list for this pregnancy is more along the lines of expandable jeans and stretchy T-shirts."

Bridget gave her a knowing smile. "Doesn't mean you can't shop for lace and ribbons for the bedroom."

Angie laughed. "Have you been talking to Darren?"

"No, but I can't wait to meet him."

Bridget took Angie's hand and wove their fingers together. "God, how I've missed you," she said. "I never should have tried to get through the cancer without reaching out. I was so scared. And humiliated," she added. A bitter look took the place of the smile. "I hate that hating Miles gives him power over me, but I don't know how to stop." She caught her breath in a hiccuped sob. "How could he just abandon me? How could he leave me the way he did? He didn't have to love me, but what did I do that made him think it was okay to walk away while I was fighting for my life? How could he care so little?"

"You only did one thing wrong where Miles is concerned. You kept thinking you could change him, that your love would turn him into a caring, thoughtful human being. Think what you gave up. Think of the years you missed getting to know yourself. Think of the opportunities you could have had to find someone smart enough to recognize what an amazing woman you are."

"You're my friend. You have to say things like that."

"No, goddamn it, I don't. I know how bad this sounds for me to actually say out loud, but what if you only have five more years, Bridget? Are you going to waste the time you have left wallowing in what might have been? Was there no one you could have called in Sacramento who would put cold compresses on your neck when you were hanging over a toilet after one of your treatments? You've always had more friends than the rest of us combined. What happened? What's the real reason?"

Bridget hesitated, started to speak, then stopped again. Slowly, inevitably, she lost her hard-won battle at composure and hiccuped through huge sobs of release. "I was hoping the treatment wouldn't work." She put her hands over her face. "I knew if I had any of you there with me, you'd talk me into caring, and I wouldn't be able just to let go."

Angie got up and squeezed into the chair with Bridget. She wrapped her arms around her and rocked her in rhythm to a silent lullaby. After Bridget stopped sobbing, Angie put her hand under her friend's chin and forced her to look up. "I'm going to make you a promise, sweet Bridget. We're going to fix you. You're going to leave here so full of life that when someone asks you about Miles Woodward, you're going to say, 'Miles who?' "

Chapter 6

Carrie artfully placed lettuce leaves on the Williams-Sonoma Poisson salad plates, impressed that even the casual dining pieces at the beach house were first-class. Someone had given a lot of thought to every detail of the finishing touches, from the Egyptian towels in the bathrooms to the assortment of magazines on the coffee table. The soaps and lotions tucked into the welcoming baskets on the beds were thoughtfully purchased, containing neutral, fresh fragrances that disappeared quickly but left a wonderful, silky feel to her skin. She didn't know the brand and had a feeling it was something custom-made for the owner of the house.

Carrie knew people who lived in that kind of luxury, but only peripherally, and most of them were clients—especially since she'd taken on the job of heading the new art brokerage division of Pearson Inc.

Danielle cut into the loaf of San Francisco sourdough bread that they'd picked up on their way to the airport that afternoon. She sliced off the end piece, put it up to her nose, and inhaled deeply. "Oh. My. God. I'm going to have drool running down my chin if I keep this up."

Carrie stepped closer. "Let me smell." Danielle handed her the slice. "This is nothing like we get at home. It actually has a tanginess to it." She broke off a piece, took a bite, and handed the rest to Danielle. "You don't even need butter."

"Oh, yeah?" Danielle reached for the butter dish. "Didn't your mama ever teach you that everything tastes better with butter?"

"It's looking at my mama and the three hundred pounds she packs that keeps me from putting butter on anything."

Danielle wound up with traces of butter on the corners of her mouth and a smile that reached all the way to her eyes. "I've been meaning to tell you how great you look. Is that part of the new job?"

"In what way?" Carrie took the shrimp and crab out of the refrigerator and started opening cupboards looking for a colander.

Danielle took one down from the cupboard beside the stove and handed it to her. "I just thought that maybe all the traveling you do now and all the wealthy people you're dealing with . . ." She shrugged. "You're not exactly in the flip-flops and cargo-pants world anymore."

Carrie didn't smile at the memory the comment stirred, she looked wistful. "I left that world a long time ago."

Danielle couldn't put her finger on what was going on with Carrie. She was not only uptight but distracted. And of the three of them, it should have been Bridget, who'd lost a baby, who would have bittersweet feelings about Angie's pregnancy, not Carrie, who'd never tried.

"Do you like the new job?"

Carrie leaned against the counter and folded her arms. "I think I do, but I'm still at the walking-on-eggshells stage. There's so much riding on this career-wise that there's no room for me to make a mistake. If it doesn't work out, I'll feel like I'm running around the city with a big 'L' stamped in the middle of my forehead."

"A little melodramatic, don't you think? With everything you've already accomplished, you're never going to be able to convince anyone that you're a loser." Danielle grinned.

When Carrie didn't say anything, Danielle pushed harder. "What's the hang-up? What could keep you from succeeding?"

"Me. The economy. Any of a dozen things I have control over and two dozen I don't."

Carrie was the one the rest of them believed without question would succeed no matter where she landed. It was a given, just like it was a given that Angie would lead the most interesting life. Despite hating cold weather, Carrie had moved to Chicago to take a low-paying job with huge potential, saying there would be time to sit in the sun when she'd put away enough money to retire early. Although she'd given lip service to the idea of settling down and having a family, Danielle had never been quite convinced by what seemed like Carrie's forced enthusiasm. She just couldn't picture Carrie changing a diaper.

"The whole thing hinges on how the clients feel about me," Carrie went on. "They have to trust that I know what I'm doing in a field where forgers and thieves are the go-to guys for information. They have to have absolute confidence that I can get them the best price whether they're buying or selling their jewelry or artwork or antiquities. Before I stupidly took this on, I managed to convince myself that having a minor in art would be an asset, but all it's done is show me how little I know."

"I'll buy that you're scared, but I hear a lot of excitement in your voice too."

Carrie gathered her hair and twisted it into a loose cord over her shoulder. "Yeah, there is some of that. Right now I'm in the process of finding an expert in Inuit art to appraise a potential client's established collection. I was hoping Angie might be able to put me on to someone, but she said the woman who was considered the most knowledgeable in the state was killed in an airplane crash last year."

"In one of Angie's planes?"

Carrie shook her head. "She had her own plane."

"I worry about Angie," Danielle admitted. "Those things scare the crap out of me."

"I know. Me too. But in her mind, it's safer being up there than the two of us driving back and forth to work every day." She reached for the wine and poured herself another glass.

"Are Inuit antiquities going to be your main focus?"

"I wish it was that easy. We're going to be handling everything from the Old Masters, which has been fairly straightforward, to Asian antiquities, which is a field rife with forgeries, to photography, which I know even less about than babies."

Danielle shook her head. "What's happened to you? You used to have more self-confidence than the rest of us put together."

"Looking at turning forty and having all those thirty-year-olds snapping at my heels." Carrie opened the package of shrimp and dumped them in the strainer.

Danielle went back to cutting a lemon. "Is it really that bad out there?"

"Which 'out there' are you referring to—jobs or dating or something else? Please tell me you're not thinking about leaving Grady. This group needs one long-term-romance success story."

"Grady and I are fine—as long as he doesn't bring home any more animals."

Carrie laughed. "You don't really think I'm buying that, do you? I remember the year you worked with a spay-and-neuter group in Charlottesville, and how you almost missed one of your finals because you were late getting back from a protest at a zoo that chained its elephants."

"It's the job market I was wondering about," Danielle said, trying to sound as casual as possible. "All you hear anymore is doom and gloom, and I was curious what it's like where you are."

"For some of us, it's downright scary. Especially the ones stupid enough to allow themselves to be talked into jumping out of a plane without a parachute." Carrie arranged the shrimp on the plates in a circular pattern, then put the crab in the strainer for a quick rinse before mounding it in the middle.

Danielle was at a loss for words. She'd gotten the impression that Carrie's new job was going to be a hell of a lot of work, but that it was also pretty much a slam-dunk—a perfect fit for her insatiable curiosity. "When are you supposed to be ready for clients?"

"According to the head of the real estate division, I'm already four weeks behind schedule. You wouldn't believe the fit he threw when he discovered I was taking a week off to come here. Didn't matter that I haven't taken a vacation in three years or that I brought my computer and will be putting in almost as many hours here as I would in Chicago."

"How long have you been working to set this up?"

"Two months of dealing directly with clients. Over a year in the planning stage."

Still, something didn't ring true. Before Carrie went to work for Pearson Inc., Danielle hadn't known such companies existed. Carrie had tried explaining that they were like a pie baked specifically for wealthy clients, with each wedge a different brokerage flavor. Those flavors varied wildly, from real estate to insurance to options to commodities. It made perfect sense that they would move into the art world; connecting a real estate client in Argentina who collected pre-Columbian art to a commodities client in Canada who was looking to sell his collection of pre-Columbian art was a commission opportunity that, until now, they'd been giving away.

Even if they were only brokering a purchase or sale for an individual client at an auction in New York or London or Hong Kong, there was a commission to be had.

Danielle mentally sorted through what Carrie had told her and finally came to a logical, if far-fetched, conclusion. "Is it possible that there's trouble in the other divisions and they need you to come up with something to bail them out? Could it be that they're using this new division as a distraction . . . that they're shifting focus hoping outsiders will get the impression the company is doing so well it's time to expand?"

Carrie threw her arms wide in a hopeless gesture. "It took you all of five minutes to figure out what the executive board has convinced itself no one, not even the reporters who write for the *Chicago Tribune* business section, will be able to see. And you're not even in the business."

"And if you fail—which seems likely the way they're pushing you to get this off the ground—where does it leave you?"

"Exactly where you would imagine. I'll be the scapegoat."

"Who's going to believe that you had that kind of power?"

"When it comes to accepting blame, these guys are experts at shoving their hands in their pockets."

"So, what if you succeed?"

For the first time since they'd come into the kitchen, Carrie's mouth turned up in a genuine smile. "That's the one thing I have covered. It's the primary reason I'm working as hard on this as I am. I figure momentum is going to give me at least a little time on top of the curve. While I'm there, I'm going to let it be known that I'm ready to move. All I need is a little luck and perfect timing and I should be able to make the jump to start my own art brokerage house before everything collapses at Pearson's."

"Won't you be blamed for the collapse?"

"Only to the point that the division fell apart because it couldn't function without me at the helm."

"I'm impressed."

"Don't be. Not until it happens. It could be that you answer a knock on your door one day and find me holding a sign: WILL WORK FOR A STELLA MCCARTNEY HANDBAG."

"Totally understandable. How can you be expected to present yourself in the best light carrying anything less?" It was the perfect opportunity for Danielle to tell Carrie what would really happen if she ever did show up in Denver. But that revelation was for another time.

Chapter 7

Bridget listened for signs that Danielle was asleep before she got out of bed, picked up her slippers and robe, and slipped out of the bedroom. As usual, she and Danielle had wound up bunking together, this time in the one bedroom out of three that had twin beds.

As the night owls of the foursome, they habitually talked until well after midnight when they were together. Carrie and Angie were morning people, rising with the sun and jogging on a trail or treadmill, believing it was possible to exchange a lifetime of morning misery for some indeterminate longevity.

Would exercise have prevented her breast cancer? As with so many other things that brought up niggling questions, she had her doubts.

About everything.

Should she have refused a lifetime of routine dental X-rays? What about non-organic food? Red meat? Milk that came from cows that were fed antibiotics as if they were food supplements?

Was there anything she had done, should have done, or could have done that would have stopped the appearance of that first aberrant cancer cell? She lightly ran her hand along the wall until she reached the living room and spotted a dim light coming from the kitchen. Before traversing the maze of furniture, she stopped to put on her robe and slippers. A minute later she was peering through the arched opening that separated the kitchen from the rest of the house. Carrie was sitting at the table, her laptop in front of her, her chin propped on her hand.

"Couldn't sleep?" Bridget asked, crossing the room to take the teapot off the stove.

"Didn't dare. It's already ten o'clock in London."

"Oh," Bridget said wistfully. "You're working." She added water to the teakettle. "I'll be out of your way in a couple of minutes."

"No need. What I'm doing doesn't require concentration."

Bridget turned on the burner and came to stand behind Carrie. "Do you mind?"

Carrie shook her head and moved the computer so Bridget could see it more easily.

Bridget stared at the screen for several seconds. "What exactly are you doing?"

"Trying to educate myself about the quality of ruyi scepters and their uses in feng shui. It's the hot new thing for up-and-coming business types to put them in their offices, both here and in China." Carrie moved the cursor to show Bridget another view of the green-and-white jadeite scepter.

"What do you know about them?" Bridget asked.

"One version has it that they originated as scratching tools for Buddhist monks—the where and how not being specified—but that's not universally accepted. What is known is that they evolved from something relatively common to objects of great value exchanged between rulers and used as gifts for imperial birthdays and weddings."

"It eventually became a symbol of power," Bridget said, moving the cursor to get a closer look at the sides and back of the scepter. The S-shaped handle was about a foot long, intricately carved with polychrome inlays of precious and semiprecious stones. The head with matching carving held a large emerald.

"I'm impressed," Carrie said. "Very few people outside of collectors know what they are."

"I had a lot of time on my hands when I lived in Hong Kong."

"Christie's London has one in an upcoming auction that's bamboo and is estimated to go for half a million pounds. I'm watching to see if the market is nearing its peak or if the Chinese are still using their new wealth to bring home the artwork that's been leaving the country for the past century."

"And you're doing this because . . ."

Carrie frowned and then smiled. "Sorry—I forgot you and Angie were outside when I was telling Danielle about my new job."

The teakettle started hissing. Bridget jumped up to turn the fire off to keep the hiss from becoming a whistle. "Tea?" she asked Carrie.

"Decaf?"

"Herb. Rooibos actually."

"Sure. As long as it doesn't put me to sleep."

Bridget left the teabags in the mugs and brought two spoons and a plate. "So tell me how you went from brokering real estate to studying Chinese art."

Carrie began to tell her. She had reached the part in her story about feeling profoundly underqualified in her new position when her phone vibrated. She glanced at the screen. "It's the London agent reporting on the sale."

"Do you want me to go into the other room?"

Carrie shook her head. "This shouldn't take long."

Bridget made a motion asking Carrie if it would be all right for her to use the computer. Carrie turned it toward her and sat back in her chair.

Opening a second search window, Bridget brought up a Chinese antiquities site, then opened two more windows to bring up two similar sites. She smiled at a photograph of a grim-faced Feng Kai, the owner of her favorite antiquities shop in Hong Kong and someone she considered a friend.

Carrie finished her call and put the phone on the table again. She yawned and ran her hands over her face.

Bridget turned the computer back toward Carrie, quickly scrolling through the sites. "Do you know any of these shops or the men who own them?"

Carrie took several minutes to study the unimpressive, poorly laid out websites before shaking her head. "Should I?"

"They're considered the go-to experts in Chinese art in Hong Kong. I spent a year following their auctions and listening to them speak at private gatherings before I approached Liu Yang about volunteering at his gallery."

"Doing what?" Carrie asked.

"Interpreting for his American customers. In exchange, I told him I wanted to learn how to spot what to him would be obvious forgeries."

"You speak Cantonese?" Carrie asked, incredulous. "Isn't that supposed to be one of the most difficult languages to learn?"

"What I know is very, very basic—on a level with a preschooler, but enough to get by. Some Arabic too. That was actually harder for me to pick up. Turns out I have an 'ear' for languages. Wish I'd known that in college. I just thought Spanish was easy."

"How could I not know this about you? Can you read and write it too?" Carrie's eyes danced with excitement.

Bridget laughed. "I'm good, but I'm not that good. I know enough not to order cow offal off a menu, but that's about it."

"You're a heaving stomach farther away from that kind of mistake than I am." Carrie leaned back in her chair, folded her arms, and stared at the computer, a place to focus while her mind cataloged this new information. "What prompted you to get involved in Chinese collectibles?"

"For my thirty-fifth birthday, I bought what was supposed to be a rare porcelain vase from someone I was told had a top-tier reputation and then discovered a couple of months later that the vase was a knockoff—and not a very good one. When the dealer refused to let me return it, I had it encased in glass and put on my desk as a reminder.

Carrie pointed to the computer screen. "Tell me about this."

Bridget smiled. "They're the experts who taught me that the only way I can tell an exceptional fake from the real thing is to turn it over to one of them."

"How do you know they can be trusted?"

"They're the men the auction houses go to for authentication on anything that lacks credible provenance."

Carrie picked up her cup and put it down again. "Why hide behind such cheesy-looking websites?"

"I don't know. When I told Feng Kai that I'd rework his, I think I offended him. I never mentioned it again, to any of them."

"Have you kept in contact?"

"Not so much this past year."

"Would you mind introducing me?"

Carrie wouldn't need caffeine to keep her awake the rest of the night. It was as if Bridget had dropped an entire roll of quarters into her adrenaline coin slot.

Bridget picked up her cup and looked at Carrie over the rim. "By phone—or in person?"

Carrie blinked. "You'd do that—go with me to Hong Kong?"

A smile radiated from Bridget's eyes. "I'd even pay my own way."

Carrie worked to control her excitement. "Are you sure? When my aunt had chemo, it took her over a year before she had any energy. All she wanted to do was sleep."

Bridget intently focused on Carrie, forcing her to make eye contact. "Listen closely, or read my lips, or do whatever it takes to hear me. I need a reason to get up in the morning, not a reason to take a nap. I'm going to sound a little full of myself here, but you're not going to find anyone better to do what you need done than me. And I can't think of anyone I would want to work with more than you. I'll give you some time to think it over, but—"

"I don't need time. You're hired."

Bridget sat back in her chair. "I promise you won't be sorry."

"We were roommates for four years. There's not much about you that I don't know."

Tears pooled in Bridget's eyes, then spilled down her cheeks. In less than thirty seconds, she'd gone from smiling to crying. Carrie reached over to wipe the tears away with her napkin. "I have a seriously important question for you," Carrie said. "Listen closely. Okay?"

"Okay."

"What did the elephant say to the naked man?"

Bridget frowned.

"It's cute, but can you pick up peanuts with it?"

What started as an indulgent smile morphed into roaring, choking laughter. Bridget covered her mouth to try to stifle the sound. Carrie grabbed the dishtowel and did the same.

A minute later Angie rushed into the room, followed closely by Danielle. "What the hell?" Danielle said.

"Sorry." Bridget grabbed the dishtowel from Carrie and wiped her eyes, then started laughing again, holding her sides and rocking forward.

Danielle looked at Angie. "What do you suppose is in those coffee cups?"

She shook her head. "I don't know, but I'm willing to bet you wouldn't find it listed on a pregnant woman's diet."

Chapter 8

Carrie took a shower while Danielle, for the first time ever, accompanied Angie on her morning run. Instead of blow-drying her hair, Carrie twisted it into a knot and pinned it into a bun at the back of her head. One of these days, probably when she was closer to fifty and she'd found a way to live with the fact that it really wasn't possible to look thirty forever, she was going to abandon her long hair and go with something short, sleek, and easy that she could blow-dry and be done with.

She hung her towel on the rack, wiped down the granite counter, opened the door, and actually took a step backward as she ran into a wall of cooking odors from the kitchen.

Carrie usually skipped breakfast. When she didn't, it was an indulgence to have a container of low-calorie fruit yogurt. Add a banana and she was on a journey into hog heaven.

But that didn't mean her senses had forgotten the smoky smell of bacon or the citrus bite of fresh-squeezed orange juice. Then there was the gentle aroma of fresh-brewed coffee weaving itself into the mix. Trailing, but not too far behind, came something sweet she couldn't identify. Cinnamon maybe?

What was Bridget thinking, cooking a meal like that when she'd told them it was everything she could do to keep Cream of Wheat down in the morning?

Carrie tossed her robe on the bed and headed for the kitchen. She heard Bridget before she saw her, singing so far off-key that it was impossible to tell what song she was accompanying on her iPod.

As soon as Bridget saw Carrie she smiled and tugged the earbuds from her ears.

"What were you singing?" Carrie asked.

" 'Help Me'—it's an Allison Krause song."

"When did you become a country music fan?"

"My friend Melinda made up a playlist for me when I was going through chemo and sneaked a couple of country artists into the mix. I fell in love with the ballads. The singers aren't bad either."

"You're always surprising me. First it was the Chinese art world, and now it's country music and"—Carrie pointed to the griddle on the stove and the bowl of pancake batter beside it—"a lumberjack breakfast."

Bridget looked around the kitchen. "Too much?"

This was one parade Carrie was not going to rain on. "Not for me. I can't remember the last time I had bacon and pancakes."

"And scrambled eggs and cinnamon toast."

"You may have stepped over the line with the cinnamon toast. Especially with the pancakes." Carrie folded her arms across her chest, her body language louder than the words that followed. "I'm going to pass."

"I used to draw that line in the sand too," Bridget said, returning the toast to the stove. "Then one day when I was sitting in my chemo chair, watching the poison drip into my arm, I thought of all the women on the *Titanic* who had refused dessert."

Carrie's jaw dropped in surprise. "Oh, my, God—you're playing the cancer card."

Bridget grinned. "Damn. Was I really that obvious?"

"Yes."

"Seriously," Bridget said. "What is it with you and food?" She held up her hand to stop Carrie from saying anything until she'd finished. "I know it's none of my business, but it seems you've got some kind of food issue going on, and I'm worried about you. I'm no expert, but it seems to me that you're going overboard on counting calories."

"It's the world I live in," Carrie said, oddly relieved to be able to talk about it. "Being overweight is the one unforgivable sin. I don't think there's one woman in the entire company who wears a size 8. Certainly not one who makes more than minimum wage."

"This is openly acknowledged?"

"Lord, no. We'd be buried in lawsuits."

"And you like working there?"

"I used to. I'm not so sure anymore."

Danielle burst through the front door before Bridget could comment.

"Where are the car keys?" she yelled.

"In my purse," Bridget answered, her heart in her throat as she responded to the panic in Danielle's voice. "I'll get them for you."

"What's wrong?" Carrie followed Bridget into the living room. "Where's Angie?"

"I left her at the park. She's having stomach cramps."

Bridget looked up from digging through her oversized purse. "Oh no"—she grabbed her sweater and scarf—"did you call 911?"

"I was going to, but Angie threw a fit. She insisted it wasn't necessary."

Carrie held her hand out for the keys. "I'll drive."

"Grab the binder the girl next door made for us," Danielle told Carrie. "It has a list of hospitals with maps and instructions on how to get to them."

Two hours later, having convinced the nurse in charge that they were Angie's sisters, Danielle, Bridget, and Carrie were crowded into an ultrasound room, with Angie lying on an examining table waiting for a doctor.

"How are the cramps?" Danielle asked.

"Better," Angie said.

"Do you want one of us to call Darren?"

"Don't you dare. His entire family would be here on the next plane out of Anchorage." Angie shifted position, trying to get comfortable, finally sitting up with her legs over the side. "I'll call him when I know something."

There was a discreet knock on the door seconds before it opened, and a woman wearing a white smock came into the room. She was followed by another woman wearing a smock covered in teddy bears and rainbows. "I'm Dr. Spurlock," the woman in the white smock said, holding out her hand to Angie. "And this is the best ultrasound tech in the hospital, Mary Boehm."

The doctor glanced at the three women pressed into the corner. "I take it these are your sisters?" she said with an indulgent smile. "I can see the strong family resemblance."

After quick introductions, Mary helped Angie lie back against the pillows, then draped a sheet over her lap. The doctor peppered Angie with questions, everything from her history with previous pregnancies (none) to her diet (all healthy, organic food with no caffeine or unprescribed over-the-counter medicines).

Danielle was beginning to relax now that she saw that Angie was being taken care of. Then she looked at Bridget and saw how pale she looked. Her hands were balled into tight fists at her sides.

How could they not have realized what it would mean for Bridget to be back in a hospital? Danielle moved closer. "Are you okay?" she whispered into Bridget's ear.

"No—but this isn't about me."

Danielle took her hand and, as discreetly as possible, unfolded Bridget's fingers and pressed the palm between her own two hands. "I'm sorry I wasn't there for you."

"And I'm sorry I didn't tell you." Bridget leaned her head against Danielle's shoulder.

Without saying a word or even glancing in her direction, Carrie reached for Bridget's other hand.

Seconds later, the room was filled with rumbling, rhythmic sounds coming too close together to distinguish individually.

"What's that?" Angie said, panicked.

"Give me a second," the doctor said, before she broke into a huge grin.

"What?" Angie prodded.

"By any chance do twins run in your family?"

Angie took the question seriously, thinking before answering. "The baby's father has—" Her eyes widened. Her jaw dropped. "Are you saying what I think you're saying? I'm having twins?"

"It's too early to see the babies with any clarity—that will take another couple of weeks. But there're two distinct shapes in there, and I'm hearing two distinct heartbeats."

"And what about the cramping?"

The doctor chuckled. "It's something you should pay attention to, of course. But my best guess is that you've gone a little overboard in the healthy eating department. Try cutting back a little on the high-fiber foods and I have a feeling the cramping will go away."

It took a second for the information to sink in and for Angie to burst out laughing. "Please tell me I'm not the first person you've treated for gas pains."

The doctor patted her arm. "And you won't be the last."

"And the jogging?" Angie added.

"For now just listen to your body. Later on your size will slow you down."

"And flying?"

"It's up to your own obstetrician of course, but with twins I wouldn't push it past twenty weeks, and only in a plane that's pressurized."

Angie's panic returned. "Even this early in the pregnancy?"

"Are you worried about getting home?"

"I'm worried about *keeping* my home. I'm a small-plane pilot. I can't afford to take off that much time."

"How important is this pregnancy to you?"

Angie didn't answer for what seemed like a long time. When she did, there were tears at the corners of her eyes. "It's everything."

"Then you have some tough decisions ahead of you."

Mary put away the ultrasound equipment and gave Angie a towel to wipe off the gel. The doctor reached into her pocket and handed Angie a business card. "Give me a call if you have more questions. I'll get back to you as soon as I can."

When the doctor and Mary were gone, Angie sat up and gave her friends a deer-in-the-headlights look. "The thought of having one baby scared the hell out of me. What am I going to do with two?"

"Buy in quantity?" Carrie suggested.

"Oh, that's helpful," Danielle said.

Bridget crossed the room and took Angie in her arms. "You adjust," she said gently.

"I'm so sorry, Bridget," Angie said. "I had no idea what it was really like for you when you lost your baby. I didn't know you could be this attached this early in a pregnancy. I hate thinking of you all alone in Hong Kong when you lost your little girl. And then your son when you were in Texas."

"Miles was with me," Bridget said. "And Danielle."

Carrie gathered Angie's clothes and brought them to her. "Like she said—it's hard picturing you alone in Hong Kong."

Carrie put Angie's shoes on the floor so she could step into them. "Do you suppose we should start working on a secret handshake to cement our promise to always be there for each other?"

"I'll do it," Bridget said, unlike the others, taking her comment seriously. "I'm good at that kind of thing."

They groaned and then laughed and had another group hug. Maybe secret handshakes weren't such a bad thing after all.

Chapter 9

They did what they could to rescue Bridget's breakfast when they got back to the beach house. The cinnamon toast was soggy and beyond saving, so Carrie made more and actually ate a piece—without butter—acknowledging that some things were worth the calories.

Adding the grounds for a second pot of coffee while Carrie and Angie cleared the table and Danielle loaded the dishwasher, Bridget asked, "What should we do today?"

"It doesn't have to be today, but I'd like to do some shopping before I have to leave," Angie said.

"And I'd like to see San Francisco," Carrie added. "Maybe we can combine a trip."

"Danielle?" Bridget prompted.

"San Francisco would be good, but today I'd just like to kick back and spend some time on the beach. Isn't that why we picked this place?"

"Sounds good to me," Angie said. "I've got a lot to think about and a lot of planning to do."

"Did you call Darren?" Bridget asked.

"Not yet. He's getting ready to fly a group of photographers to Brooks Falls, and I don't want to distract him."

"How do you think he'll take it?" Bridget asked, pouring herself a fresh cup of coffee and adding a splash of cream.

"He'll be ecstatic. He comes from a family where they just add a place at the table when another kid comes along."

"And his mother? She's got to know better."

"She's the kind of woman who sees a bump in the road as a new challenge. Nothing fazes her. But then she lives on an island where she's dealt with everything from bears destroying the winter food supply to a storm sinking the family's fishing boat. She's faced down a brown bear determined to have her favorite dog for lunch and a moose convinced that same dog was the love of his life."

Angie smiled and shrugged. "But she's so much more than the Alaska version of Wonder Woman—she loves to shop more than anyone I've ever known, including you, Carrie. She's going to be thrilled to finally be a grandmother, but she's also going to see this as an open-ended opportunity to fly to Anchorage to buy baby things every chance she gets."

Bridget poured a second glass of orange juice. "Is that good or bad?"

"Both. She's a lot of fun to be around and tries really hard not to push me and Darren about getting married, but I have a feeling that's one battle she's going to abandon when she finds out I'm carrying twins. She's going to want her son to do right by his woman. The sooner the better."

"And the age thing doesn't bother her?" Carrie asked.

"Not in the least. But you have to understand the mind-set of Alaskans. We have the highest male-to-female ratio of any state. They even have a standing joke about it up there—'Alaska is where the odds are good, but the goods are odd.'

"I think most of all she's thrilled that Darren found someone who isn't going to try to talk him into following her back to the Lower Forty-Eight."

"Why would you?" Bridget asked. "You love it up there."

"Loving the country has nothing to do with what some people go through every winter. No one knows it's going to happen to them until they experience what it's like to have the sun come up at ten-thirty and set at three-thirty. Luckily, I'm not one of the sunlamp people. I do fine whether it's six or eighteen hours of sunlight."

"Miles is one of those people who need lots of sunlight," Bridget said. "He loved living in Dubai."

No one said anything.

"Come on—I lived with the guy almost twenty years. He's bound to creep into the conversation now and then."

Danielle rinsed her coffee cup and put it on the counter for later. "Since we're already talking about Miles, the other day I was wondering whether you ever told him what really happened to his car?"

"I started to once. But then I looked up the criminal codes in Virginia, and there's no statute of limitations on theft. If he ever found out we were responsible, he wouldn't hesitate to come after us."

"Even after all this time?" Danielle asked.

"If he were on his deathbed, it wouldn't stop him." Bridget yanked off her scarf to scratch her head.

"Why don't you just throw the damn thing away?" Da-nielle said.

Angie reached out to run her hand over the soft matting. "I think you look cute this way—like a brand-new baby. And with your beautiful eyes, there's no way anyone—"

Danielle groaned. "Please tell me you're not going to be one of those mothers who makes her bald daughter wear stretchy pink bows around her head."

"Daughters, with an s," Angie reminded her.

"Or sons, with an s," Danielle added.

"Or could be one of each," Carrie said. "Which seems like the perfect solution—no sibling rivalry."

"Oh yeah?" Bridget folded her scarf and tucked it under her leg. "Miles and his sister still argue over which one of them their mother cared about the most. It's pathetic."

"Which, as I remember, is why losing the car was such a big deal to him." Carrie hiked herself up to sit on the cool granite counter, crossing her legs at the ankles.

"Remind me," Angie said. "I forgot about the sister part."

"The car belonged to Miles's uncle, and when he died, Miles's mother gave it to him. His sister threw a fit, even though she always said she hated Corvettes. Once he found out how pissed she was, he drove it to every family function he knew she'd be at, even the big get-together his family had in North Dakota every other year. He always arrived late to make sure she was already there, then he'd honk the horn all the way up the street to announce his arrival. Until—"

"We stole it," Angie finished.

"We didn't exactly *steal* it," Carrie said. "We were just borrowing it for a while."

Bridget inwardly smiled at the back-and-forth as Carrie, Danielle, and Angie manipulated the truth, creating different versions of the same story as they had for almost twenty years, trying to explain away a simple prank that could have landed them in jail.

***It had** started on a spectacular fall day with Angie overhearing Miles talking to a girl in his econ class, making plans to meet her later that night for dinner. Since Bridget and Miles had been unofficially engaged for over a year, there was no way to interpret what she'd heard as anything but what it was—Miles was screwing around.*

Angie showed up at the restaurant early, which gave her time to park so that she had a direct view of the front door. The girl and Miles arrived at the same time and were instantly all over each other, his tongue down her throat, his hand on her butt to pull her tight against him.

Angie started to get out of her car to confront them, then changed her mind. Instead, she went back to the dorm and recruited Da-nielle and Carrie to help construct a suitable retribution. Finally, after much heated discussion, they decided that Bridget deserved to know what was going on, so they included her.

Bridget desperately sought an explanation for what Angie had seen, even suggesting that she had only seen someone who looked like Miles. How could it be him? He loved her. She loved him. It was inconceivable that he would have cheated on her when they'd made love just the night before.

Angie, Danielle, and Carrie sat by silently as Bridget reasoned it out, their hearts breaking for her, but secretly more than a little happy that Bridget would finally see Miles for what he was.

Over the following week, Bridget's denial turned to acceptance, and her pain to anger. She wanted to confront Miles, but the others convinced her there was a better way.

It only took an afternoon, holed up in their favorite coffee shop, for the four of them to come up with a plan. Three days later, Bridget had succeeded in having a duplicate key made for the Corvette. Now all they had to do was wait another two days for Miles to cancel a date he'd made with Bridget.

They borrowed a car—Carrie's ancient green Volvo would stand out like a cheetah at a dog show—and followed Miles to a restaurant on the opposite side of town from the university. Almost as if it were scripted, he put on the same display Angie had witnessed the first time. Somehow Bridget managed to control the fury that rose from her chest like a dragon's fiery breath.

Five minutes later, Bridget was behind the wheel of the Corvette and headed for the hills.

The original plan had been to leave the car on a deserted road near a reservoir, figuring hikers would find it in a few days—but not before Miles had made a complete fool out of himself trying to involve every law enforcement agency in the greater Charlottesville area in the search.

While they'd scouted the area, what they hadn't paid attention to was the lack of pullouts on the abandoned, weed-choked logging road.

They finally settled on a wide spot that could be seen by a car coming in either direction, but as they started to drive away Bridget insisted the car had to be farther off the road to be safe. So they went back. Fatefully.

Bridget was unusually quiet as she reached into the driver's side and released the emergency brake. With a look of sober determination, she joined the others at the back and pushed. The car moved a lot easier than any of them had expected. And then easier still as it broke through the thick brush and picked up its own momentum, leaving the four friends gaping in surprise as it teetered on a mounded rock for a half second and then tumbled down a hundred-foot, boulder-strewn cliff. The noise was like a series of explosions as the car tumbled from one rock to another.

Wide eyes and dead silence followed. Bridget fought to control a secret smile while the others looked like they were going to be sick.

Angie moved closer to the edge, staring over the side. After scattering chrome and pieces of bright red fiberglass on rocks and in bushes, the Corvette had landed on its top, wedged between a tree and a boulder. "Oh shit," she said, struggling to take in what she saw. "Now what are we going to do?"

Danielle came up to stand beside her. Needing something to hang on to, she bent and braced her hands on her knees and then lowered herself to her haunches. "What the fuck? How could it just shatter like that? It's like it was made out glass."

"Fiberglass," Bridget said. "I knew it was fragile, but I had no idea something like this could happen."

Carrie didn't say anything as she stood and stared into the canyon, her wide eyes and frozen expression the only clue to the frantic workings of her mind.

Bridget made her way down to the first outcropping, where she stopped to examine a piece of fiberglass before stuffing it in her pocket.

When she started down again, Danielle shouted, "What are you doing? You're going to kill yourself if—"

Bridget looked up at her. "I want to make sure it's not leaking gas. There are homes down there. The last thing I want is arson on our records too."

"Too?" Angie said under her breath.

"Along with car theft," Danielle said.

Carrie groaned. "Imagine what that's going to look like on a job application."

Bridget reached the car, looked it over, and headed back up the hill. "I suppose it's a good thing it wasn't insured," she said, brushing the dirt and debris from her shorts.

"Why the hell not?" Carrie asked. "Who doesn't insure a car like that?"

"Miles doesn't. He ran the numbers and figured it made more sense to pay the uninsured motor vehicle fee while he was still in school, and not worth suing, than it was to pay what the insurance companies wanted to insure a muscle car being driven by a male under twenty-five."

"Still, it seems to me that getting a new car out of this could have gone a long way toward keeping Miles from making a big deal out of losing this one," Carrie said.

"Think about it," Bridget said with a note of impatience. "If we let Miles file a claim knowing the car wasn't really stolen—at least not the way he would report—and someone figured out later that we were responsible, the insurance company would nail our asses to the wall for fraud."

"Is that something you know for a fact? Have you actually seen it written down someplace?" Carrie asked. "Or are you just speculating?"

"What difference does it make?" Angie shouted in frustration. "We're in deep shit no matter how you look at it. I sure as hell don't have the money to get Miles another car like this one, and I know none of you do either."

"Even if we could afford a brand-new Corvette, it wouldn't satisfy him," Bridget said. "It's the power this one gave him over his sister that made it so important."

Carrie sat on a nearby rock. "Trying to come up with the money to buy him another car is a moot point because we can never let him find out we were responsible for what happened to the old one."

"Maybe it's not as bad as it looks," Angie said. "A good body shop—"

Bridget took Angie's arm and led her to the edge of the cliff. "Take a closer look. There's no way that car can be fixed. It's like a jigsaw puzzle without a picture to use as a guide or any straight edges to get you started."

Carrie and Danielle joined them. "He's going to be soooo pissed," Angie said.

"Beside himself," Danielle added.

Carrie put her arms around Danielle and Bridget. "Especially when he has to tell his sister what happened."

"Too bad we have to miss it." Bridget bit her lip to keep from laughing as she pictured Miles and his sister going at each other over the loss of the family heirloom.

Angie leaned into Bridget. "Such a shame . . . it really was a pretty car."

"And Miles did look a little like Val Kilmer when he was behind the wheel," Bridget said, putting her arm around Angie and bringing her into the group hug.

"Really?" Danielle said. "I thought he looked more like a white RuPaul."

"Oh, Danielle—that's just mean," Angie said, choking back laughter.

"I'll apologize—to RuPaul. If I ever meet him."

The offer to apologize broke the dam. It started with nervous laughter that grew and grew until it echoed off the hills.

It was either laugh or cry.

On the way home it was Carrie who said out loud what all of them were thinking.

"We can't just let this go. We have to find a way to make it right with Miles without telling him what we're doing."

"How would you suggest we do that?" Danielle asked.

"We could send him a check anonymously," Angie said.

"That would be a great idea—if any of us had any money," Danielle said.

Bridget pulled into a grocery store parking lot and turned off the car. "If anyone is going to pay Miles, it's me. None of you would have been involved with this if you weren't sticking up for me. As far as I'm concerned, that makes me responsible."

"Nice try," Angie said. "But we're in this together."

"Does it really matter if we pay him now or later?" Carrie asked. "As long as he gets paid eventually?"

Danielle turned in her seat so she could see everyone. "Since none of us has the money now, it seems like a moot point. Why don't we set a date, say five years from now, that we each have to come up with our portion. We'll get together and figure out how to send it so that it's untraceable."

"Sounds good to me," Angie said.

"Sounds like something we should do for us," Bridget added.

"I like that idea," Carrie added.

"What did you do with the piece of fiberglass you picked up and put in your pocket that day?" Danielle asked.

Bridget grinned. "When we were living in Hong Kong, I found an intricately carved, antique cinnabar lacquer box—the most expensive piece of art I'd purchased up until that time—and put the piece inside, along with a picture of Miles leaning against the fender. It was one of those poses where guys cross their arms and push against their biceps to make them look bigger. I gave it to him for our tenth anniversary.

"He asked what point I was making, and I managed to squeeze out a couple of tears as I told him that when I found out where the wreck had happened I'd climbed all the way down the cliff to rescue an important piece of his past, knowing how much it would mean to him one day."

"Oh, you go, girl," Angie said. "I've never been more proud of you."

Forever the most pragmatic of the four, knowing something had prompted the "gift," Danielle urged Bridget to finish the story.

"I caught him screwing around again," she admitted.

"What happened to the box?" Carrie asked.

"He tossed it with the wrapping. He didn't have a clue that it wasn't some cheap knockoff I'd picked up at the Temple Street Night Market. I rescued it before the housekeeper showed up the next morning. I now have over fifty boxes I collected while we were living in Hong Kong, and Miles has no idea what any of them are worth. If he did, they would have become part of the divorce settlement. But I hid them in plain sight, and he was oblivious."

"What an idiot," Carrie said.

"Thank God for small favors." Bridget smiled. "The last time I sent pictures to my dealer friends in Hong Kong, they told me that priced individually the value is well over a million dollars. Sold as a collection, it could be twice that. If something ever does happen to me and one day you receive a box of boxes in the mail. . . . Well, what you do with them is up to you. At least you know now what you shouldn't do."

Chapter 10

Danielle straightened the oversize beach towel Angie was sitting on, propped a wide-brimmed straw hat on her head, then handed her a pair of sunglasses before she tucked one plaid blanket over Angie's lap and another around her shoulders. For the final touch she dabbed a large circle of white sunblock on the end of Angie's nose. "Okay, I think we're ready."

"*Wait.*" Bridget took a quart-size bottle of water out of her bag and set it next to Angie. "Now."

Danielle tried for a vertical shot but could only get a sliver of the ocean in the background, so she turned the phone horizontal to include a broad expanse of beach. Hopefully, Carrie would wrap up her business call in time to join them for a group picture. "Ready?"

Angie nodded. "Make sure my boots show."

Danielle took a step backward and lowered herself to a crouching position. She snapped a shot, checked it, then took another and grinned. She handed Angie her phone. "There's no way Darren can think we're not taking care of you."

Seeing how ridiculous she looked, Angie laughed. "If this doesn't impress him, nothing will."

She peeled off the extra layers of clothes and sprawled out on the towel before sending the picture and accompanying text on its way to Alaska. Less than a minute later, she was deep into an electronic conversation.

Danielle reached for the sunscreen and applied a liberal layer to her arms and legs and Bridget's back. When she finished, she gave Bridget the bottle and leaned forward while Bridget reciprocated.

"Think they'll get married?" Bridget asked.

"She's going to need help with the twins."

Bridget groaned. "Oh, I hope that's not the only reason."

"Yeah, it would be nice if this works out long-term," Da-nielle said. "For her and especially for the kids."

"How's it going with you and Grady?" Bridget moved her legs out of the sun and into the shade from the umbrella.

"Fine. Once the puppy is trained, we'll go back to great."

"Whatever possessed him?"

"A sappy news story about how many animals are gassed at the shelters every year."

"I'm surprised he came home with only one."

"One *dog.* He brought home a kitten too. She's skinny and has black fur and looks like a baby bat. But she uses her litter box faithfully. I'm hoping she can teach the puppy that it's not cool to squat whenever the urge strikes."

"I'm assuming the litter box thing earned her a name?"

"Dandelion. To me she's like a beautiful weed."

"That you don't have to rush home from work to walk."

Danielle flinched. She drew her legs up to her chest, wrapped her arms around them, and propped her chin on her knees. "I should have said something earlier, but the business is no more. Grady and I made a couple of dumb decisions to try to hold on when the economy went belly up and wound up losing everything, including the building. The foreclosure sign went up the day before I left to come here."

"And you were saving this to tell us . . . when?"

"It's kind of hard to dump ordinary problems on someone who's been through what you have."

Bridget let out a deep sigh. "How long is this 'we all need to feel sorry for Bridget' crap going to go on? It's getting old."

"Then convince me I don't have to worry about you."

"I can't. If there's a colony of cancer cells hiding somewhere in my body, it's beyond my control. I'll do what I can when I can, but you're going to have to learn to live with it the same way I do." She propped herself up on her elbows to get a better look at Danielle. "Now tell me what happened to the ski shop."

"Nothing that hasn't happened to other small business owners all over the country. I wasn't prepared for the crash, and then I wasn't flexible enough to get through it. The customers who helped me build the business lost their jobs and then their homes, and when they were finally getting on their feet again, they decided that they didn't have to have new skis or boards every year and that their jackets and pants could be passed down through the family. Swap meets became the hot ticket and recycling the mantra, for everything from gloves to car racks. The final blow came when a couple of the big-box sporting goods stores moved into the area. There was no way I could compete. Customer service was all I could offer, and it wasn't enough."

"How long has this been going on?"

"Six years. We should have, and could have, bailed earlier and not lost everything, but I was convinced the economy would turn around, and with it our customers. What I failed to take into consideration was that once the pattern of shopping in the discount stores was set, it was going to take a long time—if ever—to get people to come back for the kinds of things we sold. If you absolutely have to have a Limited Edition Apex ski boot, you fly your private jet to the resorts that sell them."

"So now what?"

"I'm looking at the experience as a kick in my complacent butt to get up and out and find something new. Retail stopped being fun a long time ago. I want to have fun again."

"Come work for me," Angie said, tossing her phone back into her bag. "Darren has a pilot lined up to take over my flights, but I desperately need someone I can trust to run the Anchorage office while we're in Fairbanks."

"There you have it," Bridget said. "Problem solved."

Before Danielle could say anything, Angie sat up and added, "You think I'm kidding, but I'm not. All this time I've been spending on the phone with Darren hasn't been just about the twins. We're trying to figure out how we can be in two places at the same time, especially now that my flying time is going to end before we even get the Fairbanks office up and running. If I can't fulfill the cargo contract, I can't make the payments on the planes, and the whole thing comes tumbling down like a stack of dominos."

"I don't know anything about running an airline. The way you've described it, keeping track of the weather and being flexible on scheduling and shipping can be life-or-death matters. You need someone local who understands these things. Even with Grady there to help me, we couldn't do what you need done."

"That's not where I need you. I have people who know what they're doing who would be willing to go to Fairbanks to set things up and stay there as long as they were needed. What I don't have is someone in Anchorage to manage the office and do the billing and keep the books and handle the insurance and employee retirement accounts and all the other crap that keeps us going but that no one but me knows how to do."

"And what would Grady do?"

"What has he been doing for the past ten years?"

"Everything you just listed."

"Then what have you been doing?"

"The orders and sales and inventory and trade shows and social media."

"Oh, my, God—you're the perfect team." Angie came forward and threw her arms around Danielle. "Please, please, *please* say you'll at least think about it."

It was on the tip of Danielle's tongue to throw out another excuse why it couldn't possibly work when she surprised both of them by saying, "How soon do you need an answer?"

"Yesterday."

"Why are you hesitating?" Bridget asked. "Think of it as an adventure."

"I'll have to talk to Grady first."

Angie reached in her bag, brought out her phone, and handed it to Danielle. "The reception is great here."

Danielle looked at the phone as if it were the first one she'd seen. "Put up or shut up?"

"Not even close," said Angie. "More like down on my knees begging." She put her hands together in a pleading gesture. "You won't even have to look for a place to stay. Darren is going to move in with me. He can't sublease the house he's renting, but he can have as many guests as he wants." Warming to her subject, she added, "It's a step above your typical bachelor pad—probably because he's never there. But he's not your naked-women-poster kind of guy, so you wouldn't have to do a lot of redecorating."

Danielle laughed. "And that's supposed to excite me?"

"Am I trying too hard?"

"No . . . I understand what it feels like to fight to keep a business from going under," Danielle said.

"Is that really what's making you hesitate? Or would it just be too weird for you to work for me?"

"Weird? Yes. Too weird? I don't think so."

"That's how I feel too," Bridget said.

Danielle and Angie turned to look at her, their expressions filled with question.

"About me going to work for Carrie."

"*What?*" they said in unison.

"When did this happen?" Angie asked.

"This morning."

"Is it the Asian art thing you two were talking about?" Danielle asked.

"I'm going to be her liaison for acquiring art pieces before they're exposed to the bloated prices at the auction houses. We can save clients fifteen to twenty percent in fees, even taking the brokerage fee into consideration. Plus we're free to negotiate a better price."

"What about school?" Danielle asked. "I thought you were all signed up and determined to get your degree?"

"I am. At least I was. But how can I pass up an opportunity like this? I'm going to be stepping into something I love, with someone I trust. What could be better?"

Danielle studied the phone cradled between her hands before returning it to Angie and reaching for her own. "I'll be right back."

Angie lay down and put a hand over her softly rounding belly. "Oh, please let him say yes."

"I think my hair is coming in curly," Bridget said, purposely changing the subject. "And that's why it itches all the time. The ends are twisting around and rubbing against my scalp."

"It's not going to work," Angie said. "You can't distract me. But I love you for trying."

Seconds later she abruptly sat up and propped her sunglasses on top of her head. "Let me see."

Bridget dipped her head. "Feel free to rub it all you want."

"What the hell . . . I think you're right. How do you go from stick-straight to 'Mama made a mistake with the perm' curly just because it fell out and is coming back in again?"

"It's called 'chemo-curl' and is usually semipermanent. The last of the toxins affects the hair follicle and . . ." She laughed. ". . . And I really don't give a damn. It is what it is, and I'm going to treat it as if it were a stupid cancer gift. I've always wanted curly hair, and now I'll have it. At least for a while."

A comfortable silence settled that lasted almost an entire minute before Angie rolled onto her side, propped her head up with her hand, and asked, "Where did you say Miles is now?"

"Mumbai. Why?"

"I was just thinking . . ."

"Yes?"

"Do you suppose there's any way we could arrange for someone to steal his car?"

Chapter 11

Bridget set a large stainless steel bowl of popcorn on the counter, then went to the freezer to take out four boxes of Junior Mints. "Okay, who goes first?"

"I will," Danielle said. "I brought *Bridget Jones's Diary.*"

"Oh, good one," Bridget said, grinning. "For at least two great reasons."

"*Pride and Prejudice,*" Angie said.

"Which one?" a chorus of voices demanded.

"PBS."

"Good thing," Bridget said, giving voice to the murmur of approvals. "Carrie?"

"*TED Talks—Power Shift.*"

"Noooo—" the chorus responded loudly and plaintively.

"This is the night for mind candy," Bridget reminded her.

Carrie grinned. "Just kidding—*Breakfast at Tiffany's*."

"What about you, Bridget?" Angie prompted.

"*Ghost*."

"Oh, it seems like forever since we've watched that one," Danielle said. "Better get the tissues."

Carrie's phone rang in the other room. "I'll be right back."

"Five minutes is all you get," Danielle said to her retreating back. "Then we're starting the movie without you."

"What's up with her?" Bridget asked.

Danielle filled a bowl and handed it to Angie. "I don't know. She say anything to you?"

"Nothing." Angie sprinkled her Junior Mints over her popcorn. "But I know she's been waiting for a phone call that has nothing to do with work."

"Ah, ha—that can only mean one thing," Bridget said. "She's seeing someone."

"That can't be it," Danielle said. "She would have said something."

Angie picked up a piece of popcorn and popped it into her mouth. "It wouldn't be the first liaison she chose not to share with us."

Danielle made a dismissive wave. "That's different."

"Why?" Bridget said.

"I don't know. It just is." Danielle thought about it for several seconds. "There are some things too personal to share."

"With *us?*" Angie protested. "No way."

"Are you saying you've never done something or had something happen to you that left you so embarrassed or humiliated that you'd do or say anything to keep anyone from finding out?"

"I have," Bridget said.

Jaws dropped in surprise, Danielle and Angie turned in unison to stare at her. Of the four of them, she was the last one they would have thought capable of keeping that kind of secret.

Bridget reached up to run her hand across her bald pate in what had become as much nervous gesture as frustration over the itching. "I should have told you when it happened, but once I realized how much trouble we could get in for wrecking Miles's car, I decided it was better that you didn't know."

"And . . . ?" Danielle prompted.

Bridget took a deep breath. "I knew that cliff was on the other side of the bushes. I wanted everything to happen just the way it did."

Danielle laughed. "We all did."

"But I never should have gotten you into that mess, not when the consequences could have been—"

"You can't possibly think that's the worst thing any of us has done," Angie said. "We've been incredibly lucky not to get caught, that's all. There are more ways to get into trouble in Alaska than there are salmon, and in my early, wild-child years there, I sampled a few." She focused on Danielle. "I don't want to be pushy, but have you heard from Grady?"

"Not yet. He said he needed a little time to consider the consequences of selling the house, completely uprooting our lives, and, most importantly, leaving his golfing buddies."

"We have golf courses in Anchorage. Several of them. World-class."

"You're lying about the world-class."

"Depends on your criteria. How many places can you play golf where they give you instructions about bear safety along with your scorecard?"

"You want me to tell Grady *that*?"

Bridget came back to get the napkins, followed by Carrie. Danielle did a double-take when she saw the size of the grin on Carrie's face. "Good news?"

"The best," Carrie said. "I'm engaged."

"Wow," Bridget said. "I didn't even know you were seeing someone."

"Me either," said Angie.

Danielle studied Carrie through narrowed eyes as she held her breath for what would come next.

"So, are you going to fill us in?" Angie prompted.

"Don't leave out anything," Bridget added.

Carrie glanced at Danielle and gained courage from the knowing look of understanding she saw in her friend's eyes. "Her name is Diana Hansen."

"*Finally,*" Bridget exclaimed.

The response wasn't what Carrie had expected. Not even close. "Finally?"

"We've been waiting twenty years for you to come out," Danielle said.

Carrie struggled for words. "You've known all along? Why didn't you say something?"

"Like?" Danielle said.

Carrie was instantly crying. "Like, it's okay?"

"Come on, Carrie. How could we? Coming out is a big deal. There was no way we could tell you it didn't matter unless you said something first. It's been hard for us to be left on the outside of what's really going on with you when we can't keep our mouths shut about our own personal lives. Think of how many times we've nagged you about sending pictures of you and whoever you were seeing."

"And how we've gone on and on and on about how cute and brave and wonderful Ellen and Rachel

Maddow and Cynthia Nixon are and how fun it would be to know them," Angie added.

Danielle put her arms around Carrie and gave her a long hug. "Personally, I find it almost impossible to believe that you've never picked up on the tension between me and Bridget and Angie about which one of us you liked the best. I told them it was me, but they said no way, it had to be one of them."

Carrie burst out laughing. "Sorry—but you three are soooo not my type."

"Then tell us who is. We want to know everything about this woman who's captured your heart."

Carrie took her phone out of her pocket and scrolled through a dozen pictures. Diana appeared to be a few years older than Carrie, with streaks of gray in her long black hair. She had an infectious smile and radiated intelligence.

"What does she do?" Bridget asked.

"She's a prosecutor in the district attorney's office. Her specialty is child abuse cases."

"That must be hard," Danielle said, taking Carrie's phone and looking at the pictures again. "She looks too sweet-tempered for that kind of job."

"Early on, a lot of defense attorneys made that mistake. Now her reputation precedes her. A case is more likely to be plea-bargained than prosecuted when the defense discovers she's involved."

"When is the wedding?" Angie asked. "It's a perfectly selfish question. I'd spend the whole time feeling sorry for myself if I couldn't be there." She let out a dramatic sigh. "And you know that wouldn't be good for the babies . . . or their mother."

The rest of them groaned.

"You're really going to have to work on your delivery, Angie," Bridget said. "I'll give you some pointers later."

"Okay, so I went a little far this time. But that doesn't mean it isn't true. I really will feel bad if I can't be a part of this wedding." She frowned. "Are we going to be bridesmaids or groomsmen? I'm not up on the protocol for gay weddings."

Carrie looked from Bridget to Danielle to Angie. "I love you—all of you. Next to Diana, you are the most important people in my life. I wish I'd been braver—and more trusting—and told you about being gay from the beginning."

"Me too," Bridget said. "It would have been easier to dish about the bad relationships you've suffered through over the years if we'd been able to use the correct pronoun."

Danielle's phone vibrated. She and Angie exchanged looks before Angie crossed the fingers on both hands. "It's Grady," she said. "I'm going to take this outside."

"Can I come?" Angie asked.

"No."

"I promise I won't say anything," she pleaded.

"Didn't your mother tell you not to make promises you knew you wouldn't keep?"

When Danielle was gone, Angie busied herself getting the salt shaker out of the cupboard while Bridget poured three glasses of wine and one sparkling water. Angie's hands were visibly trembling when she tucked them under her arms and burst out crying.

Bridget handed her a napkin. "Isn't it interesting how every article you read insists that being pregnant is the happiest time of your life and in real life you're always either crying or about to?"

"Look at the bylines," Carrie said. "The articles are written by men."

"Danielle has no idea how much this means to me," Angie said.

"I don't understand," Bridget said. "Is this happening just because you're having twins?"

"I thought I had the time frame worked out. I was going to fly until the seventh month and then go to Fairbanks to make sure everything was working there and then come home a couple of weeks before the baby was due."

"Why doesn't that surprise me?" Carrie said. "I'll bet you didn't figure in morning sickness either."

"How did you ever get your doctor to approve that schedule?" Bridget chimed in.

The long silence that followed was all the answer they needed.

"Alaskan women are used to hard work," Angie said. "It's part of our nature—like the pioneer women."

"Who had ten children in order to wind up with two or three who survived," Carrie said.

"So I screwed up," Angie said. "I've never been pregnant before. That doesn't solve my problem now."

Danielle came back into the room, radiating a look of disbelief. "He said he's thinking about it. Which, for Grady, all but means it's a done deal."

"For sure?" Angie was afraid to let herself get too excited. "No trial period, or 'we'll see how it goes,' or 'we have to sell the house in Denver first'?"

"Oh, there's some of that. He wants to fly up there and meet everyone and look around. In the meantime, he bought an armload of books and has been reading everything he can find about Anchorage on the Internet. He's even arranged to have lunch tomorrow with a friend of a friend who lived in Palmer for several years."

Angie let out a squeal and threw her arms around Danielle. "I can't tell you how much this means to me."

"I think I have a pretty good idea." Danielle dug her phone out of her pocket. "One more thing before we start the movie. Puppy finally has a name. Sanuk. It's Alaskan for—"

"Fun and happiness," Angie filled in.

Danielle found the picture and turned the phone around. Sporting what was impossible to interpret as any other expression, Sanuk sat at the back door, his jowls lifted, his eyes opened wide in an ear-to-ear grin.

"I know exactly how he feels," Bridget said softly.

PART THREE
January

Chapter 1

Matthew Stephens pulled his rented Prius into the parking lot at the Monterey Regional Airport. The tires squealed in protest as he swung around a corner and dove into the first available slot. He was late, but hopefully not so late that he'd missed Lindsey getting off the plane.

He reached for his camera—a world-weary Canon 1D that was almost as familiar an extension to his hand as his fingers—and sprinted toward the terminal, stopping to scan the people in the lobby. Not seeing her, he headed for the arrival board. Rarely did he leave for an airport anywhere in the world without checking arrival times first, but there was always the exception, and this was it. With the predictable consequence. Lindsey's plane had been delayed an hour.

Matthew checked his phone. There was a text from her that he'd missed when he was climbing rocks along the shoreline photographing a couple of sea lions chasing each other in the surf. He was still operating on bush time, where checking for messages was useless.

Lindsey had told him that she'd call when the plane landed, but he'd waited so long to see her that even the forty-five minutes it would take him to get there from Santa Cruz seemed an eternity.

And now it was out of his hands. He headed for the stairs that led to the second-story viewing platform.

Monterey Regional Airport served a small, almost exclusive destination clientele. People who had business in Silicon Valley or farther up in the Bay Area didn't fly there—only those who came to play golf at Pebble Beach or to vacation on one of the most spectacular coastlines in the world. Or those who were lucky enough to call one of the towns that lay scattered around the Monterey Bay shoreline home.

The airport had the charm and friendliness that bespoke pre-9/11, when flying was still an adventure. Matthew could get candid shots there of people doing their jobs in a laid-back, friendly atmosphere without automatically becoming a terrorist suspect.

Stepping outside, he hunched his shoulders against the wind stealing up the hillside. It whistled through the bent and twisted cypress trees, gaining force as it raced across the tarmac, pushing and dragging leaves and bits of debris in an eerie display of visibility.

Matthew took several pictures, trying to capture the wind and cold. One shot had potential—a worker with leaves swirling around his feet, his collar turned up, his hat worn low over his ears—while the rest were only a small cut above mediocre.

Glancing at his watch, he was disappointed to see how little time had passed and decided to head inside for a cup of coffee. He ordered it strong and black and thought back to the days when he'd used equal parts coffee, sugar, and cream in a drink Lindsey insisted was more dessert than beverage. She'd eventually weaned him off both the sugar and cream, insisting he would thank her the first time he was given a cup of bush coffee. A handful of grounds tossed into a pot of already brown water, brewed over an open fire until it was reduced by half, was guaranteed to get you moving in the morning. It was not the kind of drink that took well to cream or sugar.

She never doubted and never let him question whether he had the talent to become the wildlife photographer he envisioned being. In the beginning, when he was still regularly losing assignments to older, more experienced photographers, she would wait until the magazine or newspaper or charity brochure was published and then go over it with him, photograph by photograph. He learned how to judge his work dispassionately and what to do to make it better.

He told her she was a natural. She insisted it was his love that inspired and supported her.

How had they drifted so far apart?

With the coffee in one hand, a recycled *Monterey County Herald* tucked under his arm, and his camera slung over his shoulder, Matthew looked for a place to settle and pass the time. He saw a woman watching him and returned her smile. She opened her hand in invitation and indicated the chair next to her. She had short hair, more pepper than salt, and a trim frame. Her eyes were sharp and questioning, her clothing expensive and understated.

"I'm here at least once a month, and this is the first time I've seen it so busy," she said as he settled beside her. "Seems none of us had sense enough to call before we came, and now it's hurry-up-and-wait."

Matthew held out his hand. "Matthew Stephens," he said.

She slipped her hand into his. "Alison Kirkpatrick."

"Are you waiting for friend or family?"

"Grandson," she said. "He took a year off before he started college to see the country. He was supposed to be in Texas by now, but met a man who was rebuilding a house in New Orleans for a displaced family and decided to stay around to help." She broke off a piece of her bagel and added cream cheese. "And you?"

"Girlfriend." Over the years he'd tried several different ways to describe his relationship with Lindsey, and even though he wasn't crazy about it, he'd finally settled on "girlfriend." He wanted more than the term implied, but how did you build a home on a constantly shifting foundation?

"I don't know much about cameras, but yours looks impressive—and well used."

Matthew put the camera on the table between them and smiled. "There's a story attached to every ding and scratch."

"Which means photography is how you make your living?"

"Some years that would be a generous assessment."

"Fashion?"

He chuckled. "In a way. I photograph the most beautiful fur coats in the world—on their original owners."

"A wildlife photographer?"

"And occasional landscapes when the magazine I'm working for needs illustration to go with an article."

"How exciting. I've always wondered about the people behind the pictures. It's hard for me to imagine what it must be like to sit and wait for just the right moment."

"Disappointed?"

"Well, I have to admit I'm a little let down that you're not wearing a safari hat."

He laughed. "Only in Africa."

"I've always wanted to go there. Is it as spectacular as I've heard?"

"Depends on where you are. Much of the continent is at war, and there's nothing beautiful about people killing each other. Botswana is the most stable country on the continent, both politically and economically, and is doing what it can to preserve its wildlife, particularly in the Okavango Delta. I don't think you would be disappointed if you made that your first trip."

"What about the Congo? I'd love to see the gorillas in the wild."

Lindsey had spent the last seven months going from an assignment in Libya to one in the Congo. It was the primary reason they'd missed their month in July at the beach house. It would have been the first time in over a year that they'd spent more than two weeks together. The coin they kept flipping, with hope on one side and disappointment on the other, was wearing thin, the letters designating the value having all but disappeared.

Matthew put off answering by taking a drink of coffee. It wasn't the worst he'd consumed in the past six months. That title went to the swill he'd been given in a kahve shop in Istanbul, one that catered to tourists looking for a genuine Turkish experience to share with their friends back home.

He put the paper cup back on the table. "About the Congo—I understand the draw. I did a piece for a German magazine several years ago after a mountain-gorilla family was slaughtered by the locals so that they could cut down the trees to make charcoal. I fell in love with that gorilla family. They really are gentle giants. But the natives who kill them aren't. You need to understand the politics in a country before you go. Right now the United Nations considers DR Congo the rape capital of the world.

"Now, that said, if you're still interested, you could do some research on tour outfitters in the neighboring countries where the mountain gorillas wander and go with the best company you can afford."

"I appreciate the advice. I knew some of this, but not all of it."

"Will you be traveling alone?"

This brought a huge smile. "I'll be on my delayed honeymoon. My grandson is coming here to walk me down the aisle this Saturday. The whole marriage thing came together so fast that we didn't have time to plan a real trip, so we're going to go to Africa as soon as I can figure out exactly what I want to see."

"Sounds like a shotgun wedding," he teased, fighting an insane feeling of jealousy.

She grew serious. "When you're sixty and you've lost people who mean the world to you, you realize how foolish it is to waste time. You should savor every moment."

It was a song he could sing without missing a note. Before he could comment, a voice came over the loudspeaker announcing the arrival of Alaska Airlines flight 2436.

"I'm going to the viewing platform," he said, standing. "Want to come?" He never invited people who weren't photographers to accompany him when he was working. He'd missed too many shots when his concentration was broken by questions. But seeing her grandson's plane dropping out of the air and taxiing toward her would be worth whatever shot he missed.

She declined. "I have this thing about watching airplanes," she said softly and stood. "But I appreciate the offer."

Impulsively, he hugged her. "Congratulations on the wedding. I'll look for you in Africa."

She smiled. "Stranger things have happened."

Matthew grabbed his coffee and sprinted up the stairs. As he passed the trash can he stopped to take one last swallow, but his throat tightened and then closed before the cup reached his lips.

He tossed the coffee and positioned himself on top of a concrete bench that allowed him to shoot over the Plexiglas barrier. The plane circled and landed, swung around until its nose pointed toward the ocean, then slowly taxied toward the terminal, where it would stop and disgorge its passengers on the tarmac.

Now blanketed by a mantle of dark clouds, the ocean had changed from deep blue to slate gray.

A portent?

He shook off the dark feeling and scanned the porthole windows on the plane knowing the odds were less than a quarter in his favor that Lindsey had bagged a window seat on the left side of the plane.

No one waved. But then, it wasn't her style to draw attention to herself. Even knowing this didn't stop him from imagining her seeking him out, a smile lighting her eyes when she spotted a not-very-imposing figure, jean-clad and wearing a quarter-century-old blue peacoat that he'd inherited from his father.

His chest ached with a volatile combination of color-laced emotions—joy, relief, passion, love. But mostly there was the profound, breath-stealing sorrow that came with knowing this could be the last time he would be there to meet her when she came home.

They'd survived ten years of hit-and-miss time together, but he'd reached the point where he was exhausted from missing her. He was lonely and wanted more. If they couldn't find a way to stop giving the best of who they were to their jobs, he would find a way to go on without her.

He'd already survived one devastating loss. Somehow, he would manage to do it again.

Before the plane landed, Lindsey caught the flicker of a shadowy figure moving across the viewing platform. She knew without question it was Matthew braving the cold, willing her plane to a safe landing by his mere presence. In all the years they had been together, she couldn't recall five times when she'd been the one doing the waiting. Somehow it was always Matthew who arrived first, Matthew who made the arrangements for a place for them to stay, Matthew who met her with open arms and a kiss that turned a long separation into a fleeting memory.

He coped with their separations by planning for the next time they could be together. She survived by escaping into whatever violent world she inhabited at the moment, having discovered early in their relationship that dodging bullets and bombs left little time to indulge the loneliness that came with missing him.

When her days or weeks between assignments didn't coincide with Matthew's, she wandered through whatever part of the world she happened to be in at the time, not realizing that what she was really doing was looking for a place for them to call home.

They'd tried an apartment in Atlanta, and one in London, picked for the major airports that served those cities more than for any love of the locations. But they found it was easier to meet spontaneously where and when opportunity presented itself. When months went by and they couldn't connect, she missed Matthew like she missed oxygen at fourteen thousand feet.

He was the ground where she sank her tenuous roots. It could be an airport where they held hands and drank coffee until one of their flights was called, or it could be a couple of days they stole to hole up in a hotel making love and ordering room service so they never had to get dressed to go out. It didn't matter in which city or country or continent they found themselves, they created their own home.

For years it had been enough. Or so they told themselves, ignoring the growing ache to share a story or a simple touch or a look that conveyed more than words could express. There were times when she looked into the night sky and convinced herself that Matthew was looking at the same star. She needed that connection to him as deeply as she needed to believe the work she did mattered.

She'd learned to patch her broken heart by summoning memories of the times when she'd stepped out of her observer role and rescued a child in desperate need of medicine or surgery, or when she'd finagled transport for a family to a refugee camp. She'd even taken solace in the story she'd talked her editor into doing on dogs adopted by U.S. soldiers while on duty and how they were forced to leave the dogs behind. She still received emails from grateful GIs, with pictures attached of their dogs, thriving in American cities all across the country as a result of the laws that were changed, in large part, as a result of that series of photographs.

Even this had stopped working. Now all that was left to sustain her fingertip hold on sanity was her constantly thinning connection to Matthew.

He was the only one she'd ever told when she started having minor meltdowns and how they had started to scare her. The last one, in the Congo—an hour of uncontrolled sobbing when she'd curled up in her sleeping bag and stuffed a sweater against her mouth—she hadn't shared with him, and probably wouldn't. To do so would be to acknowledge what Matthew had been telling her for the past four years—if she didn't find a way to heal herself, she was going to wind up locked away in some sterile mental hospital. Her parents would visit on weekends and then on the drive home ask themselves what could possibly have happened to their sweet, fun-loving daughter.

They didn't have a clue who she really was. Like her brother and sisters and grandparents, they loved her without knowing her. Only Matthew understood.

Matthew raced down the stairs and did a double-take when he saw Lindsey appear at the open doorway of the plane. In a tenth of a second, he went from confused to convinced that it wasn't actually her, just someone who bore an uncanny resemblance to her. This woman was older and a good twenty pounds lighter, her black hair was short and dull, her stride slow and unsure. Then he saw the camera bag flung over her shoulder and knew that it was Lindsey and that she was in desperate trouble.

She fought for a smile as she followed the yellow line on the asphalt to the terminal, then leaned heavily into his embrace. The wind caught her hair and blew it against his face. Finally, something familiar—the flower-laden scent of her favorite shampoo. "What in the hell happened to you?"

She hated scenes. If she put into words what she was feeling, she'd create a scene that would scare not only Matthew but everyone within range. Instead of answering, she took his arm and steered him inside.

He stopped and turned her to face him. Passengers caught in their roadblock silently parted and flowed past, like a stream finding its way around a boulder.

"What's happened to you?" he demanded again, fear radiating from him like debris from an explosion.

"Not now."

"Is it your mom? Your dad?"

"*Please,* Matthew—not now." Seeing he needed more, she added, "My parents are fine. Just get me out of here."

He shouldered her backpack and guided her toward the baggage carousel. A woman juggling two toddlers and a car seat dropped her purse in front of them. Matthew offered to take the car seat, and she handed it to him with a tired smile of gratitude.

"Want a kid or two to go along with the seat?" she joked.

He returned her smile. "Give me a couple of years."

Lindsey flinched as the innocent exchange triggered the tears she'd succeeded in controlling until then. It seemed everything made her cry lately.

"You could have warned me," he said when the woman was out of earshot.

She tried to laugh, but it came out sounding more like a choked sob. "And I could have sent a picture, but I was afraid once you saw how big a mess I am you might find a way to cancel."

Instead of answering, he clamped his jaw so tightly she could see the cords on his neck standing out. She should have known better than to try to joke about what was going on between them.

Arriving at the carousel, Matthew put the car seat against the wall and sprinted to get Lindsey's duffle bag before it made a second round.

When he returned, she tried another smile, a sad attempt to bring a little joy into her homecoming. "I've missed you." A tear raced down her cheek. "It's been so long."

"Too long," he said.

Lindsey dug in her pocket, brought out her phone, and handed it to him. "Nothing is more important than these next four weeks."

He would have been less surprised if she'd given him her camera bag and told him to toss it into the ocean. Her phone and cameras were the bible and prayer book of the Lindsey Thompson Church.

Matthew took the phone and slipped it into his pocket, appreciating the symbolic gesture, knowing it was no more than that. He picked up her backpack. Feeling its heft, he tried something easy. "Another camera?"

When she didn't immediately answer, he added, "Don't tell me you finally broke down and bought that new lens."

The smile was genuine this time. "I picked up the 70/200 before I went to Kabul last summer."

"And?"

"Other than weighing too much, it's incredible."

"I told you that you'd love it."

She came up on her toes and kissed his cheek. Fresh tears reflected the overhead lights before she could blink them away. Would she ever stop crying? "Doesn't come close to the way I feel about you."

Chapter 2

Lindsey stood in the middle of the living room while Matthew took her duffle bag into the bedroom. She glanced around and noted the small things that let her know Matthew had already settled in. There was a pair of running shoes by the sliding-glass door and a cloth on the dining room table where he'd cleaned his camera. A German edition of *GEO* magazine sat on the table beside a recliner. Next to the magazine was a coffee cup that could substitute for a soup bowl—along with a pair of glasses.

When did Matthew start wearing glasses?

She put her backpack on the table and then dug her fingers into the softness of the cashmere throw draped over the back of a chair sitting by the fireplace. If she let herself dream of houses, this would be the house she dreamed about. The walls would be painted the same sand color, the trim a soft cream. The carpet would be wildly impractical, something deep and plush and only a little darker than oatmeal. She would buy a sofa just like this one, made for naps or for tucking her feet under her legs and snuggling into the corners. Every chair would have an ottoman, and there would be lots of light for reading or doing crossword puzzles or even needlepoint.

From somewhere in the part of her brain where tender, underappreciated memories were stored, she flashed on the image of a needlepoint pillow she'd started in college and never finished. A sharp, painful ache of longing coursed through her and then, as quickly, was gone. One day she would finish and display that pillow in a home of her own, even if it looked every bit as bad as she remembered.

In her dream house there would be a fireplace with a raised hearth like this one. She could watch the flames and feel the warmth and forget, if only for an hour or two, all the children she had met who didn't know how to dream anymore.

"It's beautiful," she told Matthew when he returned. She crossed the room to look out the sliding-glass door. The clouds had lifted, leaving a narrow strip of sky on the horizon where the sun sat like a bright orange beach ball after its last bounce. "Actually, it's beyond description."

Matthew came up behind her and slipped his arms around her waist. She leaned into him. "Most of the houses in the cove are second homes," he said, "and not used in the winter, so we'll have the beach pretty much to ourselves."

"How did you find this place?"

"Remember the piece I did on the evolution of Irish Setters for *Smithsonian* a while back?"

"My mom bought a copy for me. I haven't seen it yet—but I will."

"Doesn't matter. It was just a fun piece with nothing earth-shattering in it." He leaned forward and nestled his cheek against her hair. "I became friends with one of the Setter owners, Eric, a fiction writer who used to live here with his wife before they moved to Maryland. When he found out I was looking for a place for us to rent last summer, he and his wife, Julia, suggested we stay here. Then, when our plans fell apart, Eric said we should come whenever we had the time."

"He must be pretty famous to afford houses on two coasts."

"It's complicated, but yeah, Eric's books do okay."

"Eric . . . ?"

"Lawson."

"No wonder *Smithsonian* wanted him included in the piece. I see his books everywhere." She didn't say anything for several seconds, and then asked, "How long have you been here?"

"When I asked Julia about using the house in January, she invited us to come early. There's a long-standing tradition with the year-round people to celebrate New Year's together, and since it was Eric and Julia's turn to host the party, they thought, if we came early, it would give us a chance to meet the neighbors. You weren't available, so I came alone."

Lindsey was hit with a jealousy so ugly and so uncharacteristic that it took several seconds to understand what it was.

"Was it a good party?" She thought about how she'd celebrated—after an exhausting day spent meeting with editors, she'd propped herself up in bed in a less-than-wonderful hotel room in New York, going through her pictures of the "Lost Children in the Congo" while out of the corner of her eye she watched the ball fall in Times Square on a ten-year-old television. She'd considered calling Matthew, but wasn't sure where he was or what time zone he was in and figured they would celebrate in their own way as soon as they were together again. At the time she'd thought he would call her. Now she knew why he hadn't.

"As a matter of fact," Matthew said, "it was a great party. I'm glad I took them up on their offer."

"You should have told me. I might have bailed out of my meetings sooner."

As she'd known he would, Matthew instantly responded to the *might have.*

"I didn't want to put that kind of pressure on you," he said with barely constrained sarcasm.

She waited, looking for something safe to defuse the tension. "Have you ever thought about how few mutual friends we have?"

"We've never been drawn to the same kind of people, not even in college."

"Still, don't you think it's a little strange that you know people who would give you their house for a month and you never said one word to me about them?"

"No. I know a lot of people I've never talked to you about. Are you saying I know every one of your friends?"

"I don't have the luxury of having casual friends."

"And this is supposed to be my fault?"

Lindsey shook her head as if trying to clear her thoughts. "What are we doing?"

"How I got the house doesn't matter, but you should know they didn't *give* it to me originally. At least not when we were supposed to be here in July. Once we got to know each other, they said it felt odd to accept money from someone they considered a friend, and they gave me back the deposit I'd made for July. You'd like them, Lindsey. They're terrific people."

"Sometimes I feel like a rescued dog that no one wants to adopt."

"Maybe it's because you snarl every time someone tries to pet you."

"Ouch." She flinched at the truth buried in his retort. It wasn't as if she brought anything to the party worthy of an invitation. Lately she'd found it hard to like herself. How could she expect anyone else to respond to her edgy charm?

She had treated the people she most depended on, Matthew and her parents, with careless disregard for the past two years, expecting them to understand and forgive her moods and outbursts—if not now, then once they knew what she'd been going through.

She'd taken her parents for granted to the point of abuse. They'd subsisted on sporadic phone calls and rare visits. The last time they'd seen her was almost three years ago when Matthew took an assignment for *National Geographic Traveler* about pick-your-own apple farmers in upstate New York. He was less than an hour from their farm while Lindsey was in the city trying, unsuccessfully, to get a visa extension for

Belarus. As soon as she realized that nothing she could do would make the process go any faster, she agreed to join him while she waited. Her parents were thrilled, Matthew loved having her tag along, and after the first few days she actually started treating coffee like a beverage instead of a drug.

It wasn't until she was waiting for transport out of Peshawar, Pakistan, months later, that she experienced a flash of understanding about her seeming determination to drive away everyone who loved her. If she let them in, they would see the cracks in her mental stability, and they would want to do something to help. Someday she'd be ready to accept that help. But not yet. She wasn't ready to face those consequences.

Matthew released her, walked over to the fireplace, and grabbed a section of the newspaper to start a fire. As he crumpled the paper he glanced at the date. December 26. The day after Christmas. The day a decade earlier when his twin sister, Christine, had died half a world away in Thailand. She'd gone there with her partner to formally open the clinic they'd been working on for two years, one that would focus on children with operable birth defects.

Her Christmas present to him that year—an intricately carved jade elephant pendant—arrived a week after her body was identified. Her partner was never found, assumed to have been washed out to sea along with over 37,000 others who simply disappeared with the receding tsunami. The elephant became Matthew's personal talisman and his last physical connection to his sister.

His parents had dealt with their grief by selling everything they owned and moving to Thailand to help victims of the disaster rebuild their lives. Matthew arranged his schedule to visit them as often as possible, but there never seemed to be enough time to catch up.

Matthew turned to meet Lindsey's questioning gaze. "What's really strange is why you're asking me this now. You've never wanted to know about my friends or what I do when we're not together."

She shook her head and hugged herself. "Nothing," she said. And then, "*Everything.*"

"We need to talk," Matthew acknowledged with a deep sigh. "I was going to wait, but—"

She ignored him. "What happened to us?"

"What do you mean?"

"Why aren't we in the bedroom making love? It wasn't so long ago that we could barely make it out of the airport before we were tearing each other's clothes off. Hell, I remember making love to you *in* the airport. And more than one. What's changed?"

He stared at her long and hard, struggling for the right words, something that wouldn't sound as petty as it was. "Because I'm mad at you," he reluctantly admitted. "You were in New York an entire week, and you never called."

"You could have called me."

"And interrupt one of your high-powered meetings? Fat chance."

"I don't work at night."

"Since when?"

She didn't have an answer.

"You stayed in the Congo twice as long as you were supposed to, and I suspect it was a hell of a lot longer than you needed to. Why, I can only imagine."

He put a lit match to the paper and kindling and closed the screen, waiting for the flame to consume old news and start the strips of pitch-filled pine tucked under the oak. Within seconds, the popcorn sound of the fire coming to life filled the room. Even without any immediate actual heat, the orange glow made the room seem warmer.

"You never did explain what was so important that we had to cancel July," he said. "I'd turned down an assignment I'd fought months to get. The editor was so furious she swore I'd never work for their magazine again. Then you called a week before you were supposed to meet me and canceled like I was some last-minute lunch date you could just blow off without an explanation. For the past two years I've done everything I can to find a way for us to be together, and you've acted like you can't be bothered."

Instead of answering, or trying to defend herself, Lindsey shrugged in a gesture of defeat. "I can't fight with you about this. Not now."

He'd been gearing up for battle, and she'd pulled a white flag out of her pocket. This was a woman Matthew didn't know, and it sent a warning chill through him. Their ongoing argument forgotten, he asked, "Have you thought about seeing a doctor?"

She nodded.

"Well?"

"She said I was suffering from PTSD."

Not what he was expecting, but not surprising. "What kind of doctor did you see?"

She turned away to stare at the wall as if he would be able to see something in her face that she wasn't ready to share. "A psychiatrist."

She might as well have hit him. For Lindsey to even consider seeing a psychiatrist meant as much as the diagnosis. "When?"

"After I came home from Afghanistan the last time." She'd spent almost a month photographing military field hospitals, and for some reason the shield that normally protected her from the daily doses of heartache she photographed developed a tear. Things began to slip through—a wedding ring placed in a personal property bag held for a young man who no longer had hands, a shoulder on a skinny recruit from Mississippi with half of a heart-shaped tattoo missing, a twenty-year-old girl who'd lost most of her ear and half of her face absently wondering what she was going to do with all her extra earrings.

"That was why you didn't meet me in Italy?"

"I couldn't get a flight that would get me there in time. And then you got the assignment in Uzbekistan . . ."

"Why didn't you tell me?"

"I couldn't." She looked down at her hands and saw they were curled into fists, her close-cut nails digging into her palms. With effort, she straightened her fingers and stuffed her hands in her pockets. "Every time I tried, something got in the way. You were either on your way somewhere or I was."

There was more she wasn't telling, he could see it in her eyes and the way she held herself—as if she would come apart if she let down her guard for even an instant. He crossed the room and took her in his arms. "If I gave you the impression I don't want you, then we have a problem bigger than either of us imagined."

Without waiting for her to reply, he cupped her head in his hands and kissed her, trying to express in touch what he'd clumsily failed to do with words.

She dug her fingers into his thick brown hair to bring him closer still. Tears slipped from her closed lids and gave their kiss a salty taste. "I love you, Matthew," she whispered. "No matter what else you know, you have to know that."

He picked her up and cradled her against his chest, fighting a wave of fear at how little of her there was to hold. "You're the one constant in my life, Lindsey."

Chapter 3

Not trusting that the bedroom door would close without creaking, Lindsey left it open. She checked one last time to see that Matthew was still asleep before she picked up her jeans and backpack and went into the living room, torn between wishing he would wake up and go with her and looking forward to a morning without the pop of gunfire to put her on edge and only the fog for company.

Their lovemaking had gone long into the night, first with a seemingly insatiable need and then with an exquisite tenderness that left her not only sated but consumed by a feeling of hope.

Afterward, in the darkness, with the only light stealing past the curtained window from a shrouded full moon, she'd felt safe again. Safe enough to remember . . .

When Matthew *had texted that they would have to postpone meeting in Italy for two weeks because of snow leopard kittens his guide had discovered in Uzbekistan, Lindsey allowed David Ambrose, her editor, to talk her into going to the Congo to cover the waves of children crossing the country in a desperate attempt to reach the relative safety of a refugee camp.*

This time it wasn't just frantic boys trying to escape the marauders who would turn them into soldiers—it was terrified girls looking to escape what the United Nations had called "the Rape Center of the World." Word reaching the outside said that several refugee groups contained girls barely past infancy. It was the girls David wanted photographed. The more desperate and heart-wrenching the better.

For all of five minutes, she had tried to turn down the assignment, saying the stabilizer on her primary lens needed fixing and her camera had major electronic problems. David countered with an offer to overnight a new camera and lens. Finally, she pled exhaustion. David immediately jumped to the inducement he only brought out when he was desperate: how often in her lifetime would she be given the chance to make a real difference?

When even that didn't work, he finally settled on the single argument that Lindsey could never set aside, no matter how pressing her own personal needs were. The children were dying—now. If someone didn't find a way to draw the attention of a world already saturated with photographs of infants with distended bellies being held by mothers whose breasts were as dry as their tear ducts, then it would be impossible to save even one of them.

If not her, then who?

How many children would die because Lindsey needed time off?

How important could that time off be compared to the life of even one child?

In the end, she did what they'd both known she would do all along and agreed to photograph the children who flowed over the landscape like blood from a mortally wounded promise of peace.

She left for the Congo as soon as the new camera and lens arrived, hopping on a cargo plane carrying medical supplies for Doctors Without Borders. Instead of sleeping, she thought of images of the carnage from a civil war that had gone on for over half a century and ways to bring a fresh eye to the story.

Without something eye-catching, she would lose the nano-second attention span of a world that preferred newspapers and television newscasts that concentrated on the latest celebrity news—divorces, drunk driving, homicides, suicides. Those were the stories—the ones that took the rich and famous down a peg or two—that people talked about at work the next day. Stories you could walk away from and not feel a lingering, haunting sadness.

She needed a photograph that could eclipse a picture of Donald Trump's hair in a windstorm. Without it, the donations the aid workers needed to provide a life-sustaining cup of beans for a three-year-old would disappear.

The story couldn't wait while she waited around for Matthew to come back from Uzbekistan. What was her life, or even her sanity, compared to the opportunity to save an eight-year-old girl who was wandering the jungle, wondering not if she would be raped but when? Didn't every child deserve to know, if only once in his or her life, what it felt like to be safe?

She'd left a message for Matthew with his agent that she was postponing their trip to Italy and she would be in touch as soon as she had cell service.

They managed to connect by phone ten days later. She told Matthew she was going to be in the Congo even longer than she'd told his agent. He'd seemed okay with it at the time and said he would go to South Africa to cover the trial of a group of rhino poachers—it was a rare event that anyone had even been arrested. He was hoping for the perfect ending to a story he'd been working on for two years—a conviction.

Lindsey and the fixer David had arranged to accompany her in the Congo found and joined a group of thirty children, mostly girls between nine and thirteen. They'd been traveling without adults for more than a month. Some had been forced out of their homes by parents who could no longer feed them, some had been separated from their families during a militia attack, and some were the lone surviving members of what had once been extensive families. All journeyed with one goal in mind—to reach a refugee camp in Yida. They'd been told that they weren't wanted, but they knew they would be given a bowl of beans to eat and, at worst, a piece of cardboard to sleep on. It didn't matter that the hut that would shelter them was vermin infested, it was safe.

What none of the parents who'd set these young girls on their journey had understood was that they would become targets for bands of men who treated even the youngest like members of a transient brothel—put on the road solely for their entertainment.

Without an adult to guide them, the children chose their own leader, Sittina, a wisp of a girl as determined *to get them to the camp as a mother leopard with cubs to feed on the trail of a wounded wildebeest. With the innate ability of a child born in the bush, she taught them to turn into ghosts, scattering and fading into their surroundings at the sound of a distant vehicle or a single footfall on dry grass. This extreme caution kept them alive, but it also slowed their progress, and that eventually took its toll on the weakest and sickest as they went days and then nearly a week without food. The end was inevitable for some of them when, out of desperation, they turned to eating indigestible grasses.*

At night they huddled together in whatever shelter they could find, uselessly covering their heads with their arms at the whistling sounds of aerial bombs, taking turns standing guard with sticks they had fashioned into weapons to use against opportunistic lions looking for an easy meal.

There were some children—mostly the ones who carried infants and toddlers on their backs like cords of wood—who were the last of their families. Their stories were different yet had a familiarity that, after a while, made them all sound the same—families slaughtered for no other reason than the misfortune of having built their grass huts and raised their sheep and cattle herds on the wrong side of an imaginary dividing line between the least developed nations in Africa.

Although Lindsey was there as a photographer, not as a writer, she asked endless questions, mostly to try to make sense out of the insanity that had inspired the children's journey from one side of a war-torn country to the other.

Even after what had happened to her in Afghanistan, she believed that she was as removed from the possibility of becoming a part of the story herself as she was from the possibility of switching careers. This time, though, something changed. Sittina walked up to Lindsey, insisting that she was ten but looking no older than five or six because of acute malnutrition, and found a permanent home in Lindsey's heart.

Days later, when they crossed a dry gully and Sittina reached for Lindsey's hand to keep from falling, a folded piece of orange cloth held together with a single piece of knotted grass fell out of the tattered pocket of Sittina's dress. Lindsey retrieved the cloth from a crack in the parched dirt and turned to hand it back. She was startled to see Sittina's expressive black eyes widened with challenge.

Even after the week they'd been together, Sittina had automatically assumed Lindsey would keep the small treasure. Tears of gratitude slipped from her eyes as she tucked the bundle into her whole pocket and carefully buttoned it closed.

"It was my mother's," she said as they moved to rejoin the group. "The men could only find one earring after they killed her. They were so angry that they cut her into many pieces with their machetes. They were drinking and singing very loudly when they left our home. They were proud of what they had done to my mother. They danced and sang as if they had faced a pride of lions to capture that one small circle of gold."

The connection between the young woman soldier in Afghanistan who only needed half of her earrings and Sittina's mother haunted Lindsey for days. She stayed in the Congo less than two months—six weeks longer than the original assignment but shorter than the time she needed to tell the story. After five days in New York going over her work with the new photo editor who'd been assigned to the piece—a woman wearing a pencil dress and Christian Louboutin pumps trying to explain her indefensible rationale for pulling photographs that were too "difficult" for their readers—Lindsey felt as emotionally empty as a plastic bag caught on a barbed-wire fence.

She didn't call Matthew while she was in New York because she had nothing to offer him.

Listening for sounds coming from the bedroom that would indicate she hadn't sneaked out successfully,

Lindsey stood in front of the sliding-glass door and stared into the night, seeing nothing but an impenetrable gray-tinged blackness. Slipping into her jeans, she opened her backpack, which contained at least one of everything she needed when she traveled, including a toothbrush. The first thing she pulled out was the tightly woven wool sweater she'd picked up at the duty-free shop the last time she'd been in Dublin. She had to dig a little for the rain jacket to put over the sweater. There were good and bad things about clothing that disappeared into its own stuff bag—small might be convenient, but it could also mean hard to find.

She loved the idea of Ireland, but like most cities in peaceful parts of the world, she knew the airport, not the country. Years before she became part of the press corps that chased wars and bloodshed, the Good Friday Agreement had been ratified and Ireland had moved toward a shaky, but eventually triumphant, peace. There was no reason to send someone like her on assignment to a country where people died of natural causes.

One day she would go back and experience the serenity of the countryside and the boisterous pub evenings she had only imagined. She would lose herself in the culture and not duck for cover if a car backfired. These were the kinds of places she went in her mind to try to put herself to sleep at night while bullets and bombs exploded around her. She allowed herself to fantasize about such things even if she didn't believe in them.

With a stealthiness that belied the background of a girl who'd broken both of her arms once and one leg twice falling out of trees and down gullies and ski slopes, she slung her camera bag over her shoulder and headed for the beach, anxious to see what picture opportunities would appear when the sun finally penetrated the fog.

As she'd expected, she had the beach to herself. It was still a good half hour before even the hardiest fisherman would arrive. Time enough to explore once her eyes adjusted. She was looking for a stretch of undisturbed sand where she could leave relatively deep footprints that wouldn't immediately be washed away. Maybe a few unbroken shells for a focal point or just a ragged line of foam. It was a picture that had already been taken a thousand times, and that was the challenge. She wasn't going to get what she really wanted—a baby sea lion following the footprints, erasing them as he reclaimed what was rightfully his. But that was for another day. This was plainly not a beach where sea lions hauled out for a day in the sun.

Propping her backpack against a log resting well above the high-water line, she sat with her arm looped through the strap and her back firmly planted against the pack, a trick she'd learned after losing her first camera to a ten-year-old thief in Kabul when she'd stopped to rest by sitting against a tree and promptly fell asleep. Even though there was no chance of that happening now, old habits were . . . well, they were old habits.

Lindsey woke to the sound of laughter. Giggling, to be more precise. The sun was still nowhere to be seen, but it was light enough to detect the outlines of three people walking along the shoreline. One was a girl no more than four or five, judging by her size and the high-pitched squeal when she misjudged a wave and the water climbed her legs. As she came closer Lindsey saw that she was wearing pajama bottoms and a coat that hung lopsided from having been closed one button off.

"Not too close," the woman accompanying the girl warned.

The man laughed. "You might as well be talking to the sanderlings."

Lindsey shifted and sat up straighter. There was something decidedly strange about this threesome. She reached for her camera. Because there were times when her life and the lives of those around her depended on being as quiet as possible, she always had her camera set to silent mode. When she started shooting, she didn't get so much as a glance in her direction.

As always, she and the camera instantly merged, her world reduced to the image she saw through the lens, her focus laser-sharp, her peripheral vision gone.

The adults who accompanied the child were old, too old to be late-in-life parents. More likely grandparents, maybe even another generation out. They followed the girl's every movement, allowing her the freedom to explore, ready to intercede if needed.

With a palpable joy, the girl let out another squeal as she stopped to pick up something left behind by a foamy wave. She ran to her guardians with her arms outstretched, turning over her prize when she reached them. They said all the right words, too softly for Lindsey to make them out, but the child's delighted reaction was enough to fill in the blanks. She clapped her hands and spontaneously hugged them before skipping back across the packed sand to hunt for more treasure.

A distant voice, female and frantic, shattered Lindsey's focus. She had no sense of time when she was working. Her only clue was when she glanced at the camera to see how many shots she'd taken and was startled to see it was over five hundred.

With one part of her mind aware of the woman's voice, but seeing no reason to become involved when the resolution was only moments away, she went back to shooting, capturing the child's concerned look and being surprised to see the grandparents' relieved expressions. Again it struck her that there was something strange about the three of them.

This time the voice that shot through the fog was a man's, loud and insistent. "*Abbey*—where are you?"

The girl stopped exploring and looked behind her. Her chin dropped to her chest. "I'm here, Daddy," she said, barely loud enough for Lindsey to hear.

But plainly a father seeking his daughter's voice was tantamount to a soldier listening for an ambush.

"Abbey?"

"I'm by the water, Daddy. With my friends."

It wasn't Abbey's father who first materialized, but her mother. She ran to her little girl and scooped her into her arms. Seconds later, her father joined them. Abbey tried to talk as they pummeled her with questions, but every sentence she offered was crushed by one from her parents.

"What friends?" her mother insisted.

Abbey looked around, but her protectors had disappeared. Even Lindsey had missed seeing them leave.

"They have my presents," she moaned. "I found the pretty shells you told Daddy you wanted to take home, and they were keeping them for me." Dejected, Abbey walked over to the spot where her companions had last been.

"They're here," she shouted seconds later. "They left them for me on this pretty scarf." She ran back to her parents, the red-and-blue scarf fluttering behind her. She grabbed her father's hand. "If we hurry, we can find them."

Through it all, Lindsey continued taking pictures, unnoticed against the dark log, in her usual position of being a witness to life rather than a participant.

Abbey's father hoisted her to his shoulders. "That pretty scarf is your sister's," he said. "And unless your imaginary friends broke into our house—"

"They aren't imaginary," she insisted. "They talked to me and everything. They told me my shells were beautiful. They said I was beautiful too," she added softly.

They walked away and the tenor of her parents' voices changed from naked relief to stern reprimand. Abbey plainly listened to neither as she took advantage of her perch and intently swiveled her head back and forth, seeking the uncritical man and woman who had shared her magical morning.

Matthew rolled to his side, taking up even less space in the king-size bed than he had the night before.

He was accustomed to narrow cots and sleeping bags and had trouble adjusting to a bed big enough to hold a small family. He wasn't surprised to find Lindsey missing. She might fill his heart and his mind, but she'd never truly filled his life.

He ran his hand over her side of the bed, seeking warmth that would indicate how long she'd been gone. The sheet was as cold as the room. The five days he'd been there alone were days lost from the month they had planned to be together, but it had given him time to grocery-shop and unpack and wash his basic traveling clothes.

Surprisingly, his favorite purchase was one he almost didn't make—bathrobes. He bought two, one for each of them, imagining them sitting together drinking coffee on the deck or by the fire at night sipping hot buttered rum out of ceramic mugs.

He did this kind of thing a lot lately—imagining a life that had little reference to reality. For years he'd walked a narrow line down the center of reality and fantasy when it came to Lindsey. He accepted that he would never love anyone the way he loved her and that she would never change. She would fight the good fight with her camera until she was too old to shoulder her pack and climb a mountain. And then she would die.

Her crusade for justice was her lifeblood. Without it, she couldn't breathe. Her pacemaker was her conviction that no one else would tell the stories that needed to be told. She honestly believed there was a world of innocents who could not and would not survive without her ability to communicate their plight in ways that drew attention.

It wasn't ego so much as recognition that, to touch someone's heart, your own heart had to be breaking when you told the story. She insisted she knew how to protect herself from the pain, but Matthew knew better. When their separations were as long as the last one, the changes in her were dramatic and irrefutable.

The sound of the sliding-glass door softly opening roused Matthew. Lindsey was back. He climbed out of bed and into his new bathrobe, knowing if he didn't beat her to the kitchen he'd have to drink her coffee. That was a torture he'd rather not endure.

But instead of heading for the kitchen, Lindsey had gone for her computer. She looked up and smiled when she saw him. As he came closer she reached out with a hand rosy red from the cold. "Good morning."

He gave her a kiss. Her face was slick and salty with moisture, and her hair dripped water onto her sweater. He glanced at her backpack and rain jacket and shoes sitting on the throw rug by the door.

They were soaked too. "I'll make the coffee while you get into something dry."

She smiled. "Two for one. You get to nurture me and protect your coffee sensibilities at the same time."

He put his hand over his heart. "I'm wounded."

"And I'm freezing," she acknowledged.

"Take a shower and I'll build a fire. I bought you a present. It's hanging in the closet."

She put her laptop on the dining room table and shrugged out of her sweater, shivering when her bare flesh hit the cold air. "Let me guess—a robe."

"How did you know?"

"You're kidding, right? You've been trying to domesticate me for years now. How much more domestic can you get than matching bathrobes?"

"Not exactly matching—" He brought her into his arms and gave her a longer kiss, one he hoped would provide a different kind of warmth. Again, he was startled at how easily he could count her ribs.

She responded with an intensity that told him he'd stumbled into another of her emotional storms. They were as mysterious and unpredictable as a summer cloud that moved innocently across the sky until it dropped a fierce funnel to consume everything in its path.

Usually, Matthew just held on for the ride. This time he took her head between his hands and stared deeply into her eyes. "Talk to me," he insisted. Even as she'd opened her heart and told him about Sittina, he'd sensed there was more she was holding back.

"Make love to me," she answered.

"First tell me what's got you hanging on by your fingertips."

The playfulness left her eyes. "I can't."

"Can't or won't?"

"This is one of those times when it's the same thing." She pulled free and headed toward the bedroom, then turned back, hugging herself against the cold. "Why did you start this when what you really wanted was to interrogate me?"

Her fierce response told him more than her words. She was hiding something. "Cut the offense crap, Lindsey. Despite its reputation, it really isn't the best defense. Remember, I'm the one who knows how you operate."

"You don't know as much as you think you do."

"Oh? Then tell me where I went wrong."

"You think I'm—" Instantly, she was crying again. She wiped the offending tears with her fingers as if they were scalding her cheeks. "You look stupid in that bathrobe."

He stared at her. "No, I don't."

This time she sobbed. "I'm sorry."

"For what?"

"For everything."

"That covers a lot of territory." He went to her and lifted her arms to put them around his neck. He'd seen her in pain, but nothing like this. A clamped jaw, yes. A seemingly unending well of tears, never. Even if it was impossible to go back to what they'd once had, he couldn't let this be the period at the end of their life story. "Are you talking sorry for the time you shipped my new camera to South Africa instead of South Dakota, or for the time you used ketchup instead of tomato sauce when you made spaghetti?"

The smile she gave him was achingly sad. "I thought you forgave me for the camera thing."

"I did. It's the spaghetti I'm still working on."

She buried her face in his neck. "I can't tell you. Not now. Maybe never."

"Okay," he said softly. "I'll let it go—until you're ready." He had to give her more. "But first you have to apologize for that crack about my new robe."

She wrapped her arms tighter around his neck. "I love you," she whispered. "You are my everything."

He had it on the tip of his tongue to say something about corny song titles when it struck him that there was nothing corny about what she'd said.

Chapter 4

Matthew listened for the water to stop in the shower before he fixed their coffee. He was in the middle of adding the repulsive hazelnut flavoring Lindsey had adopted after talking him out of his cream and sugar when he caught a flash of movement out of the corner of his eye. He turned to see her standing with her arms outstretched.

"Pink?" she questioned. "As long as you've known me, have you ever seen me wear anything pink? And who did you think you were buying this for? A Macy's Christmas balloon?"

"Okay, so it's a little big."

"And the color?"

"It's you, babe. As a matter of fact, now that I've actually seen it on you, I think you should consider switching everything over, including your flak jacket."

"What were you thinking?"

"That I only had twenty dollars in my wallet and this was the one on sale?"

"I don't believe you. You did this on purpose. You've always secretly wanted a woman who would snuggle up to you in pink chenille after you brought home the bacon."

"Not true—at least not since I became a vegetarian."

The playful look disappeared. "You *what?* When did that happen?"

"The last time I was offered snake stewed with fish heads. I'd been leaning that way for a long time, and I finally reached the point where I decided it would be a lot easier to just commit. This way I can stop making excuses for filling up on beans and rice when I'm offered giraffe."

"What about when you're home?"

"I thought about doing that, but then—" He shrugged. "I feel better not thinking about it. It's easier all the way around."

"I'm not in the same place on this, Matthew. I don't know if I ever will be."

"I'm not asking."

"I know. It's just that I don't want to feel guilty chomping down on a hamburger while you're munching on sprouts."

He laughed. "I hate sprouts."

"You haven't stopped drinking coffee, have you? Please promise me that's not going to happen. Or at least promise me that if you do, you won't stop making it for me." She reached for the cup he offered and took a sip. "I'm in heaven."

"Coffee's still on the list. As long as it's fair trade."

She rolled her eyes. "It's only been nine months since we saw each other. Why no mention of any of this vegetarian stuff in your texts or emails?"

He could have pointed out that he'd been moving in this direction a lot longer than nine months, but she'd been too consumed in the world she occupied when they were apart to pay attention to something as mundane as his eating habits. Catching up on things they no longer shared was a conversation for another time. Instead, he nodded toward her camera and asked, "Did you get anything this morning?"

"I hope so."

"Want to show me?"

"Yeah—as a matter of fact, I'd like your opinion on something."

Although he knew dozens of photographers, Lindsey was the only person he went to for criticism. It was the same with her. They both dealt with editors who judged their work in the context of the story they were working on, and luckily, they'd both had several who were the best in the field. But Matthew had never gone to any of them with his personal work, and Lindsey had never shared the pictures she took for herself with anyone but Matthew.

She rolled up the too-long sleeves on her bathrobe and pulled the belt tighter around her waist before she opened her laptop and turned it on. With the memory card in the card reader, she sat on the sofa, angling to give Matthew room to sit beside her. In the time it took to download the pictures, he added another log to the fire.

She put her hand possessively on his thigh when he sat down. He liked it when she showed this kind of natural and easy communication, and he hungered for it more often than he had in their early years, when being apart was an exciting novelty. This easy intimacy was the way his parents interacted. They saw each other every day, but it seemed they were as excited when they were together as he and Lindsey were when they saw each other after months apart.

Lindsey clicked on the first picture, the one that out of habit she always took to check exposure and settings and to be sure the camera was operating the way it should. She moved to the second picture, stared at it for several seconds, and then wordlessly turned the screen toward Matthew.

What he saw was a mist-shrouded child, no more than four, her arms flung wide, her face glowing with unmitigated delight. "She's beautiful," he said, struggling for a better word. "What was she doing out there?"

"Gathering seashells to surprise her parents."

"Where were they?"

"I'm assuming they were still asleep."

"She was there alone?"

"Her grandparents were with her." Lindsey turned the laptop back to search the picture more closely. She frowned and clicked on the next picture. And then the next. "They were right here," she said. "They were right beside her the whole time." She enlarged the picture and looked for aberrant pixels. "She talked to them. She gave her grandmother the shells to hold."

Matthew took the laptop and made some adjustments to bring out details hidden by the fog. "There's nothing here, Lindsey. Not even a shadow."

She ran her hands through her wet hair. "I saw them, Matthew. I can describe them down to the kind of shoes they were wearing."

He went through the remaining pictures, carefully searching the hundreds of images. What he saw was a child filled with the pure, raw joy that comes with the innocence of not knowing how bad the world can be and believing love doesn't have to be earned, it just is. "Is this them?"

Lindsey glanced at the screen. She shook her head. "That's her parents."

"Did they talk to the old couple?"

She considered his question. "No . . . they were gone by the time Abbey told her parents about them." She started to get up. Matthew tugged on her sleeve and brought her back down.

"Look at this." He scrolled through the images until he found the one he was looking for, then pointed to the girl. "She's definitely talking to someone."

Lindsey stared at the screen and then scrolled further back. "Here," she pointed. She skipped to another picture. "And here. She's plainly listening, Matthew. And she's laughing in this one."

"Maybe she's one of those kids who have imaginary friends."

"And where does that leave me? Remember, I saw them too." She enlarged another picture and studied it. "Look at this one—her hand's outstretched. She's giving something to someone." She enlarged the picture further. "It's a shell."

Lindsey flipped back and forth between the picture of Abbey holding her hand out and the ones that came before and after. She'd been shooting on burst, and yet she hadn't captured the actual handoff. In one frame Abbey was holding something, in the next she wasn't. Lindsey enlarged the picture even further, looking to see if the shell was sitting on the sand. It wasn't—at least not that she could see. Lindsey turned to look at Matthew. "What's going on?"

"Beats the hell out of me."

"Mutual hallucinations?"

"More likely ghosts," he said jokingly.

"I don't believe in ghosts," she said, staring at the screen.

"You have a better explanation?"

Before she could answer, her cell phone rang. She handed Matthew the laptop and headed for the kitchen, where she'd plugged in her phone the night before. She hadn't even tried to hide what she was doing. Matthew had known there was no way the gesture of handing over her phone at the airport was anything but a way to say how sorry she was for all that had gone before. "It's me," she said in lieu of hello.

"No, I haven't been watching CNN, David. We don't have a television here. Just tell me what's going on."

Matthew closed the laptop and put it aside. Calls from David were never good news.

"Shit." The word was more an expression of pain than profanity. "When?"

The silences were followed by rapid-fire questions until finally there was a silence longer than the others. "I can't," she said, her voice dropping low. "I mean it, David—I can't." This was followed by, "All right, then, I won't. You're going to have to find someone else this time."

Matthew opened a cupboard door on the wall opposite the fireplace, touched a button, and stood back while a large-screen television came forward and angled itself toward a pair of recliners. He hadn't been hiding the fact that there was a television at the beach house, he just hadn't gotten around to telling Lindsey.

He glanced at the cable lineup and tuned in to CNN. Familiar faces filled the screen behind the reporter, one was a writer Lindsey had worked with in Afghanistan and another was a photographer she'd shadowed when she had her first assignment in Iraq. The third face that scrolled across the screen was a young Arab journalist Matthew didn't recognize, and the fourth hit him with the force of a physical blow. Ekaterina Bradford was the wife of Matthew's best friend, Zach. She was an award-winning photographer who specialized in human-interest stories, not battlegrounds. What in the hell was she doing in Syria? He turned up the sound.

"—missing almost forty-eight hours. Their bodies were found in a dump site near Damascus just days after Syrian forces again proclaimed they would kill any journalist who set foot on their soil. Early reports say it appears Bradford had been tortured and sexually assaulted. We're waiting for confirmation of—"

"Turn it off," Lindsey said, covering her ears with her hands. When he didn't move fast enough, she raced for the remote control and frantically searched for the off button. Looking up and seeing the depth of his concern, she tried to cover her reaction with a shrug and a weak explanation. "They're past any real news. All we're going to get now is salacious retellings."

He took the control from her and hit the off button. "Are you all right?"

Even as she answered him, she backed herself into a corner and collapsed into a fetal position, burying her face against her knees and covering her ears again, as if the television were still playing.

Matthew was too stunned to move at first and then, slowly, not wanting to scare her, he lowered himself to his hands and knees and approached. How could he have missed what was happening to her? Shouldn't he have recognized the PTSD symptoms, even over the phone? "What do you want me to do?" he said softly. And then, "Do you have meds?"

"I threw them away."

He put his head back in frustration and stared at the ceiling. "Why?" he asked, already knowing the answer.

She was trembling noticeably now. "They made me groggy."

Not knowing what he should do, he did the only thing he could and brought her into his arms. She was shaking so badly now that, at first, it was hard to hold her.

"I'm sorry," she sobbed.

"Say something smarter," he insisted.

Surprising them both, she laughed. "You're sorry?" she said.

It broke his heart to hear the desperation in her voice. She didn't want to be in the dark place that held her. He would give everything he had to help her, but he didn't know how. So he simply rocked her and whispered words of love and softly sang her favorite songs. Eventually Lindsey stopped shaking.

She sat up and looked at him, working hard to gift him with a smile of appreciation. "I'm okay now."

He kissed her tearstained cheeks. "Hungry?"

She nodded.

"Can we talk about this?"

"Later?"

He nodded. "I'll fix us something to eat, and then I really need to call Zach."

"You won't reach him." She unfolded her limbs like a flower reluctant to face the sun. "He left for Beirut this morning."

"They know for sure it's her?" he asked, his throat tightening as he fought to hold back his own tears. "There's no doubt?"

"None," she answered so softly he had to strain to hear her.

"Were they able to get them out?"

"Someone in the rebel forces arranged transportation to Beirut." She ran her hands through her hair and then over her face. "David said their bodies are on the way there now. The Syrian army is celebrating this as a great achievement, doing everything they can to get as much attention as possible. They actually think it will keep journalists out of the country, at least female journalists. No one believes we have the stomach for this kind of thing, especially for seeing our women raped and tortured."

Matthew knew without question where this was headed. "David wants you to go."

"Of course."

"Seems to me you've earned a pass on this one. Their story is going to be told a hundred times before you step on a plane. By the time you get there, they'll be little more than a footnote on a page listing all the journalists and photojournalists who've been killed covering the Middle East." He reached for her.

"It's my job. I don't have the luxury of going to work only when I feel like it." What was she saying? She'd already told David she wouldn't go. What screwed-up part of her mind couldn't accept that?

Instantly, he was angry beyond reason. "That's bullshit. When have you ever turned down an assignment? You're going to have to come up with something better if you want me to believe you." He stood and paced, trying to control the stupid urge to put his fist through a wall or to throw something. "Are you sure the real reason isn't because no one would draw the same attention as a Pulitzer Prize–winning female photographer martyred for the cause? Is that what you're after? Go down in a blaze of glory?" He started to walk away, then turned and came back. "Have you considered that when they find your mutilated body, there won't be anyone left to cover the story the way you think it should be covered?"

She answered him with an achingly sad smile. "Is that the best you can do?"

He flung his arms wide. "I give up."

This was why on particularly lonely nights he was tempted to walk away, why it didn't matter how much he loved her or admired her or knew his life wouldn't be the same without her. "Do what you want—I'm out of here."

"I told him I wouldn't go," she said defensively.

He gave her a withering stare. "But did you tell him in a way he would believe?"

Chapter 5

Lindsey picked up her phone to see who was calling. It hadn't stopped ringing since Matthew left. As she'd expected, it was David again, the third time in the past ten minutes. He wanted a chance to talk her into changing her mind.

Losing friends and colleagues in battle wasn't something she would ever get used to, but since losing Asa it had gotten even harder, more personal. Why else would she have had that embarrassing meltdown in front of Matthew?

She understood Matthew's reaction. He was scared, and he was tired of being scared, especially after what she'd just put him through. The episodes were something she'd been dealing with for a couple of years. Until today, she'd always managed to control them until she was alone.

In the field, she never had complete control over her environment, but she managed to maintain the illusion that she had options. Matthew had nothing but an occasional dispatch from wherever she was, assuring him that she was all right and that the IED or suicide bomber or riot she'd been assigned to cover had taken place miles away or before she arrived. They were mutually agreed-upon lies that protected them from the truth. For a man with Matthew's imagination, waiting to hear from her was its own kind of hell.

It didn't matter if he himself was in an isolated part of Botswana doing a piece on wild dogs or in the Amazon Basin tracking jaguars through hostile Shaur headshrinker territory, he worried about her. He tried to deny it, insisting that he understood her need to follow her own path and that he was okay with it. It was another all-consuming lie that had sustained their relationship for ten years.

The phone rang again. She didn't have to look. It was David. He didn't know how to back off or give up any more than she did. She bristled when someone called them adrenaline junkies, reducing their passion to tell the truth to the level of a video game.

This time she answered.

"You think this story is going to wait while you futz around with Matthew?" he said by way of greeting.

"Too far, David."

He ignored her warning. "Matthew's a nice guy, Lindsey, but what he does is cotton candy compared—"

"Stop right there, David. I've let you get away with talking about Matthew's work that way in the past because you have the sensitivity of a slug and have never been in a relationship without a price tag. But no more. If you want me to keep taking assignments from you, then things are going to have to change, starting with accepting the fact I'm not taking this one."

"When this gets out—"

It was everything she could do not to scream at him. Only the knowledge that losing her temper had never worked in the past kept her voice at a relative calm. "Just who did you have in mind to tell, David?"

"These people were your colleagues. They deserve to have their story told by the best. And that's you."

From manipulation to bullying, then back to manipulation. She hung up on him.

She tossed her phone on the recliner and headed for the kitchen to pour herself another cup of coffee. Her mother had always claimed that whatever inheritable domestic gene existed in their family had skipped Lindsey and doubled down on Rachel. Her sister made her own curtains, whipped out a five-course meal as if it were hot dogs on the barbecue, and made a room she'd decorated from Target close-outs look like something out of *Architectural Digest.* She did all of this while mothering three intelligent and well-adjusted kids.

Knowing this about herself was both a blessing and a curse. When some latent urge to do something domestic bubbled to the surface, it always took Lindsey by surprise, then left her confused and at loose ends.

Like now. Why was she looking at the kitchen with this stupid urge to bake something? Why was she noticing the uncluttered granite countertops and the polished wood cupboards? Most of all, why did she wish this was her kitchen in her home when she'd fought Matthew for years over owning their own place?

Foolish questions when she already knew the answers.

She knew the exact moment when this latest longing to set down roots had hit her—when she'd had to leave Sittina at the refugee camp.

She had a thousand pictures of Sittina, only a few of which she'd had to go through as potential shots for the syndicated story. Her contract gave her control of her photographs once the agency chose the ones it wanted to use. She knew there were potential award-winners in the mix, but she couldn't bring herself to look at them. Not now. Not when the mental image of Sittina watching as Lindsey left the camp remained burned into her consciousness.

There hadn't been anything accusatory or condemning in the look Sittina gave her. There wasn't even a silent plea. It was the acceptance on the girl's face that broke Lindsey's heart. Sittina might have had the bad luck to be born in a country that had been at war with itself since assuming self-governance over fifty years ago, but that didn't mean she was automatically denied hopes or dreams or ambitions. It was fundamentally wrong that she should accept being abandoned again, as if it were a warped kind of birthright and as natural as seeing her family slaughtered.

Before she left, Lindsey had made arrangements with a friend who worked for Save the Children to do what she could to find Sittina's grandmother, even though she knew that finding the grandmother was as likely as finding a beloved family heirloom floating in the Japanese tsunami debris field headed toward North America.

A tear dropped from Lindsey's chin to her chest. She grabbed the kitchen towel and wiped her cheeks. How could she not know when she was crying?

She poured her coffee, added creamer, and went to her computer, opening it and waiting for the familiar humming sound and the flash of color. A picture of Matthew blowing her a kiss came up first. He'd made it her wallpaper a couple of years ago after a trip to Holland, surprising her when she opened her computer on the plane. Corny, but effective. She'd taken a lot of teasing about it from people she knew would trade places with her in a heartbeat. In her circle of photographer and reporter friends, a long-lasting relationship was about as easy to come by as a double-indemnity accidental-death insurance policy.

She opened her Photoshop program and clicked on the picture of Abbey twirling in foam left behind from a wave, her arms clutching her sides, her head thrown back, and her mouth open wide in a smile. Lindsey tried to reconcile the images of two little girls half a world apart—one absolutely convinced she was the pearl in the oyster, the other knowing without question she was the gritty grain of sand.

Lindsey abandoned the computer and went outside to sit on the back deck, ignoring both the wet chair and the fog that eventually left her as wet as if she'd gone swimming.

Matthew wasn't surprised when he returned and found Lindsey missing. He'd originally gone outside to walk off his anger. Almost before he knew it was happening, the walk became a run. He ran blindly, trying to escape what waited for him back at the house. He'd always believed he knew what drove Lindsey, why she felt compelled to tell the stories no one wanted to see. Her passion and compassion were what had attracted him to her in the beginning.

With the insulation of youth, he hadn't understood that every battle Lindsey would fight would claim a part of her soul. Slowly, over their years together, he'd watched the laughter disappear as profoundly as the playful light in her eyes. She was dying in infinitesimal pieces, and he didn't know how to save her.

What he'd come back from the run knowing was that, despite the need to protect himself, he couldn't just walk away. He would do what he could, when he could. And he would love her as he'd always loved her, even if, in the end, they wound up taking separate paths. Until then, he would take his cues from her, letting her decide whether being bound to him was a benefit or a curse.

He took a shower and dressed, then headed for the kitchen to start lunch. Almost by accident, he spotted Lindsey on the back deck.

For several seconds, he considered not disturbing her. Plainly, she was still in the middle of working things out. Then he remembered how cold he'd been when he was running, even uphill. She was too mentally and physically fragile to do something this stupid.

He stepped outside and planted himself on the foot of the lounge chair. "Don't you think—" When she looked up, he saw the red circles around her eyes and the rest of what he'd had to say stuck in his throat.

"Goddamn it, Lindsey. When are you going to tell me what's really going on with you?"

She came forward and put her arms around his neck. "I can't do this anymore," she sobbed.

Her robe instantly soaked his shirt. "Me either," he said, both relieved and defeated. "Seeing you like this is killing me. Maybe if you stop trying so hard to make *us* work, you'll find a little peace alone. Maybe even a little happiness."

She stiffened and pushed him away. "Are you saying what I think you are? You want out?" Her face became a mask of agony. "When did you decide this? Is it because of the Syria thing?"

Shit. He'd completely misjudged her meaning. "Come inside." She slapped his hand away when he reached for her.

"Why?"

"So we can talk."

"What do you call this?"

"Freezing our asses off." He stood and pulled her up beside him. She didn't come willingly, but she didn't fight either.

They went into the living room, where Matthew took off her robe. "I guess this should have been a clue," she said, moving to the fireplace. Her teeth chattered a ragged Morse code. "Do you think it was some subliminal kind of thing—a way for me to keep warm when you weren't around anymore?"

He actually laughed. "That has to be one of the dumbest things you've ever said."

Her shoulders sagged. "Yeah, I'm not at my best right now."

He grabbed a blanket off the back of the sofa and wrapped it around her. "So what is it that you can't do anymore?"

"Why do you want to leave me?" She was good at using anger to cover hurt, but there were wide cracks in her defenses this time. "What did I do?"

He held her closer. "You didn't do anything. You've stayed true to who you are. It's me. I'm the one who's changed."

"Why?" She stopped trying to hold herself rigid and melted against him, pressing her face into his chest. "How?"

"I don't know," he answered honestly. "I didn't recognize what was happening for a long time, and then I woke up one morning missing you so badly it felt like my heart was in a vise. I don't want to live like that anymore. It hurts too much."

"And you think leaving will make you miss me less?"

All the resolve and direction he'd gained on his run disappeared like Halloween candy in a dorm room.

"I've been using hope like a drug where you're concerned. If I get off that drug, maybe I'll be able to get on with the rest of my life."

Looking up at him, she said, "Don't you know I am who I am because of you? You're the only home I know. Without you, I'm like those kids in the Congo—looking for something I'll never find because it isn't there anymore."

"It isn't here now," he said as gently as he could. "Think about your life, Lindsey. What you are and who you allow into your circle are of your own choosing. You have a wonderful family, and you treat them as if they were objects you could shelve and pull out when it's convenient. I've never understood why you treat them the way you do."

"I'm their big disappointment, their one failure in life." She pulled the blanket closer. "I don't fit their mold, and I never have. From the time I was a little girl, my father would tell his friends he was sure they'd made a mistake at the hospital and that I really belonged to someone else. He'd laugh and say things like, 'Can you imagine how those people feel, raising the sweet, compliant, ruffle-wearing daughter they wound up with?' You can only hear things like that so many times before you stop thinking where you grew up is home."

Lindsey's cell rang before Matthew could reply. She crossed the room to retrieve her phone from the recliner, the blanket trailing behind her as if she were Linus walking away from a bruising confrontation with Lucy. Skipping the amenities, she said, "Find someone else, David. I'm not going. And don't call me again until I tell you it's okay. I'm going to take some time off."

She dropped the phone back into the chair and looked at Matthew. "I'm assuming you were telling the truth when you said you still love me?"

"I'd stop if I could, but I don't know how."

She gave him a sad smile. "As it turns out, I may know a way to take care of that for you."

Chapter 6

Matthew added a log to the fire, laying it on the bed of glowing embers, where it immediately caught fire. He considered making coffee or tea or anything to delay whatever it was Lindsey wanted to tell him. Instead, needing contact to soften the blow for both of them, he brought her down to sit next to him on the sofa and allowed her space to burrow into his side. She chose to keep her distance, sitting forward instead, her hands covering her face.

"You've suspected something was going on for a long time, haven't you?" she asked.

His mouth went dry, and his throat tightened in an unfamiliar fear. "I'd rather not play that game, Lindsey. Why don't you just get it over with and lay it out for me."

She took a deep breath, then sat back and stared at the flames, the fire taking and giving at the same time. "When I told you I couldn't meet you in Italy last year, or in Cyprus, and then in Turkey, because I had assignments, I was lying. It's why you could never reach me at where I said I would be."

She spoke as if she were reading lines from a speech she'd given a hundred times, betraying none of the guilt that had controlled her life for two agonizing years.

Matthew was too stunned for words. Trust was the fuel of their relationship. Without it, everything stopped working.

She glanced at him and winced at the look in his eyes. "Say something," she pleaded.

"If you weren't where you told me you were going, where were you?"

"Virginia."

"Here? In the States?" The idea that she had found someone else and had gone there to be with him was so far out of the realm of possibility that it couldn't even gain a toehold in his mind.

"I told you that I had seen a doctor. What I didn't tell you was that the doctor was connected to a hospital."

"And you felt you couldn't share this with me because . . . ?"

"You would have tried to rush to my rescue like the knight in shining armor that you are. And you would have tried to talk me into quitting. I wasn't ready then. I was convinced I could work through it with a little help. You probably never saw it, but I even talked David into doing a piece on PTSD in returning vets so I could get inside the military hospitals where they were treating it."

Matthew got up and started to walk away, but immediately came back. "You're right. If I'd known, I would have dropped everything to go wherever you were. You would have told me you weren't ready to quit, and we would have fought about it, and in the end you would have won, like you always do. What was different this time? Why did you leave me on the outside?"

More importantly, what was different now? *Why had she actually shown up at the beach house instead of making up another excuse? She sure as hell wasn't cured.*

Lindsey used the corner of the blanket to wipe tears from her cheeks. Speaking through hiccuped sobs, she said, "I thought it would be so obvious. This time I *want* you to win. I can't go on this way. I discovered I have a breaking point, and this is it."

She held her hands out in a pleading gesture. "But I don't know how to stop. I can't let go, Matthew. I've tried.

And it always comes back to the fact that what I do can make a difference. How can I turn my back and walk away from all the Sittinas of the world? Who is going to tell the stories of the soldiers who go through three tours of combat and then come home and put a gun in their mouth?"

He sat next to her and pulled her into his arms. Snapshot memories of his disappointment when she'd canceled seeing him at the last minute merged with imagined images of her in a hospital room huddled in a corner, desperate to find a way out of the dark world she now inhabited.

"What finally pushed you over the edge?"

"I was flying back to base camp in a helicopter with a kid who was barely old enough to vote. A couple of medics worked on him as if he actually stood a chance and then just stopped and turned to help another medic working on a girl who'd lost her leg. I couldn't stop staring at the tattoo on the dead kid's arm—FOREVER. Eighteen years is a long way from forever. He had so much life ahead of him. And it's not as if he died in isolation. The dreams of all of the people who loved him died with him. His parents might learn to cope with his loss, but they will never recover. They will spend the rest of their lives looking into the eyes of babies, and before they go to sleep at night, they will wonder and imagine, and their hearts will break all over again.

"One of the medics told me later that by the time we landed I was unresponsive and they had to carry me into the hospital. It was my first big breakdown."

Her doctor in Virginia had taken her back to that day a dozen times, practicing cognitive behavior therapy and then eye movement desensitization while prescribing a variety of antidepressant medications. Hating the way the antidepressants made her feel, she stopped taking them.

"I'm not going to pretend I know what to say or what to do to help you," Matthew said. "You're going to have to help me help you."

"Make love to me."

"Is that really what you want?"

"More than anything. Right now all I want is to be lost in a world where you take care of me in every way possible. I'm so tired of being brave and strong."

He cupped the sides of her face with his hands. "I am your new forever, Lindsey."

"I'm sorry I didn't tell you before. We'll live a lifetime of regret if we don't try to work this out. We have a month, and if that's not enough, I'll do whatever it takes to get us more time."

"Define 'whatever it takes.' "

"I understand why you don't believe me, but I know how to say no. And I will. My photography might be my passion, but you're my life. I can't do what I do without knowing I have you to come home to."

"You're the most independent person I know. You only think you need me." Matthew tucked the blanket closer around her. "It's hard at first, but you find ways to survive."

"You learned the wrong lesson when you lost Christine. You think you survived, but you've always refused to recognize that a part of you died with her. You have a hollow place in your heart. You guard it like it contains something precious, when all it holds is loneliness and fear."

They weren't her words. Lindsey didn't talk or think that way. If she weren't sitting so close, keeping him from escaping, he would be gone. "Sounds like you and the psychiatrist talked about more than your PTSD," he said, his anger tangible. "You had no right to—"

"What? Tell her about my life? About yours? We're a couple. There's nothing either of us can do or say that doesn't affect the other."

"You should have said something to me."

"I am."

"A long time after the fact."

"What are you afraid of?" she almost shouted.

"Nothing."

"Liar."

He tried to move her. She refused to go. "You had no right."

"Yes, I did," she said softly. "You want to know what pushed me over the edge the second time, Matthew? It's so simple it's almost laughable. It was in Pakistan when I believed I was going to die and that I would never see you again." She pressed her cheek against his arm. "That was when I decided I had to find a way out of my dark place. I thought all it would take was a month in the hospital to get my miracle cure. You can see I misjudged it by quite a bit."

Long moments passed with only the distant sound of the waves and the crackling fire to break the silence.

Finally, standing, he held out his hand. "Come with me."

"Where?"

"For a walk."

She couldn't hide her disappointment.

"For a very short walk," he added, his voice husky with wanting her.

"What should we do today?" Lindsey asked, bringing the down comforter up to her chin. They'd let the fire go out the night before and forgotten to turn on the heater. It was cold in the bedroom even with her head resting on Matthew's shoulder and her bare leg lying possessively across his. Her hand on his chest, she absently outlined the edges of the jade pendent his sister had given him.

He propped a second pillow behind his head and gave her a satisfied grin. "More of the same?"

"Sounds perfect. Then what should we do tomorrow?"

"What would you like to do?"

"Something normal people do when they come here. I want to see if I can remember what it's like to be a tourist. You know, one of those people who take pictures to show off to friends and family when they get home. I was trying to figure out how long it's been since I sent my parents a picture of us and thinking about how excited my mother would be to hear from me."

"We could head down the coast to Big Sur. Maybe stop in Pacific Grove to see how many monarchs are still wintering over. Tonight we can go for pizza. Julia told me we can't leave without going to Pizza My Heart at least once."

"Can you handle a half meat and half veggie? Or are you one of those vegetarians who—"

"Careful," he warned. "You're about to stumble into fighting territory."

She laughed. “I figure if you’re still eating cheese you can’t be a complete fanatic.”

“She also told me about Gayle’s Bakery. Supposedly it’s right up there with the pizza.”

Lindsey propped herself up on her elbow and looked down at him. “Pizza and a bakery in the same day? You’re going to make it your mission to fatten me up, aren’t you?”

“I’ll make you a deal—I’ll match you pound for pound.”

“And that’s supposed to impress me? You can drop twenty pounds in a month by running an extra half mile and cutting ice out of your diet.” She kissed him. “Tell me you love me.”

“I love you.” He returned her kiss. “We are so connected I honestly don’t know where I end and you begin. If I ever commit a crime, they’ll send my DNA out for testing and it will come back that I’m the guy who loves Lindsey Thompson.”

“That’s pretty impressive.”

“It should be. I’ve been working on it for hours.”

Suddenly serious, she said, “I’m scared.”

“Me too,” he admitted.

“But not for the same reason I’ll bet. We were so cocky ten years ago when we told my parents that we were different, that our love was so special we would succeed with our long-distance relationship even though everyone else who tries ends up failing. And now look at us. Turns out we're no different than any other egocentric couple."

How could he argue with her? They'd given themselves four weeks to figure out how to make something work that they both knew had no real solution. Take away all the fancy words and proclamations of love and what they were left with was nothing more than two people looking for a painless way to say good-bye.

Chapter 7

Lindsey put on a pair of jeans and Matthew's old sweatshirt that had a picture of a pair of elephants with locked trunks. The caption read: WAS IT AS GOOD FOR YOU AS IT WAS FOR ME? He thought it was hysterical. She thought it belonged on a frat house wall.

Even though she knew Matthew wouldn't be back from his run for at least an hour, she glanced out the front window anyway. It seemed impossible, but the fog was even thicker than it had been the previous morning. Too dense for anything but close-up shots, maybe some macros of the foam or the moss on the log she'd been leaning against when she saw Abbey.

There was no sign of Matthew, just as she knew there wouldn't be. Running was as much escape for him as exercise. Despite his seemingly easy acceptance, he needed time to absorb what she'd told him the night before. Intellectually, he might understand how she'd reacted, but he was creative and imaginative, and there was nothing he could do to keep images of what she'd gone through from insinuating themselves into his thoughts.

Enough. She would not go there this morning.

She'd spent two years agonizing over whether or not to tell him about her duel with sanity. Now she had, and there was no going back. He would either accept the lies she'd told him about not being able to meet him, and the reasons for those lies, or he'd add the lies to the list of reasons they were better off separating.

She grabbed her camera bag and Matthew's tripod and headed outside, where she stopped to inhale the cold, salty air, taking it deep into her lungs. She could live here, she suddenly realized, feeling a kind of deep bond with what was wild and free that she hadn't felt since standing on top of Mount Kilimanjaro with Matthew, watching the sunrise, and sharing a hotel-room-size bottle of really bad wine. Slowly, she moved toward the sound of crashing waves, trying to remember where the stairs were. She found them, then almost stumbled over a girl sitting on the top step, tucked tightly into the folds of an oversize gray hoodie and sweatpants, her back pressed to the railing.

"My fault." The girl popped up and moved out of the way. "I didn't hear you coming."

"Don't worry about it," Lindsey said, moving to step around her.

"Hey, wait—are you the photographer?"

Lindsey studied her, noting the lack of makeup and generous spray of freckles. She had a feeling that somewhere under that wool cap and hood was a shock of deep auburn hair and the stubborn personality to go with it. "I'm *a* photographer. I don't know about being *the* photographer. Are you looking for anyone in particular?"

"Lindsey Thompson?"

She didn't like it when someone she'd never met knew her name. "That's me," she said reluctantly.

The girl brushed the sand off her sweatpants. "I'm not a stalker or anything. Grace told me about you."

"Grace?"

She turned and pointed toward the house behind her. "My sister. She takes care of Julia and Eric's place when they have renters."

"Oh." Lindsey relaxed. She vaguely remembered Matthew telling her about the girl who lived next door. "I wasn't the one who made the arrangements so I—"

"I looked you up," the girl said. "You're really good, even if what you do isn't my thing. I did volunteer work at a free clinic when I was in high school, and I saw enough of the messed-up things people do to each other to last me a lifetime. I can't imagine taking pictures of it day after day."

"You learn to distance yourself."

"What about when someone's shooting at you, like those journalists who just died?"

Lindsey didn't want to go there with this girl, still she felt compelled to answer. "It's hard to explain, but you become so focused on what you're doing that your world is reduced to the image you see through the viewfinder. You hear the bullets and bombs, but convince yourself they're not meant for you." Matthew understood this feeling of invincibility and knew there was nothing he could say or do to change it. The most dangerous thing she could do was to think too much about being cautious. And it wasn't as if he worked in a zoo.

"Sorry, still not my thing."

Lindsey laughed. She liked Rebecca's attitude, but especially appreciated her moxie.

"I looked up your husband too. His stuff blew me away. Not that yours didn't. It's just that—"

"It's not your thing."

"If I could take pictures of animals that were one-tenth as good as his, I'd be camping on the doorstep to *National Geographic*."

The husband part was a natural mistake, but the assumption usually came from someone older. "I'll let him know he has a fan."

"Do you think he'd talk to me? No one around here knows anything about what it's like to be a real photographer. My teachers keep telling me I need to be practical and learn how to shoot weddings and babies as a backup. Oh, and let's not forget 'architecture,' which is a euphemism for real estate brochures and websites. Can you imagine anything more boring?

"My freshman counselor even tried to get me interested in fashion by telling me I could meet celebrities. Who in their right mind would want to take a picture of Kim Kardashian when they could go to Canada for Spirit Bears or Sumatra for tigers?"

Obviously, the girl had done her homework. Both stories had been award-winners for Matthew, the Sumatra-tigers piece winning the Veolla Environment Wildlife Photographer of the Year Award. "Do you want me to ask him or would you rather do it yourself? He should be back from his run in an hour or so."

The girl hesitated and then smiled. "To be honest, I'd rather you did it. But what kind of photographer am I going to be if I can't be a little pushy when I need to be?"

A seagull walked past Lindsey, almost stepping on her foot. "I think I've just witnessed a new way to describe fog."

"It usually doesn't hang around too long, at least not this dense and not this time of year." She nodded toward the tripod. "If you wait, it should start clearing in a couple of hours."

"Which leads to lesson number one—sorry, I didn't get your name."

"Rebecca—actually Becky," she sheepishly admitted. "Rebecca just sounds a little more the way I like to think of myself now that I'm pushing twenty-one."

Lindsey raised an eyebrow.

"Okay, so I just turned nineteen a couple of weeks ago. It's the 'teen' part that drives me nuts."

"Doesn't matter what age you are. The photograph is all anyone cares about." The more Lindsey traveled, the more people she met, the more she'd come to believe the old cliché: age doesn't matter. A starving two-year-old looks at the world through ancient eyes, while the centenarians of Okinawa seem childlike in their joie de vivre. "So, Rebecca it is."

"You were saying something about lesson number one?"

Lindsey laughed. "Lesson one is that you never let the weather dictate the shoot. Animals still have to feed and drink and mate and take care of their young, whether it's raining or snowing or so foggy you can't see your hand in front of your face. Think of the emotional response to a picture of a puppy left out in the rain. Or an elephant looking for water in a burned-out, dust-filled landscape." The images were hers from her early career. Remembering them gave her a surprisingly bittersweet yearning for that all-too-brief time before she joined the crusade to change the world.

"I thought you took pictures of people."

"But as you know, I live with someone who is one of the world's best nature photographers. Some of that is bound to rub off."

Rebecca grinned. "Want another roommate?"

"First we'd have to have a house."

"Everyone talks about being footloose and free, but I've never actually met anyone who is. Do you have any idea how exciting that sounds to someone like me? What's it like when Matthew is getting ready to go out on a story? Has he always been as good as he is now? Was he born that way? I know there are prodigies in everything, so I would imagine photography has them too."

"I didn't know him when he was a kid, but I'm sure he always had potential." Lindsey finger-combed her hair out of her eyes, wishing she'd thought to bring a cap. "I don't think he'd be all that excited about the prodigy thing. He works hard to get those 'lucky' once-in-a-lifetime shots."

"I love hearing that."

Lindsey knew there had to have been a time when she was this young and enthusiastic, but the memory was buried too deep to easily summon. Impulsively, she asked, "I'm exploring this morning. Want to come along?"

"Are you kidding?" Moving backward, Rebecca held up her hand. "Give me just one minute. I'll get my camera. It's right by the back door." Even in the gray of the fog, Lindsey could see Rebecca blush. "I was hoping you'd ask," she admitted. "You don't mind, do you?"

Lindsey shook her head and waved her on. She hadn't believed for a second that their meeting was accidental. "Bring a tripod if you have one."

She was back in the promised minute, and they started down the stairs. Rebecca had to work to keep up with Lindsey's long stride as they crossed the beach, following the sound of the ocean to the packed sand where the walking was easier. Lindsey unerringly wound up at the log she had been leaning against the morning she'd photographed Abbey. There were times her life depended on such instincts, and she never took her sense of direction for granted.

"Do you know many of the people who live around here?" Lindsey asked, adjusting the tripod legs for a low shot of two fishermen working the waves with long, heavy poles.

"Everyone but the renters. I've baby-sat or house-sat for most of them."

"What about a little girl named Abbey?"

"Her parents are renters, but they come for a couple of months every year. I think the house belongs to a relative, or maybe a friend. Someone told them I baby-sit, so I got to know them fairly well last year."

"What's Abbey like?"

Rebecca gave her a puzzled look, but didn't question how Lindsey would know someone's name and not know anything about her. "She's really smart and really curious. Loves to play games and dress up in this box of costumes her mother bought at an after-Halloween sale."

"So she has a good imagination?" It was a question that implied Abbey had been the only one to see the couple on the beach. If they had been figments of Abbey's imagination, where did that leave Lindsey?

She checked her camera settings and passed them on to Rebecca, with quick explanations about the reasons for the adjustments. Rebecca's Canon was five or six years old but had been the top of the line for entry-level

35mm cameras at the time. "I saw her on the beach yesterday morning. She had an older man and woman with her."

Rebecca eyed her warily. "You mean *really* old, like in their eighties, but they act like they just started dating? He's a head taller, and she does most of the talking? He wears one of those European hats. And she always wears a blue-and-white scarf."

"That's them."

"Yeah, I see them every once in a while, but I've never known anyone else who did. I tried talking to my dad about them, but I could see it made him sad, so I never brought it up again. I figured the way he acted, something weird must have happened."

"Do you have any idea who they are?"

"Yeah—Joe and Maggie. They're the people who used to own the house where you're staying."

"Why do you suppose no one believes you when you talk about seeing them?" Lindsey tried to sound casual, but could see by Rebecca's reaction that she'd failed.

Rebecca hesitated. "Maybe because they died like five or six years ago?"

This Lindsey hadn't anticipated. It left her slack-jawed. "I don't believe in ghosts or apparitions—or anything I can't actually touch," she said. "There has to be some other explanation."

"Let me know when you figure it out, because I don't believe in ghosts either. Makes it kind of hard when you actually see them, though, doesn't it?"

The images Lindsey had captured of Abbey handing her shell to someone and her obvious delight in what turned out to be her invisible companions wasn't something she was ready to share with anyone but Matthew. "We do seem to be an odd threesome to share the same delusion—you, me, and Abbey."

"Maybe it's a girl thing." Rebecca toed the sand into a mound. "It seems they only come around when someone needs them, and I wouldn't be surprised if Abbey was headed for trouble that morning. She thinks she's going to grow up to be Wonder Woman and isn't afraid of anything, including things she should be, like the ocean."

"What about you?"

Rebecca was slow to answer. "I had a hard time going with the idea that my mom chose cocaine over me. It's a common story for kids like me and my stepsister Grace. Joe and Maggie helped me see my anger was really screwing up my life. I had no room for the people who loved me and wanted to take care of me. What about you?"

"I'm going to save that for another time."

"Fair enough. You never know, I could be some tabloid spy."

Lindsey laughed for the second time that morning. It felt . . . good, like something normal people did.

Rebecca rechecked the settings on her camera. "Why is it that I can never get my pictures to turn out the way I see them in my head?"

"You have to become so familiar with your camera that it becomes a part of you. When that happens, you take pictures intuitively. You even look at the world differently. Your curiosity is heightened by little things, like seeing a broken spiderweb and wondering what it would look like with the sun behind it, or whether to bring in the barn at the back of the property. You try to arrange happy accidents where something happens, like catching a hummingbird stealing the silken threads for its nest."

"How would you do that?"

"Go somewhere with lots of hummingbirds during breeding season, find a good web, and wait.

"I went to an autograph party for a writer I know, and during the question-and-answer part of the program someone said something about writers being born, not made. My friend said that every writer he knew had served an apprenticeship of writing a million words. I feel that way about photography. If you want to be a good photographer, go on a couple of trips a year to fabulous places. If you want to be a great photographer, go out in your own backyard every day. Eventually, you will have taken enough pictures to know what works and why and you'll be able to set up your shots as naturally and effortlessly as you blink."

"I can't even imagine what that must be like."

"You stop seeing the world the way you do now and realize how powerful a single image, frozen in time, can be. There isn't a video, no matter how dramatic, that can compare to a still shot that has captured human emotion at its peak. What makes a great photographer is the ability to anticipate those moments, to set yourself up so that you're ready when the action takes place. You develop a sixth sense of sorts.

"This kind of shot is a given at sporting events, but the truly great images are rarely, if ever, taken by an amateur, unless it's an accident. You have to know what's going on to anticipate what's going to happen.

"Sometimes the best pictures are off the field. Fans and parents of athletes are great human-interest subjects, especially at nonprofessional games.

"If you can capture someone sleeping through a political speech or yawning in a Batman movie or a soldier standing guard over a friend who died and waiting for a medevac helicopter, you can tell your story with one image."

"I want to see the world the way you do."

"First you have to train your mind to go there without conscious thought. Then you have to accept that you don't see the world around you the way others do. There will be times you feel like you're speaking a language from a country no one knows exists." Lindsey laughed. "That's when you start looking for another photographer to talk to just to prove to yourself that you're not going crazy."

"I had a teacher in high school who singled me out to tell me that my pictures suck. I know I have a long way to go, but there's no way I'm going to let someone like that walk all over my dream."

Lindsey had a theory about people who put themselves in the position of crushing budding talent rather than nurturing it. She laid it off to unrestrained jealousy on one side of the coin and frustration on the other. Someone or something had walked on that person's dreams, and it was impossible to resist the urge to pass it on by doing the same to someone else.

Rather than haul out the soapbox, Lindsey changed the subject. "Another thing—don't let yourself get caught up in having to have the latest camera or lens or whatever. There's always going to be something coming out that's bigger and better and more expensive. More than anything, it's the photographer who makes a great picture, not the camera."

She'd carried a camera that was little more than a point-and-shoot into every conflict she'd ever covered, using it as a backup because she could hide it in her "working" bra—one a full cup size larger than she normally wore and padded to hold not only the camera but batteries and memory cards when the temperature was below freezing. Without it, she would have come out of the Kunar Province in 2010 with nothing to show for two months' work.

A tribal leader she and Asa had gone to for safe passage out of the mountains had taken them to a village where he demanded her cameras and equipment as payment. She'd tried to bargain with him, offering her insulated boots in exchange for his sandals and the memory cards in her pack. He could keep the cameras. All she wanted were the cards. Afraid to show how angry she was over the shakedown, she turned to Asa and saw the silent plea to let it go. She realized then that she wasn't bargaining for her images but for their lives.

"What you have now is more than you need for the shooting you want to do. It will teach you how to get in close and not rely on a long lens for everything," Lindsey told the girl. "Great photographs have been taken with a lot less."

Rebecca took the cloth Lindsey had given her and wiped the moisture off of her camera. "I want this so much, I get ahead of myself."

Lindsey had driven her mother and father crazy with her hunger to leave the farm and see the world—at fifteen. There was no way she was going to reel in the string that let Rebecca's kite soar. Especially not today. Today it seemed fitting, a tribute in a way, to nurture Rebecca's dreams for all the dreams that had died with her friends.

Lindsey pointed toward the fishermen. "Tell me what you see. And then tell me how you're going to tell their story. Pretend you're working for a PR firm that wants something subtle, but evocative, to sell their rubber boots. And then pretend you're doing a story for *National Geographic* on global warming."

"Cool."

Chapter 8

An hour later, with both of them soaked to the skin, Lindsey scrolled through the images on Rebecca's camera, sat back on her heels, and proclaimed, "Well, now we know. You definitely don't suck. You have an artist's instinct for zeroing in on where the focus should be, and you're creative at finding new ways to tell an old story."

Rebecca grinned. "Thanks—I think."

"You said something about teachers. Where have you gone to school?"

"I took a class last summer at the community college before my regular classes started at UC Santa Cruz. It was really retro. The guy who taught it seemed to think the only way to become a *real* photographer was to start with film. We spent the first half learning how to operate old film cameras and take black-and-white pictures. The second half we learned how to process the film. Did you know the chemicals they used to use were toxic? I'm surprised all those early photographers lived as long as they did.

"I thought the class was a waste of time, but my mom and dad wouldn't let me drop it. They have this thing about making their kids see things through once we start them."

Rebecca's cell phone played a short piano riff. She looked as if she was going to ignore it, then gave in. "It's probably my mom. I'm supposed to work at the nursery this afternoon." She glanced at the screen. "Yeah, she's looking for me." She sent a return text, not bothering to look at the phone.

"That's pretty impressive," Lindsey said, thinking of the number of times that particular skill would have been useful on the road.

Rebecca shrugged. "It was something I taught myself in high school. I was the only one of my friends who never had her phone confiscated." She backed away from the cameras, which were still on the tripods, and brushed the sand off her sweatpants.

"I know it's really pushy," Rebecca said, "but is there any way we could do this again? I can arrange my schedule at the nursery to fit yours." When Lindsey didn't immediately answer, Rebecca added, "If you've got something going this week, I don't mind waiting until you're free. School doesn't start again for a couple of weeks, and even then I have holes in my schedule I could work around."

"I don't know," Lindsey said.

"It's okay. I understand."

"It's not what you think. I don't know if I'll still be here."

Rebecca frowned. "I thought you were staying all of January."

"Something's come up." Why not just say what it was? "Matthew and I lost a good friend in Syria, and we're going back east to her funeral."

Rebecca was hit with a spark of understanding. "Oh, wow—I'm sorry. I saw the story on the news. It's really sad what happened to them. Are you going to be taking her place after the funeral?"

"No one can take her place. She was a special woman who got caught up in an ugly war and died trying to tell the world what was happening."

"I'm sorry," Rebecca said. "Grace is always telling me I'm skinny because food can't get past the foot in my mouth." Her cell phone went off again.

"Don't worry about it." Lindsey had planned to stay on the beach a little longer, but realized Rebecca wasn't going to leave until she did. She picked up Matthew's tripod and slung it over her shoulder, not bothering to detach the camera or collapse the legs. He was as fanatical about sand getting trapped in the locking rings as he was about his coffee and preferred doing the cleanup work himself. Heading for the stairs, she said, "If I'm still around tomorrow, how about same time same place?"

"Are you serious?" Rebecca said. "I'd go anywhere—anytime—for another morning like this." She spontaneously hugged Lindsey, nearly dislodging the tripod. "Oh my God," Rebecca moaned, "I promise you that I'm not usually such a klutz."

Out of nowhere, an image of Sittina appeared in Lindsey's mind, crowding out where she was and who she was with. For a breath-stealing moment, she tried to reconcile a world where two young women could lead such different lives. Neither could have truly understood the life of the other—they had everything and yet nothing in common. It would have been impossible for Sittina to imagine a kitchen with food for the taking, a place where fruits and vegetables were tossed in the garbage because they were less than perfect and where leftovers were scraped into a disposal. Rebecca would have been horrified at the thought of chasing vultures from a lion kill to rescue scraps of putrefied meat.

"What kind of nursery?" Lindsey asked. The area between Santa Cruz and Monterey was known as the salad bowl of the world, with growing conditions perfect for crops as wide-ranging as artichokes and strawberries.

"Orchids."

"A perfect place for a lesson on macro mode—if I'm still here."

They were at the top of the stairs when Rebecca turned to Lindsey. "This is going to sound totally selfish, but even my mom and dad take vacations and they're the hardest-working people I know." After another quick hug, this one more careful, Rebecca gave a little wave, held her camera and tripod with both hands, and took off at a run.

Lindsey lost sight of her in the fog, but could hear her open the door to her house and call out that she was home. For the second time that day she thought about her parents and how casually she took for granted that they too would always be there to welcome her home.

Wasn't it a birthright for all children? Wasn't home the one place that you could, that you should, be able to count on? If so, where did that leave Sittina and all the other children of the world lost in refugee camps who had no one to welcome them when they rolled out their ragged pieces of cardboard to sleep on each night?

Chapter 9

Matthew greeted Lindsey at the door. Relieving her of the tripod and camera, he automatically started cleaning both.

"How was your run?" she asked, giving him a quick kiss.

"Interesting. I took a wrong turn somewhere and wound up at this great doughnut shop. I must have looked pretty pathetic because the owner gave me a cup of coffee and a doughnut on credit."

"Why didn't you call me? I would have—" She thought about what she'd been about to say. "I probably should do something about getting a new phone."

"What happened to yours?"

"I buried it."

He cocked a questioning eyebrow. "And you did this because . . ."

"I got up to get a drink of water last night and heard it vibrating. There were fifteen messages from David. He's not going to let go, because he thinks he can wear me down. Why wouldn't he? I've played Pinocchio to his Geppetto for five years."

Matthew grinned. "And now you want to be a real little boy?"

"Okay, so it wasn't a great metaphor."

"You could always dig it up and take it in to have the number changed."

She shook her head.

"I'll bite—why can't you?"

"Because I smashed it before I buried it."

"I see we have to add littering to your growing list of petty crimes."

She put her arms around his neck and planted a kiss on his cheek.

"You missed."

But he didn't. He captured her mouth in a kiss that took her to a place she longed to be—safe and warm, where the problems they faced were mere bubbles that rode the waves to shore and then disappeared. In this place there was no pain or longing or sorrow, only love.

He swept her up in his joyful passion. It was where she wanted to be, but she had to stop pretending that what separated them could be buried because it was inconvenient, or even damaging. But not yet. "I need you to know that I'm working hard on walking away from my job, but it's more complicated than simply turning my back. It's even more than recognizing that there are kids in school now who will graduate with cameras in their hands and go to war-torn countries and send back pictures better than anything I ever did. I have unfinished business with some of it that I can't turn my back on, that I can't walk away from.

"Remember the girl I told you I met in the Congo? I let her in, Matthew, and I can't stop thinking about her."

"She was the reason you stayed there as long as you did?"

Lindsey nodded. "When I tell you about her, you'll understand."

"Long story?"

"Kinda."

"Then you should probably change into something dry, don't you think?"

He was the only person she could lean on without feeling weak, the only one she had ever shared her most intimate dreams and ambitions and fears with and not felt vulnerable. How had she convinced herself it was okay not to tell him what she was going through? She'd been so stupid.

Before he let her go, he asked, "Are you okay?"

She looked deep into his eyes and knew with absolute certainty that he would be as alone without her as she would be without him. "I will be."

She started toward the bedroom. "I'll make us coffee as soon as I'm changed."

"I'll do it."

Self-preservation—she could always count on it where Matthew and coffee were concerned. She smiled.

For almost three hours, Lindsey sat cross-legged, tucked into the corner of the sofa, drinking Matthew's coffee and telling the rest of Sittina's story. At first she fought to find words with more meaning than the ones she'd used the first time she'd told Matthew about Sittina, and then she gave up and got her laptop to let her pictures tell the story. He winced when she showed him the photograph of Sittina hiding in a bush, her back to the other children, methodically chewing the small portion of the energy bar that Lindsey had given her into a mash and slowly feeding it off the tip of her finger to a six-month-old boy whose brother had died earlier that day.

Sittina hadn't complained or cried, not even when she talked about her mother and little sister and how they died. One night when she and Lindsey were on lion watch together, she talked about the dream she'd had of being a doctor who traveled from village to village taking care of children. It was beyond Sittina's capability to imagine anyone ever taking care of her again, not even her grandmother, who had been lost to the family for over a year.

"I may know someone who can pull some strings, at least to help us find Sittina's grandmother," Matthew said. "I did a piece on Roger Grayson's work with the Raise Your Hand Foundation a couple of years ago, and we've stayed in touch. He's one of the most compassionate people I've ever met, and he loves challenges."

Her heart swelled at how easily he'd said "us," immediately and automatically assuming that whatever burden she carried was his to carry too. "This isn't just a challenge. Finding anyone in one of those camps is like looking for a wildebeest with a chipped hoof in the middle of migration. There are over thirty thousand refugees in Gihembe alone. A quarter of them are children. Finding Sittina could be as hard as finding her grandmother."

"So we don't try?"

She put her hand over her heart as if she could contain the powerful swell of emotion his words created. "Will you marry me?" she asked, almost as surprised as he was.

"I thought—" He studied her. "You're serious?"

"Yes."

"After all these years? Why now?"

"Because it's the only way I know to tell you how much I love you. There are no words to express how I feel."

"You don't have to—"

She stopped him. "And it's something I want, more than I've ever wanted anything else in my life. I met a girl today who told me my *husband* was an awesome photographer. Only half of that was true. I want it all."

"A ceremony isn't going to change anything between us, Lindsey."

"Why are you fighting me on this? I thought you wanted to get married."

"Maybe I don't trust that two or three or ten months into it you won't change your mind. And then where would that leave me?"

Lindsey handed him her laptop. A picture of Sittina in profile, staring at a shallow, open grave where the baby she'd fed her rations was about to be laid, filled the screen. "What I know is that I can't do *this* anymore. It's killing me."

He stared at Sittina's picture a long time before he said, "Grab your camera."

"Where are we going?"

"We're going to see if you can survive two weeks of taking pictures of the otters that hang around Elkhorn Slough."

"Piece of cake. I love otters. Give me five minutes for a shower and I'll . . . unless you'd like to join me. Then I'll need ten."

He laughed. "I'm not that fast."

"I was counting on it." It was on the tip of her tongue to remind him that he hadn't responded to her proposal, but she decided to let it go. Pushing for an answer before he was ready could get her the wrong one.

Lindsey's initial impression of Elkhorn Slough was less than wonderful. She'd expected something more sanctuary-like. Instead, when they pulled into the harbor at Moss Landing, where they were renting a kayak, the active harbor and massive power plant made the site seem almost industrial. Twin exhaust stacks, just short of two hundred feet tall, dominated the landscape.

Opposite the power plant were two large marine research vessels from the Monterey Bay Research Institute, and next to them were commercial fishing boats. Rows of privately owned skiffs and aluminum boats were moored next to million-dollar yachts and a pontoon boat. The harbor was a bouquet of fish and salt, a cacophony of gulls and seals, and an eclectic assortment of people who loved the sea.

She absorbed the ambiance while she waited for Matthew to make the arrangements for the kayak, then spotted a glass-covered board filled with tourist information about the slough. She was drawn to trivia the way she was drawn to a really good book—compulsively absorbing both.

She studied the map first and saw immediately that the harbor was only the cork in the bottle. The far-reaching slough extended seven miles inland. Outside of San Francisco Bay, Elkhorn Slough was the largest tract of tidal salt marsh in California. Over seven hundred varieties of plants and animals lived inside the marine reserve, and it was considered critical habitat for several species of migrating birds.

Matthew came up behind her. "Have enough 'did you know?' details to get us through the day?"

She was an information junkie. Obscure bits of information were like fine Belgian chocolates to her—morsels that could be savored selfishly but were more fully enjoyed when shared. "This place where we are isn't part of the sanctuary. It's called Moss Landing."

He slipped his arm around her shoulders and waved a piece of paper in the air. "I know. I picked up a map."

He guided them across the parking lot. "I'll bet you don't know this one," she said. "When a female otter is hunting, there are some male otters that have learned to kidnap her baby while she's underwater. They make her pay a ransom of the food she just brought up before they'll give the baby back."

"Seems a little coldhearted and lazy."

"It's why we'll see moms with pups off by themselves. Imagine how exhausting it would be for the female to try to feed one of those big males plus her pup."

"Plus herself."

Lindsey couldn't imagine anyone not finding this kind of information as fascinating as she did. "Did you know otters are considered among the world's best mothers?"

"Plainly the males fall short in the dad division," Matthew said, pointing to a ramp.

"Not only that, they bite the female's nose during mating, sometimes pretty viciously."

"The ugly side of cuteness."

Matthew tossed her a life jacket when they arrived at the kayak. "Front or back?"

"Front—I'm the student, after all."

Matthew laughed out loud. "As if."

"And while we're on the subject of students, remind me to tell you later about my morning." Sitting on the dock, she slid into the kayak, then held it steady while Matthew got in. "I met the next-door neighbor's daughter."

"Grace?"

"No, the older one, Rebecca. She's the one I told you about who thinks you're the world's best wildlife photographer."

"Smart girl." He pushed them away from the dock and turned the kayak south, headed for the entrance to the slough. Sea lions were everywhere, using the seawall and fishing docks to rest as they sought shelter from their main predators, orcas and white sharks. Others waited in the water for a prime spot to clear, heads bobbing like glass fishing floats.

She ignored him. "This isn't about her, it's about me."

"Ahh . . . I didn't catch that part."

"I discovered something I never knew about myself. I like teaching." She raised her arm to point to a raft of otters fifty-strong.

"It's a bachelor party," Matthew said. "The guys hang out together in large groups while the females and their pups usually gather in smaller rafts."

"Do you suppose they're trading information on effective kidnapping methods?"

"Could be, but I doubt it. My guess would be they're bragging about how many noses they've bitten lately." He let the kayak drift closer while he slowly lowered his camera to just above water height. "Now tell me about this teaching thing."

"I could see myself being a mentor." Lindsey focused her camera on a brown pelican coming in for a landing.

"Really? Do you think you have the patience for something like that?"

"I'm sure it would depend on the student. Rebecca reminds me of myself when I picked up a camera for the first time. Boy, what I would have given for a little one-on-one time with someone who knew what they were doing."

"Shhh . . . listen."

"What?" she whispered.

"I think I just heard a door opening."

Lindsey smiled. "You know, I think I did too."

Chapter 10

Matthew rolled over in bed and, for the second time since they'd been at the beach house, found Lindsey's side empty. He glanced at the clock. Three-thirty. Too early for her to be wandering around outside. He listened, and seconds later heard her voice. While she'd destroyed her actual phone in a wonderfully freeing gesture, her practical side had taken over and she'd removed the SIM card at the last minute. No matter what direction she chose to go, she'd be lost without her calendar and contacts. On their way home that afternoon they'd picked up a new phone, which she'd had up and running before they left the store.

He tried, but couldn't make out what she was saying. It was the tone of her voice that concerned him. He looked for his robe but couldn't find it, so put on a flannel shirt instead. The height of fashion—hairy legs topped with red plaid.

She was at the table, her open computer the only source of light—the candle of the twenty-first century. She glanced up and saw him. Grinning at his outfit, she poked her hand out of the rolled-up sleeve of his robe and waved him over. It seemed she'd taken to the robe thing after all. If he was ever going to get his returned, he'd have to make sure hers made it out of the washing machine.

"Are you sure it's her?" she asked. "Marial is a pretty common surname, isn't it?" She waited for the answer. "Yes, I can hold." She reached for Matthew's hand, and whispered, "Barbara—the woman I told you about with Save the Children—thinks they've found Sittina's grandmother."

"Why would someone claim to be her grandmother if they weren't?"

"Every refugee camp has a criminal underground. Some specialize in preying on orphaned children, using them for everything from prostitution to thievery."

"Right now I'm going with the idea that it's really her grandmother," he said. "This girl needs something good to happen to her—other than meeting you."

The gentle kindness made Lindsey smile. "They won't know for sure until they find Sittina.

Barbara said she took off a couple of days ago to look for her grandmother, and they haven't seen her since."

Abruptly, Lindsey sat up straight and swung the phone back toward her mouth. "Yes—I'm here."

Matthew got up and went into the kitchen to make coffee and check out the sweet rolls they'd bought that afternoon. As he passed the computer he saw that it wasn't pictures of war or refugee camps or even Sittina that filled the screen. It was a mother otter grooming her baby. The picture wasn't there for him to discover, she'd been working on it before he came into the room.

The discovery was a gift.

Minutes later Lindsey came into the kitchen and wrapped him in the folds of his bathrobe. "She's going to call me back as soon as she hears something."

Matthew gave her his own update. "Roger's assistant said she'd get back to me as soon as she could reach him," he said. "Seems he's somewhere over the desert in Mongolia in a balloon. In the meantime, she's contacted the people they have working in Gihembe to see what they can do on their end."

She kissed him. "Have I told you lately that I love you?"

He responded with a kiss of his own. "Actually, you have—and in some rather creative ways that I'd like you to remember for a repeat performance."

She put her head against his chest, feeling both his heartbeat and the gentle pressure of the jade elephant. “Something brought us here. This house is more than a place to stay. There’s something special about it.”

“Still thinking about the old couple on the beach?”

He wasn’t teasing her or dismissing what she’d seen, and it didn’t matter that apparitions were rock bottom on his credibility scale—he believed in her and that was all he needed. “That’s part of it, but there’s so much more.”

“Like?”

“This is going to sound strange.” She tilted her head back to look at him. “Okay, it’s going to sound even stranger than ghosts. I have this feeling that I belong here. I’ve never felt this way about any other place we’ve stayed, not even the apartments in Atlanta and London. We’ve been here three days, and it’s like we’ve always been here, like it’s home.”

“It wasn’t home for me until I picked you up at the airport,” he admitted.

“See? Something was leading us here, and it had to be now, not last summer. I’ve always thought it didn’t matter where we were, as long as we were together. Now I have this weird hunger to set down roots.”

“How big a role does Sittina play in these feelings?”

Lindsey frowned. “In what way?”

"You want to give her something you don't have."

"It isn't me. I want her to have what Rebecca has—a loving home, stability, education, even a full cupboard."

"So you're thinking about adoption?" Matthew asked, betraying none of the conflicting emotions he felt.

"It's been on my mind almost constantly since I left her," she admitted. "But it wouldn't work."

"Why not?"

"The adoption process is in as much chaos as the country. And for some bizarre reason, several of the agencies have decided to deal only with children who are under five. They claim that older children don't transition well to living in the States. There are five million children without parents or family members to take care of them, most come from traumatic backgrounds, are malnourished, plagued by parasites or other medical conditions, suffering from abuse, abandonment, and complete loss of hope."

"Plainly you've done more than think about it."

"Look at us. No agency would take us seriously once they found out what we do for a living. And as much as I hate to admit this, Sittina needs a constant in her life, not parents who visit her between assignments. Every reason we've ever had for not adopting children applies double when it comes to her."

"And yet?"

"I can't let her go."

"We're getting ahead of ourselves," Matthew said. "First we need to find Sittina and see if this woman really is her grandmother. Then we'll talk to her and see what she wants to do." He drew Lindsey closer. "In the meantime, we'll check into what it would take to get her and her grandmother to the States. That could be easier than adoption, and they'd have us to help them get settled. Do you know if they have any relatives living here, someone who could sponsor them?"

"It's not something we ever talked about."

Matthew's phone rang. Despite the hour, he didn't even consider letting it go to voice mail. He checked the name and told Lindsey, "It's Zach."

She nodded. Knowing it would be a long call, she slipped out of his robe and draped it across his shoulders, then pressed a kiss to his temple and headed back to bed.

Lindsey could see light coming through the window when Matthew gently shook her awake. She rolled away from him. "Ten more minutes," she pleaded.

"Okay—but you should know there's a bright-eyed, freckle-faced young woman hopping from one foot to the other, waiting for you in the living room."

"Oh my God," Lindsey groaned. "I forgot I told Rebecca I'd meet her this morning." She swung her legs over the side of the bed and grabbed her shirt. Running her hand through her hair was about as effective as trying to eliminate static electricity with an inflated balloon. "Give me five minutes. No, better make it ten." She stuck one leg into her jeans. "Teach her something. Remember, she thinks you're the world's best nature photographer. Impress her."

"With my charm or my wit?"

She smiled. "With your talent, of course."

"When you get back, we need to talk."

She stopped her frantic hopping. "Zach?"

"He wants me to give the eulogy at Ekaterina's service."

There were a hundred, a thousand, things Matthew did well, some of them better than anyone she knew. This wasn't one of them. He was an incredible public speaker, able to captivate an audience in a couple of short sentences, but he could not get up in front of a crowd and talk about what it meant to lose someone as full of life as Ekaterina. The loss of his own sister had been too profound to separate from the loss of others.

The thought hit her like baseball-size hail falling from a cloudless sky, stunning her both mentally and physically. How could she have been so stupid as not to recognize the depth of the fear he must go through every time she left him? Matthew didn't share the illusion that protected most people when they told a loved one good-bye—that they would see them again in the prescribed time and their lives would go on as before. He knew it could be a lie as big as the ones that led to most of the wars she covered.

"What did you tell him?"

He passed his hand over his face, then stood with both hands tucked in his back pockets. "When you get back. It's too long to go into now."

"I'll postpone. Rebecca will understand."

"No, don't. I need some time to think about this anyway."

She nodded. "Whatever you decide, I'm—"

"I know."

She crossed the room and took him in her arms. "I'm so sorry, Matthew."

"This isn't about me."

But it was. How could he stand in front of hundreds of people and talk about what it took for someone to do Ekaterina's job and not be haunted by the realization that every time she and Mathew kissed good-bye at an airport Lindsey was headed into the same kind of danger. "I'll make this fast."

He nodded and gave her a quick kiss. "I'll be here."

Rebecca was sitting on the edge of one of the ottomans, her hands clasped between her knees. She stood and picked up her tripod as soon as she caught sight of Lindsey.

"This is a bad time," she said. "Why don't we wait until you get back?" Realizing she'd said more than she should, she added, "I'm sorry, but I couldn't help overhearing you and Matthew talking."

"Then you also must have heard that he wants some time alone."

"No, he doesn't," she said with conviction. "Not really. I say that too all the time, but I don't mean it."

Lindsey gave her a questioning look.

"Six years ago, my mother and my little brother died in a house fire that started because she was heating the oil to make popcorn and forgot about it when a friend dropped by with some blow. They went down to the basement to get high. By the time I smelled the smoke, the flames were climbing the stairs to my room and it was too late to do anything but get outside and find someone to call the fire department. I broke my brother's window to try to reach him, but it only made the fire worse.

"Later, everyone listened when I told them I wanted to be alone. I didn't have anyone to talk to about the bottle of pills I stole from my first foster mom. She found me and got me to the hospital, but she didn't want me to come back because I was a bad influence on the other kids.

"When you have something bad happen, you say you don't want to talk about it, but you really do."

"I'm sorry." Lindsey didn't know what else to say.

"It turned out okay. I got to move here." Rebecca blinked away the tears that had formed in the corners of her eyes. "And I got to see Joe and Maggie. They don't talk a lot, but they're really good at listening."

Rebecca headed for the door. "Let me know if you still want to do this when you get back. If not, I understand." She found a smile. "Don't worry, it won't slow me down."

Lindsey followed her. "Maybe next time we'll get Matthew to go with us."

"I'd like that."

"He would too. He's a teacher at heart. If you get a chance, look him up on TED."

"I will." Rebecca turned to give a wave as she headed across the brick walkway. "I'm sorry about your friends."

"Yeah, me too," Lindsey replied, not sure Rebecca had heard her before she disappeared into the fog.

Chapter 11

Lindsey replaced the latest issue of *Wildlife Photographer of the Year* book on the table in front of her and went to the sideboard to fix a cup of tea. She'd have thought a New York City agency as prestigious as Lind Brothers would have a receptionist who brought drinks out on a tray.

A note in a plastic sleeve on the cover of the book had attracted her attention. It said that six of the photographers in the current book were represented by the agency, including the top prize-winner of the year, Matthew Stephens. Curious, she'd looked to see which of his pictures were included. There were a dozen, with over half devoted to the work he'd done on rhinos. He never entered contests himself, but the agency felt it was important enough for name recognition that they "encouraged" him to participate, doing everything short of choosing the pictures.

She wasn't surprised that he hadn't told her. Matthew's satisfaction came from his work in the field, not from the awards. Still, according to his agent, the awards brought in enough assignments that he'd finally reached the point where he could choose the projects that interested him rather than having to take ones that simply kept him employed.

She heard someone coming and turned to look. It was another agent escorting another client—undoubtedly, if her own rumbling stomach was any indication, out somewhere for lunch.

She smiled as they passed and took her tea over to the window to look at the people working in the building across the street. The agency had a great address, but that didn't always come with an equally great view, especially in New York.

Surprisingly, considering she hadn't shared Matthew's enthusiasm for spending a month in California, all she thought about now was getting back. The service for Ekaterina had been subdued, but heartbreaking. Fittingly, they'd celebrated her life with photographs, devoting a portion to her work, but the majority to her life with Zach. There were childhood images and pictures from family gatherings and others with her dozens and dozens of friends. Her infectious smile had reached into the hearts and minds of the mourners. It didn't matter how often they were told that the service was a celebration of her life—there were no dry eyes.

No display of past joy could erase the images that had turned viral on the Internet, pictures put out by her captors showing Ekaterina's terror-stricken face before she died. Images of the actual violence done to her would have gotten the clip removed immediately, but the people behind it were too clever for that and the video stayed up for almost a week—plenty of time to be copied onto other sites and talked about on blogs and passed from computer to computer on email loops. Ten million official hits. Not close to the Sneezing Panda or Justin Bieber or a skateboarding dog, but enough to make Ekaterina more famous in death than she'd been in life.

Matthew did what Zach had asked him to do—he told stories that made people laugh. Ekaterina loved practical jokes, none more than the ones pulled on her. He told the stories behind the best and the worst, not breaking down himself until he looked at Zach and saw him smiling through his tears.

Except when he was speaking, Matthew sat next to her, hanging on to her hand so tightly his fingers left marks in her palm. For most of the service, he kept himself together through sheer will, and she was the only one who knew what was happening to him inside.

This time when the door to the agents' offices opened, Matthew appeared. He had an expression that vacillated between bewilderment and incredulity, topped off with a lopsided grin. He took her cup and put it back on the sideboard. "Come on—let's get out of here. I have something to tell you and it can't wait."

"Me too," she said, almost running to keep up with him. "I'll flip you for who goes first."

As soon as they were in the elevator with the doors closed, he kissed her, long and hard and with toe-tingling passion. He didn't stop, not even when the elevator doors opened several floors later. A man started to get in, gave a little bow, and said, "This one is all yours."

"How long have we got?" Lindsey said breathlessly.

"Not long enough."

"Want to bet?" She reached for the STOP button.

Matthew grabbed her hand. "Look up."

She did and saw a security camera perched too high for either of them to reach. "Damn."

He put his arms around her waist, lifted her in a bear hug, and swung her in a circle. "I'm sure there must be a utility closet somewhere."

"Tell me," she pleaded.

"Not yet."

The next time the doors opened they were on the first floor. "Drinks or the hotel?" he asked.

She laughed. "You're kidding, right?"

Matthew had the cab driver stop by a liquor store on the way to the hotel. He asked for their best champagne and was given a bottle of Louis Roederer Cristal Brut. When they reached their room, he filled the sink with ice, put the bottle in to chill, and joined Lindsey on the bed.

"Now?" she asked, yielding to his enthusiasm. What she had to say was beyond the moment, it was forever.

He brought her to him for a kiss. "First, I owe you an answer to your proposal." He opened his hand and showed her the jade elephant. "I know it's not traditional, but nothing could mean as much to me as this does. Is it okay? Will it do for an engagement ring until we can find one you like better?"

She caught her breath. "Are you sure?"

"I've been thinking about it for days. I just didn't know how you'd feel."

She tried, but couldn't stop the tears. Taking the elephant from his hand she put her arms around his neck. "There is nothing better. I don't know how to tell you how much this means to me."

"It doesn't bother you that it's associated with something sad?"

"Christine sent this to you in love, not sadness. It's time her gift represented what she intended."

"I still miss her."

Lindsey touched his cheek. One day she would tell him about Joe and Maggie and how she'd come to be a believer in things she'd once dismissed as easily as the magic of double rainbows. "She's here, Matthew. Just as Ekaterina is there for Zach."

He couldn't help but smile. "You do realize how certifiable you sound."

"Afraid I'm turning new age on you?" She twisted so that he could put the necklace on her. Pressing the pendant to her chest, she was overcome by a wave of emotions. "Now it's my turn," she said.

"Not yet."

"There's more?" She wasn't surprised, just anxious. What she had to tell him would be as life-altering as their engagement.

He took a deep breath. "I've been offered a dream assignment, something I never imagined was possible."

When he hesitated, she said, "Am I supposed to guess?"

"You couldn't. Hell, I couldn't." He started to tell her and then stopped, lost for the right words.

"Before I say anything more, I want you to know that I countered their offer with what I told them was a deal-breaker. They have to give me time off whenever you have free time."

She grinned. "That's easy."

"Since when?"

"Yesterday."

He frowned. "Does this have something to do with what you have to tell me?"

"It's everything. I quit. Officially. Actually put it in writing. I'm no longer working for the agency—not covering any war, anywhere, anytime." She tried to force a smile, but failed. Walking away was the right thing to do, but it didn't make it any easier. She was leaving a job that had allowed her to make a difference. And going . . . where?

"I don't understand." Matthew studied her for some reaction. He prodded her with one of his own. "I can get out of this. I haven't signed the contract, and there's plenty of time for them to find someone else."

"Why would you do that?"

"Isn't it obvious? For the first time we have a chance to be together. There's no way in hell I'm going to blow that for—"

"First tell me what exactly you would be giving up. What is it about this job that has you so excited?"

He wiped his hand across his eyes as if it would help him see what was going on more clearly. "It's a documentary that's being funded by a consortium of environmental and wildlife rescue groups. The goal is to create a film that shows what 'endangered' means in a way that reaches an audience beyond those already converted. Environmentalists have been preaching to the choir too long. They need new recruits to get done what needs to get done."

"Playing devil's advocate here," Lindsey said, "what could you possibly say, or show, that hasn't been done a dozen times already? How are you going to get someone to care about some obscure frog in Australia when they don't care that there are children all across the world being sold into brothels by their own parents?"

"Self-interest. We're going to connect that frog to the fires that consume Australia every year and show the ongoing consequences of inaction.

"Wealth anywhere depends on consumption. Take away the consumer, for whatever reason, and industry collapses. Just look at what's happening in China. They have a glut of consumer goods that no one wants because no one can, or will, buy them. People are listening to the doom and gloom on the news every night, and they're reacting in the only way they know how."

Rarely did Lindsey get caught up in Matthew's passion for the environment. Privately, she was like most people who believed the earth was capable of perpetual self-healing and that focusing on a specific owl or whale or wolf turned people into tree-hugging fanatics who then turned people like her into skeptics.

"So what will you be doing?"

"They want a still photographer to focus on the behind-the-scenes animal shots for the text and coffee-table books. Right now I'm it. They're looking for someone who can capture the people behind the cameras, but—"

"I can do that," she said, surprising him almost as much as she surprised herself.

"What?"

"I'm a whole lot better taking pictures of people than you are." It wasn't bragging, it was fact, something they'd talked about since college. She'd tried, but had never been able to capture the animal shots Matthew took as intuitively as breathing. It was the same for him trying to capture human emotion.

As fast as the thought had arrived, it struck her that she might not be wanted. "Could you work with me? Would that be a problem? I wouldn't just be stepping into your territory, I'd be going there in combat boots."

"I'm having trouble wrapping my mind around this," he said, truthfully. "Give me a couple of minutes."

"We've never been together longer than a couple of months. What if we started getting on each other's nerves?" The more she embraced the idea, the more questions she had, most of them hypothetical. "How long is this assignment?"

"Two years."

"Wow." It was all she could think to say. And then, "When do they want you to start?"

"The film crew is leaving for China in four months. They want me with them to document their arrival."

"Four months . . ." It wasn't as long as it sounded. Half of that time would be spent getting ready.

Matthew leaned forward to take his phone out of his pocket. He went through his contacts until he reached his agent, then handed Lindsey the phone.

"Put up or shut up?" she said. "You don't think we should talk about this some more?"

"No—I'm afraid you might change your mind."

She smiled. "Could it really be this easy?"

"You haven't got the job yet." He was having trouble containing his excitement.

"Want to place a little wager?"

"Do I look that dumb?"

Chapter 12

Propped against the headboard with pillows at their backs, wearing their new bathrobes, Matthew tipped the bottle of champagne, dividing the last splash between his and Lindsey's glasses. "Congratulations," he said.

"To both of us," she added.

"We're employed."

"Together."

He grinned. "What a concept."

"I've been thinking . . ."

"Yes?"

"Where do we go from here?" She put her glass on the nightstand and curled into his side.

"Meaning?"

"Should we postpone getting married until we get back?"

"Fat chance. There's no way I'm giving you that kind of time to change your mind."

"I should tell my parents. A long time ago"—she looked up at him and smiled—"waaay back when I was positive there was no way I was ever going to get married, I promised my mother she could help plan my wedding."

"Something small, I hope."

"Just family. It's time you got to know them better. I should probably warn you that my father thinks it's your fault that I never see them. It doesn't matter whether it makes sense, he can't imagine his precious daughter would stay away for any other reason."

"Oh great. And all this time I thought we got along fine."

"Then my sisters and brother and their families. My sister-in-law isn't crazy about me, but she'll come around. After all, what's not to love?"

"Anyone else?"

"There are some cousins my mom will want to invite."

"Sure you don't want to elope?"

She shook her head. "I owe this to my mom. I haven't been the best daughter to either of them since I moved out. Maybe I can make up for it a little now."

"What else needs to be done before we leave?"

"Sittina. I'm going to do whatever it takes to get her and her grandmother to this country." They'd gotten a call an hour before Ekaterina's funeral telling them that Sittina had been found and reunited with her grandmother. A small victory in the midst of all the sadness that had surrounded them.

"You're going to need an advocate for them while we're gone. My understanding is that with this kind of thing it's hurry-up-and-wait and then you have days, sometimes only hours, to meet a deadline."

The proverbial lightbulb turned on in Lindsey's mind. "My dad would be perfect. He's been driving my mother crazy since he retired, and this would give him something to do. Something he would love doing."

"Next?"

"What do you mean?"

"There has to be something we're forgetting."

"You mean besides California?"

"I don't see how we can fit in going back there. Not with—"

"Then we skip something else. The beach house is where we found each other again. Besides, I made a promise to Rebecca that I'm going to keep, come hell or high water. Not going back isn't an option."

"It means that much to you?"

"It means everything."

"Then we'll call it our honeymoon."

Matthew unlocked the door to the beach house, turned to pick up Lindsey, and before she could say anything, carried her across the threshold. "How do you suppose this tradition got started?" he said as he put her down and turned to flip the light switch.

"I happen to know this one," she said, "and you're not going to like it. Your choice—either it's to represent women who were kidnapped and raped who did not go to their new husband's home willingly, or as a way to demonstrate the bride's virginity by her reluctance to cross into the room that contained the marriage bed."

"Can we go out and do it again? This time you can come in on your own two feet."

She laughed, something that was becoming as easy as it had been hard in her old life. "How about if we go with the reluctant virgin thing instead? That way we could head straight for the marriage bed."

"You're insatiable."

"I'm on my honeymoon."

He took her hand. On her third finger was a plain, recycled platinum wedding band, one Lindsey had discovered in an eco-friendly jewelry store in New York.

He wore a matching band, sized and polished and inscribed inside with the word FOREVER.

During the ceremony, when he put the ring on her finger, she'd leaned forward and whispered, "This does not mean I'm going to become a vegetarian."

He'd winked and smiled slyly. "Should have made it part of the vows."

Epilogue

The end of February arrived with a gentle breeze and a scattering of cotton-tufted clouds in an azure blue sky. For two weeks the single universal topic of conversation in the Santa Cruz area was the beautiful weather. Unspoken, but recognized by those who lived in a water-thirsty state, was the underlying feeling of guilt that permeated time spent enjoying the sunshine on the patios of restaurants and taking long bicycle rides along the shore.

More often than not, whenever the people who called the area home were outside, they sent quick glances to the horizon, looking for the gray that would indicate an incoming storm. As two weeks turned into three, they stopped talking about how lucky they were to live in such a mild climate and turned on the news each night for updates on the weather.

By the middle of March, water and fire districts were holding special meetings on how to deal with what they foresaw as an upcoming drought season.

And then the end of March arrived—not on slippered feet but in hobnailed boots. A storm that meteorologists had tracked and predicted would hit the Bay Area and bypass the area from Half Moon Bay to Monterey entirely, stalled offshore and then veered right.

Trees were uprooted, shingles stripped from rooftops, and streets flooded. Entire neighborhoods were isolated. People benefited from the generosity of those living around them or went hungry.

The beach house stood firm, protected by the original shutters that had been stripped and painted and reinforced during the refurbishing the year before. The walls withstood hits by a half dozen branches from a neighbor's eucalyptus tree, but the flower garden lost most of the perennials.

Andrew and Grace took inventory as soon as there was a lull in the storm, checking for cracked windows and any leaks that might have developed around the chimney. It became a routine for them as storm after storm hit, all the way through April and into May.

A three-week break was followed by another round of storms, not as fierce as the first, but without even a day's break to clean up.

Julia called several times, and Andrew reassured her that all was good with her beloved beach house.

What neither he nor Grace had been able to see was the cracked shingle near the valley in the roof that separated the kitchen from the living room. For three months water had been entering the crack and running along the support beam above the kitchen cupboards, dripping behind the drywall, saturating the insulation, and warping the plywood flooring under the travertine tile.

Grace discovered the hidden damage when she tried unsuccessfully to open one of the kitchen cupboards. She grew sick to her stomach the more deeply she looked and the more damage she discovered. For the rest of the afternoon she tried to convince herself that it would be better if her father called Julia to tell her what had happened. She was sure to have questions Grace couldn't answer.

In reality, Grace couldn't face Julia's dismay—not so much because of what had happened to the house, but over her disappointment in Grace.

But she couldn't do that to her father. This was her job. She'd received the paychecks. What had happened was her responsibility.

Thankfully, Julia was home when Grace called. It wasn't a phone call she wanted to make twice.

"The whole back wall in the kitchen?" Julia said in response to Grace's initial description of the damage.

"And the cupboards. I took out the dishes and put them in the dining room just in case."

"Thank you," Julia said. "And you're sure it isn't something that could be fixed easily?"

"I don't think so," Grace answered, a catch in her voice.

"Don't do that," Julia said. "Don't you dare feel guilty over what happened. It wasn't your fault. You can't fix what you can't see."

"But I should have—"

"Okay, I'm going to tell you something that I don't want you to tell another soul." Julia paused. "Promise?"

Grace nodded and then realized Julia couldn't see her. "Promise."

"This whole thing happening the way it did is like some screwy gift that I didn't deserve."

"I don't understand."

"I hated that kitchen."

Grace turned to look at the polished granite counters, the sleek walnut cupboards, and the stainless steel stove. "Me too," she said, incredulous. "It doesn't fit the house."

"There was no way I could tear it out and start over once I realized what I'd done. I was afraid I was going to have to live with it for the next twenty years."

Grace grinned. "Not anymore."

A loud crashing sound came from the kitchen.

"What was that?" Julia asked.

Grace peered around the corner. "The cupboard over the stove."

"Time for you to get out of there. Tell your dad that I'll call him when he gets home from work."

Julia sat at her desk for several minutes after reassuring Grace again that nothing she'd done or hadn't done had caused the leak. Her hand still cradling the phone, she thought about the upcoming home show she'd seen advertised in the newspaper. It wasn't often that second chances like this one came along, and it was hard to believe it was pure coincidence.

While she didn't believe in ghosts or spirits—never had, never would—it was comforting to imagine Joe and Maggie having a hand in what had happened at the beach house.

Comforting was good.

She'd go with that.